The Ocean in My Ears

The Ocean in My Ears

Meagan Macvie

Ooligan Press
Portland, Oregon

The Ocean in My Ears
©2017 Meagan Macvie

ISBN13: 978-1-932010-94-7

Ooligan Press
Portland State University
Post Office Box 751, Portland, Oregon 97207
503.725.9748   ooligan@ooliganpress.pdx.edu   ooligan.pdx.edu

Library of Congress Cataloging-in-Publication Data
Names: Macvie, Meagan, author.
Title: The ocean in my ears / Meagan Macvie.
Description: Portland, Oregon : Ooligan Press, Portland State University,
[2017] | Summary: In small-town Alaska in the 1990s, high school senior
Meri's determination to escape for a more exciting place wanes as she
struggles with family, grief, friends, and hormones.
Identifiers: LCCN 2017005062 | ISBN 9781932010947 (pbk.)
Subjects: | CYAC: Coming of age—Fiction. | High schools—Fiction. |
Schools—Fiction. | Dating (Social customs)—Fiction. |
Friendship—Fiction. | Grief—Fiction. | Family life—Alaska—Fiction. |
Alaska—Fiction.
Classification: LCC PZ7.1.M2588 Oce 2017 | DDC [Fic]—dc23
LC record available at https://lccn.loc.gov/2017005062

Cover design by Taylor Farris & Leigh Thomas
Interior design by Maeko Bradshaw
Illustrations by Riley Pittenger

Excerpt from "Circe/Mud Poems" by Margaret Atwood, included by permission of the Author. Available in the following collections: In the United States, SELECTED POEMS I, 1965 – 1975, ©1976 by Margaret Atwood. Published by Houghton Mifflin Harcourt; In Canada, SELECTED POEMS, 1966 – 1984, published by Oxford University Press, ©Margaret Atwood 1990.

References to website URLs were accurate at the time of writing. Neither the author nor Ooligan Press is responsible for URLs that have changed or expired since the manuscript was prepared.

Printed in the United States of America

For Olivia

Contents

Last year I abstained
this year I devour

without guilt
which is also an art

—*Margaret Atwood*

1
The Flesh

"Fornication," says Pastor Dan, staring down at us, "is more than just sex out of wedlock."

I cross my legs. The sanctuary is suddenly too hot, and the pew's pea-green wool pricks at the undersides of my thighs.

"Fornication," he says, "is a range of evils between unmarried people."

The word *fornication* is a serrated blade, smooth and bumpy at the same time. Shiny. Dangerous. Sharp enough to knife a heart or cut through bone. Fornication is love's sinful cousin, wicked and wild. It is Joaquin's bare shoulder. Dark and powerful.

If I could, I'd jump out the window and run in my kitten heels all the way to Joaquin's trailer. I'd remind him about our Spring Fling slow dance, and he'd say I was unforgettable, and we'd...

I let my breath out in a loud gush. Mom's finger flies to her lips. "Shh, Merideth!" Her whisper turns my name into a reprimand. Because sighs in church are a hideous crime.

Maybe Joaquin's forgotten me—he never called like he said he would—or maybe he lost my number. Either way, I can't ditch church to find out. I'm wedged between my mom and little brother. Alex is on the end, one long leg jutting into the aisle. He's reading the Batman comic he's hidden inside a hymnal. Mom's shoulder crowds me on my other side, and next to her, my six-foot-five dad is blocking my escape window. A shaft of sunlight sparkling with dust motes shines in on Dad's shoulder. I crane my neck and catch a glimpse of the clear June sky. It was still half-filled with drifty morning clouds when we came in.

Beyond the window, the land drops off to where the Kenai River flows into the Cook Inlet on its way to the Pacific Ocean. The inlet is edged by the high bluff upon which our church perches light-house-style, complete with an illuminated neon cross in place of a warning beacon. Below us, fishing boats come and go like seabirds to and from their nests, and along the shore, colorful tents sheltering cannery workers dot the beach like downed kites.

But I can't see any of it.

Like every Sunday, I'm holding down our pew—second from the front—listening to Pastor Dan explain scripture and what God actually meant when He said this or that. I generally disagree with our pastor's interpretations, but I have to swallow my opinions. Sermons aren't discussions.

The Kenai Believers Church is small. Sixteen benches on both sides of the sanctuary angle toward the center aisle—I've counted them a million times. Upright backs discourage slumping. Polished wooden sides are carved with crosses like ornate bookends. Pillowed wool seats look more comfortable than they feel, and where each seat and back meet, a hungry crease devours the remains of past parishioners: Tic-Tacs, paper scraps, lint, fingernails.

Pastor Dan's neck reddens as he yammers on and on about the church being Christ's body—I'm probably the equivalent of Christ's eyelash, something small and sloughable. He likes extending metaphors, but they never go deep enough, and his answers only lead to more questions. Plus, he mixes metaphors like crazy. For example, how can the church, of which I am a part, be Christ's body, and my body also be God's holy temple? Totally confusing.

Guaranteed there was nothing holy about my temple last night when I was doubled over on the couch suffering through period cramps. At the memory my abdomen twinges, and I groan.

Mom clears her throat at me and mouths the word "listen."

Yeah, I wouldn't want to miss out on Pastor Dan's warnings against our sinful nature. We have fallen, blah blah blah. He stares directly into the eyes of every teen in the congregation and pleads with us not to give in to fleshly desires. I feel his gaze on me but deny him the satisfaction by feigning interest in my own finger, as I pick at a growing run in my nude-colored tights.

How weird that "nude" describes both a color and the state of being unclothed. I picture Joaquin in the nude. Muscled back, black hair hanging long. Shorter hairs curling in places I shouldn't imagine. A holy temple.

My heart races, and I tug at my jean skirt.

"This is how the devil works," Pastor says. "He seduces you."

My head tilts to one side and my lids droop. How would Joaquin seduce me? I imagine his lips pressing against my exposed collarbone.

Pastor Dan's voice snaps my head up and springs my eyes open. His sermon has circled back, as all sermons do, to an earlier refrain. "You are the precious Body of Christ!"

Body. Joaquin's hands with those bumpy calluses. His forearms twice the size of mine. "Mm." The sound escapes, but I follow it quickly with a cough. Dad pulls the box of Luden's cherry cough drops from his shirt pocket and reaches over my mom's lap to hand it to me.

I take the box and dig inside—as quietly as possible—breaking a stuck drop from the congealed red mass inside the waxed liner.

"Thanks," I mouth as I hand it back to Dad. He nods, and the box disappears into his pocket. The most interaction we've had in weeks.

"Scripture tells us," Pastor Dan booms, "that 'the flesh lusteth against the Spirit and the Spirit against the flesh: and these are contrary the one to the other.'"

This is old information, but today when I hear it, I feel more aggravated than usual. What does this even mean? I know the Spirit—that small part of God inside me, the part I curl into when I'm afraid or beg for help when I'm in trouble—is good. That is my God part. Strong and forgiving. The flesh—my flesh—is bad. Flesh is weak. It is the pounding want. Lust.

But when I think of Joaquin, I don't *feel* bad. More curious. Excited to be close to him. Not like being lured by the devil, more like being cold and wanting a blanket.

Alex leans toward me, pointing with his pencil to the gallows he's drawn on the back of the church bulletin. I take the pencil and paper, and under the gallows I draw five dashes. Playing hangman with Alex is better than riding Pastor Dan's shame train or daydreaming about some hot guy I barely know.

The sermon has run over the usual stop time, and the whole congregation is getting antsy at this point—even my dad is shifting in his seat—so Mom pretends she doesn't notice our surreptitious game. In five minutes I easily hang Alex—I even draw hair and shoes before he can guess my word.

"Dumb word, buttface," he writes below the hung stick guy.

I *am* being a little unsportsman-like. I should have given the poor kid a chance. No fifteen-year-old dude would guess the word "flesh."

But isn't that the point? To hang the man?

After church is over and Mom is done gabbing with the ladies, I suggest we go to Diary Queen for lunch. Today is Charlie's last day on the job, and what kind of a best friend would I be if I wasn't present for her important moments? She's always been there for me.

Dad prefers the Garden of Italy, but caves easily. He's been home from the oil fields only a few days, so we're still in the Slope-worker honeymoon period. Plus, the Garden is pricey, and as Mom likes to remind us, we're on a budget. Her budget somehow manages to fund eating out every Sunday so she doesn't have to cook. She says it's the Day of Rest. I never mention how the restaurant people aren't resting.

When we get there, Alex runs ahead and holds the door for Mom. He's all arms and legs in his button-down shirt and pleated slacks, but there's a tautness to him that's new this spring. His shoulders have widened, and his once-rounded jawline has hardened into muscles and bone. It's weird that my little brother will be a sophomore in the fall, driving by the end of the school year.

I breeze through the entry behind Mom. "Ladies first," I say.

Alex rolls his eyes.

"Thanks, son," says Dad, bringing up the rear. He takes over holding the door and ushers Alex through, as if playing the role of doorstopper is a very serious male responsibility.

The second I smell greasy burgers frying, my mouth starts to water, and I stride ahead, equally driven by hunger and my anticipation of seeing Charlie. The smell reminds me of the first time we met. Hamburger day in the Soldotna Junior High lunchroom.

"You in line?" she had asked. Her hair was big and blond and stylish.

I was neither stylish nor in the hamburger line but wished I was both. "I'm out," I said. "Of line, I mean. I'm not in line."

"I'm definitely out of line." She laughed. "But I do need a burger." As she assessed my faded jeans and T-shirt—the same basic outfit I wore every day—her lips did this twisting thing that I've watched her do a million times since. It's her weighing options face.

When her eyes reached my zipper earrings, she grinned. "We have Bagley's science class together, right?"

We actually had both science and PE together. That was my first year in public school, and for some reason, Charlie took me on as her project. She claims now that she saw potential in my zipper earings. In less than one semester, she had transformed me from the Christian school weirdo into a normal-ish teen. With an awesome best friend.

Charlie's working the register today and waves when she sees me. The Day of Rest instantly becomes a zillion times better. Her uniform is a shade off from chocolate—closer to dog poop—and is edged with a yellow plaid that makes her already pale face look sickly. There's no line, so I bound up, grin extra wide, and say, "What a lovely brown."

Charlie scratches her nose with her middle finger before my family files up behind me to the counter. "Welcome to Dairy Queen," she says sweetly. "May I take your order?"

"Double burger, fries, rootbeer, and a hot fudge sundae in a helmet," says Alex, who's decided he needs to collect those ridiculous mini-baseball-helmet bowls.

"The usual," I say, delighted that Charlie knows the food I like. She seems equally pleased to be able to anticipate my wants. This is partly what makes us best friends: knowing so many little details about each other. Fritos are Charlie's favorite food, she's obsessed with her hair being perfect, and she has a secret crush on Kenny Clark. Next year, Charlie and I are going off to college together. We don't know how or where yet, but we have definite plans to be roomies someplace.

"Hello, Charlie," says Mom, who's always been soft on Charlie in spite of—or maybe because of—Charlie's wild nature. Mom accepts Charlie for Charlie and saves her judgments for her own children.

"Her nametag says 'Charlene,'" Alex points out, knowing how much Charlie hates her full name.

"At least she has a nametag, slacker," I say. A low blow—for weeks Alex has been applying for summer jobs to no avail. I wouldn't have heckled him if he wasn't antagonizing Charlie for no reason.

"Shut up," he says, trying not to sound wounded.

"Your sister's right," says Dad. "Better step up on those applications." Dad's been amping up his lectures to Alex about being a man and needing a job so that he can support a family one day. Alex says he's never getting married.

After we order, we cram into a booth, and Mom goes on about the nice weather for the grueling five minutes it takes for Charlie to call out that our order's ready. Dad tells Alex to help carry the food, so they both trudge up to the counter. As Alex follows Dad back to our booth, he scowls down at the brown plastic tray loaded with drinks and ice cream treats. Alex is obviously still in a sulk after being reminded that he's not measuring up to Dad's dumb expectations.

A kind of slow motion takes over when Dad halts to set the burgers and fries on the table. Alex, whose head is down, bumps his tray into Dad's back. Two of the sodas and Alex's sundae-in-a-helmet waver and topple off, falling heavy, like air missiles. All three explode when they hit the floor. Liquid artillery splashes cold and sticky on my tights and shoes underneath the table.

Alex's body goes rigid. His eyes flash shock and fear and shame in rapid fire. Mom reaches across me, her hand flying up to steady the two drinks. Her sundae and my Blizzard are still upright on the tray Alex is gripping.

"What are you doing?" says Dad, his eyes narrowing. "Are you even paying attention? C'mon, kid."

Alex's mouth has frozen open. The almost-man who held the door twenty minutes ago has been demoted to the oversized kid who spills drinks.

"Howard..." says Mom, as if invoking Dad's name will somehow calm him. Dad shakes his head and stalks through the dark soda sea back up to the counter.

Soon Charlie appears, pushing the wooden handle of a mop submerged in a rolling bucket. "I'll take care of it, Mr. Miller," she says in a too-chipper voice that I know means she'd rather ram that mop handle straight up Alex's clumsy ass.

Alex sets the tray down and reaches for the mop. "I can do it," he says, but Charlie pulls the handle away. His outstretched hand hangs in the space between them.

"Sit down, son," says Dad.

Alex slumps into his seat next to Dad, and we eat in silence, save the squishy sounds of Charlie sopping up ice cream and soda. Another employee brings us new drinks and offers to remake Alex's spilled sundae, but he says no, he doesn't feel like it anymore. I grab an extra spoon and try to share my Blizzard, but he shakes his head.

Beside our table, Charlie squeezes gross gray sludge from the mop into the bucket.

"Just think," I say, "next year at this time we'll be packing our bags and deciding how to decorate our dorm rooms." Neither of us has any idea how we'll pay for tuition and everything, but getting out of Alaska has been our shared dream since eighth grade, and that dream is sometimes the only thing that gets us through a bad day.

She lifts her head, but her eyes don't meet mine. "Hope so."

Charlie needs this job. Needs *a* job. Her mom barely makes enough for both of them as it is. She told everyone she quit because the brazier grease was making her face break out and her mom was sick of shuttling her back and forth, but I know Charlie's really quitting because of her manager.

He's this gross thirty-something guy, always "accidentally" bumping into her boobs. He also refused to schedule shifts long enough for her to get paid lunch breaks, so she was barely working ten hours a week anyway. Chances are slim that Charlie can land something else now that summer's here. Every teen and college student on the Kenai Peninsula is desperate right now for seasonal employment.

When the floor is slick and shiny with drying bleach water, Mom thanks Charlie.

"It's my job," Charlie says, setting Alex's empty, mini Yankees helmet on our table.

Was. Only one more hour until her fast-food career is officially over.

6/10/90

After church, I told Pastor Dan that the Kenai Believers Church is going to slide off the bluff and into the inlet someday. He patted me on my shoulder in this really annoying way and said, "God willing, I have faith it won't happen in my lifetime." I said erosion doesn't need his faith. It just is.

6/11/90

Dad's flying back to Prudhoe Bay in a few days. I'm glad. Two weeks without his hounding about our filthy house and his tyrannical TV monopoly. Even Mom's ready for him to go. Newsflash, Dad: We survive just fine when you're gone. AND WE WATCH MACGYVER.

6/12/90

Tonight a stray cat showed up at our door, meowing really loud. It's super fat and looks like a Siamese with glassy blue eyes. Mom said she could feel babies inside that big belly, so Alex and I named the cat Mama Kitty. Dad said she had to stay out in the barn.

A survey lady called today wanting to know how many
hours we watched TV and when and what shows. Very
ironic. I wanted to tell her I'd watch more if my dad
wasn't always hogging it up, but I answered her questions
like normal because I had nothing better to do. Soldotna
is so lame the survey lady couldn't even say it right. I
pronounced it for her like five times. Sull-DOT-nuh. In fifth
grade Ms. Livingston told us it's actually the Russian word
for "soldier." Charlie calls it Slowdotna, for obvious reasons.
It might as well BE Russia.

6/14/90

Mama Kitty had her babies in the barn. We followed the
sound of their mewing to find them. They're so cute, but
Dad said we had to get rid of them before the summer
ends. He said they'd be too young to survive winter in the
barn.

2
Bright Like Comets

Summer has already turned boring. Sunday church is the one routine I'm forced to follow, and usually I work a few shifts at Jay Jacobs during the week for gas money. Besides that, I'm either stuck at home or, whenever humanly possible, I figure out a way—usually by half-lying to my mom—to cruise around town with Charlie and search for something to do.

Tonight I'm going out with Charlie.

When I pull up, she doesn't emerge after two honks, so I have to run in and get her. I leave the Bug running, because I'm feeling optimistic. The girl has no excuse for not being ready. She has no siblings, her mom never makes her clean her room, and she doesn't even have a job anymore.

She has no good reason, but *still* she makes me wait. The chances she'll come bouncing out to meet me decrease with every step closer to her porch until finally I'm nose to nose with her kitschy brass door knocker. The thing's useless, so I rap my knuckles against the unforgiving oak as I watch the Bug idle in her driveway like a vibrating orange, wasting gas money.

Her mom swings the door open, and I almost gag because the house reeks like fish and burnt oil. Mrs. Taylor hugs me, tells me Charlie's getting ready upstairs, and holds out a plate of salmon patties. I shake my head, and she sets the plate down on the coffee table. She picks up her wineglass and raises the pale liquid as if toasting me. "Last summer as a high schooler, Miss Meri. Ready for your big bad senior year?"

No. "Ready as I'll ever be," I say, sliding my Jansport from my shoulder and stashing it behind the stereo. The beginning of summer is no time to worry about summer's end or the finality of twelfth grade. That's why fall was invented. Days darken, leaves die, and everybody gets broody. Right now, I need to make my Summer of Seventeen memorable, which is why I'm here at Charlie's and not at home where my parents exist in a timewarp. Charlie's mom may not always be clued in, but at least she gives Charlie her space. "Thanks for letting me stay over, Mrs. T."

She takes a swig from her glass. "Anytime, honey."

I nudge my toe against my overnight pack as the room grows quieter than Sunday church, and I can actually hear the gulpy sounds of Mrs. T.'s swallows. My fingers fidget with the frayed hem of my denim mini. I'm wishing Charlie would get the lead out and that I hadn't left my car running.

"Cute skirt," says Mrs. T. "You look like D. J. Tanner."

No, I don't. I definitely don't.

"I'd marry that John Stamos in a heartbeat," she says and launches into an excruciating play-by-play of the *Full House* season finale. All I hear is my gas money sputtering away.

After forever, Charlie flies down the stairs in cutoffs and a red tank. The summer evening is warm for Alaska but not tank-top warm. She checks herself in the hall mirror, then grabs my arm. "C'mon, Lame-O. Let's roll!" Her energy is as bouyant to me as helium. I'd probably float away if she wasn't holding me down.

Charlie blows her mom an air kiss, and we blast out into the half-light of the never-setting Alaskan sun.

"Charlene Louise Taylor!" Mrs. T. yells after us. "Be good! I can't afford to bail you out of jail."

Charlie jumps into the Bug and rolls down her window. "Don't worry your pretty little head, darling! I'm always good!"

I pray I don't hit their mailbox with Mrs. T. watching.

Tonight we could end up at a rager or beach bonfire, or I might see Joaquin or make out with some college guy working in a cannery. Maybe I'll swim naked in the Cook Inlet and get hypothermia. Who knows? The best part of a night out is the beginning, because anything can still happen and nothing terrible has already happened and not knowing makes me buzz with endless possibilities.

We turn off the Spur Highway into the gravel lot next to 7-Eleven, where a dozen cars are already parked. Speaker boxes blare music from the popped trunks of tricked-out cars. Kids stand in clusters, talking and laughing and swatting at invisible mosquitos. A few are tipping back Nalgene bottles probably filled with Everclear. If Charlie and I are going to find anything worth doing tonight, we'll find it here in Kenai, ten miles away from boring Slowdotna.

Students, graduates, and even some of the younger teachers from SoHi and Kenai High pack this vacant lot every Friday and Saturday night. We're like caribou gathering at the river flats. We graze a bit, then move on. To the woods or a gravel pit or a private house party or wherever. It's not safe for the herd to stay out too long in the open.

As we drive by a couple making out, Charlie lunges over and honks my horn. The two jump away from each other, wide-eyed. We're totally cracking up. The guy flips us the bird and yells a bunch of obscenities, but in two seconds they're back to swapping spit. Typical.

The Kenai Peninsula is known for two things: salmon fishing and the teen birthrate. Highest per capita in the nation. Charlie likes to say, "If you're not fishin', you're fuckin.'" I can only speak to that first one. I've been fishing more times than I've been to the movies, and that's the third most popular thing to do around here. But she's kinda right about the second one, too. During those dark months—winter's curse in exchange for summer's infinite light—you can either go outside and freeze, or lose your mind being bored in your house. I imagine getting it on with someone is less boring, but I wouldn't know. There's a lot I don't know. Alaska's like two thousand miles away from anywhere cultured. No offense, Canada.

We circle the edge of the gathering, and I barely see the raven pecking at something dead on the gravel before we're on top of it. I swerve, and black wings take to the air just before we collide. Charlie and the raven both shriek.

"Drive much?" says the girl riding in *my* car without her driver's license.

I'm still annoyed at her for making me wait. I want to tell her she should be grateful that I always cart her ass around and maybe she should offer to pay for gas once in her life. Instead I huff, "The bird's alive. We're alive."

But Charlie's already moved on. One major difference between us is that she lets stuff go. She lives in the present, inhabiting every moment with gusto. Like a clock's sweeping hand, ticking forward with each new second, Charlie doesn't get hung up. Unlike me, who's always worried about tomorrow and last week and five minutes ago, Charlie doesn't cheat herself out of right now.

She points though her open window at a low-slung, silver sedan and says, "That's Matt Selanof's Probe!"

Familiar custom black racing stripes catch my eye. "Didn't he go off to some fancy flight school in the Lower 48 like the instant he graduated?"

She shrugs. "Maybe he already got his pilot's license."

"Why would he come back?" A big-shot pilot returning to the Kenai Peninsula? That's like an exonerated prisoner intentionally returning to incarceration. Almost as crazy as the idea of SoHi's 1990 Partier of the Year piloting an airborne machine filled with actual human passengers. Who knows, though; stranger things have happened. Just the fact that Matt got out of town for a year seems like a miracle to me. Anyway, he's way beyond our league, so even if he *is* back, it's not like Charlie or I will ever be in a position to ask him why.

I search the crowd for a recognizable face, secretly hoping I'll see Joaquin with his shaggy black hair, slim jeans, and that gray tee, softer than baby moth wings—the way I remember him from the SoHi Spring Fling dance.

It was only one dance—the last of the night. Half of Journey's sappy ballad, "Lights," was already over by the time Joaquin walked me out to the dance floor. I was so relieved that he'd finally asked. I didn't know his name, but I'd been eyeing him all night, watching the way he moved. He was the best guy dancer I'd ever seen. While we were dancing, though, I was so nervous. I kept my eyes focused on his shoulder as Steve Perry crooned about loneliness.

After the song ended Joaquin leaned in close to introduce himself, and his breath tickled the tiny hairs on my neck. His lips were right there next to my cheek. I wanted to kiss him, but instead, I wrote my name on the back of his ticket with my phone number, hoping. He never called, but that was my Junior Year Fairytale Moment. I'm not sure why he was at the SoHi function, since he's a Kenai student, but I've spent more nights than I'd care to admit driving around Kenai aimlessly and still haven't seen him.

Maybe he doesn't go out. I scan again for his signature black ponytail. Relief washes over me when I spot Kenny Clark's mouse-brown head bobbing above the crowd.

"By the Bronco," I say. "Isn't that Ti—I mean, *Kenny*?" Charlie hates when I call him Tiny, even though it's the nickname Kenny's had for as long as he's been taller than everyone else—basically forever.

But the Bug's engine rumbles louder than a demon-possessed lawnmower, so Charlie misses my almost-slip. Her eyes are locked on the teeny, rectangular mirror recessed in the visor. "Crap," she says.

I hold my breath, worried she's discovered a puss-filled zit or sprouted a hairy mole, both certain to wreck my night.

"My bangs have completely fallen!" She whacks my thigh. "Where's that butane curling iron you keep in here?" She smacks me twice more. "Park in front. In front!"

"Bitch!" I shout. "Stop hitting me!" Her bangs do look kinda flat, but I draw the line at assault. I swerve away from the cars, toward the lined spaces at the front of 7-Eleven.

Charlie's freaking out, slapping the air and the seat and me, indiscriminately. "Your curling iron!"

I point to the glove box, but her eyes remain focused on her reflection.

"This," she points to her perfectly ratted perm, winging out on either side of her face like it has since eighth grade, "is what happens when I have to use my mom's crappy mousse." Charlie narrows her eyes at me, "Because a certain *slut* forgot to bring back my hairspray."

I don't mention that she's the one who left her precious Finesse Super Hold at my house. The truth is, I love her tantrums—she only freaks out on you if she really likes you. Plus, Charlie has this power. She can turn the worst profanity into a term of endearment. "Fuck you" becomes "I love you" and "slut" is her version of "sweetie."

Charlie begins rifling around in the back seat.

My eyes track to the glove box where my "emergency" curling iron is stashed, as well as the videotape of *Overboard* that we're supposed to be watching right now. I push away the guilt for lying to my mom.

Luckily, I've seen the film a dozen times and will be armed with movie details when she asks tomorrow. An image of Goldie Hawn bitching out the newslady pops into my mind, and it occurs to me how improbable that scene is. As if this is a profound realization, I say, "A TV crew would never go to a hospital and interview some random amnesia lady."

"Focus!" she says, her hands on either side of my face. "Your friggin' curling iron."

I tap my finger on the glove box knob, which is nubby and black and reminds me of a miniature tire. She twists it open and digs around. *Overboard* falls to the floor, followed by my Margaret Atwood *Selected Poems* and several wadded gas receipts. I lean across the gap between our seats, scoop up the fallen things, and shove them all back in next to the mileage diary I never use. Sorry, Dad.

Charlie pulls out a pack of Big Red and rolls it over the back of her thumb—the same trick she does at school with pencils. "Finders keepers," she sings.

I shake my head. "Sorry, Charlie."

She gives me the stink eye for using the Dreaded Phrase, and the gum stills.

"That's breath deodorant for my swampy-mouthed brother," I say. The pack belongs to Alex, and honestly, I just don't want Charlie to take it.

"Your brother's nasty." She pulls out a single stick, unwraps it, and pops the gum into her mouth. I stifle the urge to defend Alex as Charlie stuffs the gum back into the magic box. She finds the curling iron, slides it inside her bomber jacket, and blows cinnamon breath in my face. "Score me a Diet Coke, will ya?" She leaps out while the Bug is still in motion.

"Get a job, mooch!" I say.

Charlie swings open 7-Eleven's glass door, and the mechanical bell tones twice like "uh-oh."

The Bug's engine stalls as my front tires bump against the curb. I hope I'm not out of gas already—the gauge shows a quarter tank, but it isn't always reliable. In my head Dad starts lecturing about saving money for that amorphous black hole ahead of me: My Future. There's not much light at the end of that tunnel.

Since I was sixteen, I've spent more than twenty hours every week straightening clothes rounders and complimenting middle-aged ladies on their dumpy-butt spandex, but my wages as a Jay Jacobs fashion consultant cover gas, my school clothes, weekend incidentals, and not much else. I'll probably make assistant manager by graduation, but even if I never buy another skirt or soda again, there's no way I can save what college costs.

It is entirely possible that I'll be working as a retail slave in our crap mall for the rest of my days, which is a prospective hell I'd rather not ponder. Because right now it's summer. And I need a life. And it's my money. And I'll spend a little if I want.

When I jerk my keys out of the ignition, I notice a guy leaning against the firewood stacked along 7-Eleven's side wall. His stained jeans, rubber boots, and blood-shot eyes tell me the dude's a cannery rat—probably just got off a twelve-hour shift. At least I'm better off than *him*. He's likely sleeping on the beach or in the woods.

He lights a cigarette as he watches me walk to the door. His hungry eyes both unsettle and fill me. I lift my chin, step up onto the concrete, and swing my hips. You couldn't look away if you wanted to, buddy.

The familiar bell chimes twice as I sashay inside, but this time it sounds like "hel-lo." My nose fills with the delicious mix of hot dogs and gasoline. Food and freedom. I head first to the blue tide charts by the register, pick one up, and flip to today's date. The tubby cashier behind the counter is eyeing me but pretends he's not. Like I'd steal a tide book, you gonad.

Ocean tides are one of the most reliable things in this world. Back when Dad and I used to go out on the boat in Kachemak Bay, times for high and low used to matter because fish care about tides. Mom would sometimes take Alex and me to the beach to watch the tide change. We'd huddle under a blanket as the Cook Inlet rose above the seaweed line and swallowed the dark gray sand. But now the tide makes no difference; I just want to know.

I run my finger down the page. Tonight's high—seventeen feet—is at 10:20. Where will Charlie and I be at 10:20? A million answers pass through my brain like comets, each one brighter than the one before.

Around me, the coolers whir and a chest freezer full of bait herring gasps as I pass by on my way to the fountain machine. I fill two red cups with soda, then cut through the candy and chip aisle, where the packages glow under the fluorescent lights. Oranges and blues, greens and yellows.

I grab Charlie's poser chips, and for myself, a roll of SweeTARTs and my favorite healthy snack, Bit-O-Honey. Practically a granola bar. I open the Bit-O-Honey before I pay, peel a piece from the wax paper, and set it on my tongue. The nutty taffy grows pliable and fills my mouth with sweetness and saliva. I smile at Gonad like I own the place.

Charlie appears from the bathroom, bangs revived, and we hustle over to the register.

"Have a good night, ladies," he says, as he separates the four dollars and sixty-two cents—an hour's worth of fashion consulting—into his till drawer compartments.

Charlie flips him off on our way out, just because she can. I consider flipping him off, too, for acting like I'm a klepto, but my hands are preoccupied with not dropping the chips and candy and two pops that Charlie's not helping me carry.

Outside, the stench of cigarettes and salmon lingers even though the cannery rat's gone. I hand Charlie her Diet Coke and the bag of Fritos. "Don't say I never gave you anything."

"You've given me plenty." She tallies on her fingers. "Pubic lice, crabs, herpes..."

I punch but she dodges my half-hearted fist.

Back in the Bug, we hold our drinks between our legs as I steer us into the lot beside 7-Eleven, weaving through the rows of parked cars. I keep an eye out for Joaquin and hunt for a spot.

Charlie points. "There! There's Kenny!" She sits back and fans herself with her hand. "Straight up fine, that boy."

Kenny's square nose, scrawny neck, and bony elbows don't add up to fine for me, but Charlie's into him. He's one year older than us, though in ninth grade his parents divorced, and he stopped going to class. He missed so much school that the administration held him back. Now he'll graduate next spring with us—class of 1991. Charlie takes it as a sign that they're meant to be together. I can't argue, since I've made my own bargains with destiny, and who knows how those will turn out.

Tiny sees the Bug and waves us over. He's talking to a guy I've never seen—probably a Kenai guy, like Joaquin, but this guy looks older than high school. He fills out his stonewashed 501s, not with a slight boy body, but with a grown man's. He's resting one of his hightops on the chrome wheelwell of his towering blue Bronco. All the Bronco's glass surfaces are mirror tint, and as we drive by, its reflective rear window transforms the Bug into an itty-bitty orange Skittle rolling across the gravel.

One of the few perks of owning a tiny car is ease of parking. Near the end of the row, I squeeze between two trucks and park in the extra space the drivers probably left as a door-ding safety zone.

Charlie takes a long swig of her Diet Coke to make room for rum or whiskey, then starts cuffing her shorts so they show more of her thighs. I get out and check myself in the side mirror, hiking up my jean skirt. My boxy sweater hides the bunched denim at my waist, which is a small price to pay for making my legs appear longer.

Charlie is already speed-walking toward Tiny. I almost trip catching up to her, my toes pinching and my heels smooshing into the gravel with every step.

Tiny yells at us over the music pumping out loud from the Bronco. "Hey, pretties!"

Call him Kenny. Call him Kenny. I say, "Yo, Kenny."

Charlie hip-checks his thigh. "What's shakin', Kenmeister?" She looks up at him through the waterfall of her bangs. So obvious.

But Charlie and her short shorts and her tight red tank may as well be invisible to Kenai Guy, who's staring straight at *me*. His dirty blond hair looks good sticking out under his Miami Dolphins ball cap. "Gonna introduce me, Tiny?" he says. "I go crazy for hot redheads."

"You couldn't handle this," I say with manufactured confidence. I flick my side pony over my shoulder to prove I don't give a flying crap.

He twists the cap around backwards and reaches to open the Bronco's passenger door. A familiar bass—Beastie Boys' "Brass Monkey"—thumps out like an invitation. "Wanna go for a ride?"

3
First Time on the Shitter

Music vibrates against my body. I've seen this Bronco around the peninsula a zillion times and always wondered what it looked like inside. Maybe tonight I'll find out.

Kenai Guy stands like a freaking footman holding the door. I reach into the shadowy cab and slide my hand over the furry blue passenger seat. My skirt rides up as I step onto the running board. I lean as if I'm going to get in, but instead I hop down and shake my head. "I'm not supposed to get into cars with strangers."

He pulls something from his back pocket. Holds out a Bit-O-Honey. *A sign?*

"Serious? You're bribing me with candy?"

"If it works," says Kenai Guy.

"Miladies," says Tiny, swooping an arm as if he is about to introduce the Duke of Kenai, "meet Brett Hale."

"Hey," says Charlie.

Tiny puts his arm around Charlie. "Hale, this exquisite blonde is Charlie...."

My hand flies out, and I nick the Bit-O-Honey from Brett's slack fingers before Tiny can say Taylor.

Tiny shakes his head. "That depraved ginger is Meri Miller."

We stand around bullshitting. Brett gets all technical about how he installed subwoofers and a new multi-disc CD player. He's talking to Tiny, but his eyes keep shifting to me. Tiny pulls a flask from his jacket and pours whatever's inside into Charlie's red cup. She whispers in my ear, "That Brett guy graduated in like '87. I bet he can *buy*."

Brett's cute, clean-cut, and filled out in a way Tiny isn't. Plus, there's this attitude. Like he knows something the rest of us don't. Whatever Brett says, Tiny punctuates with "yeah, dude" or "right on, Hale."

The crowning moment is when Matt Selanof walks by holding a bottle wrapped in brown paper. Matt is tall and tan, with a black crewcut and a muscled body from his years playing hockey. He sees Brett and stops. "Bro!" he yells, and struts over. Matt has never said two words to us before.

Charlie and I give each other The Look.

Matt grins in our direction and takes a swig from his bagged bottle. "Christ, Hale," he says. "That system's boomin'!"

Brett watches my mouth as I chew on my straw.

I can't believe this older guy is interested in me. His attention is intoxicating, as if the girl he sees isn't some small-town, high school girl. Reflected in Brett's unwavering gaze, I become uncommon and fascinating and worth pursuing.

I'm feeling bold, so I ask Matt about flight school.

He turns to Brett. "Who's the jailbait?"

I want to crawl under Brett's giant Bronco.

Brett winks and bumps his shoulder into mine. "This is Meri."

"Well, Merrrri, there's a party out the North Road tonight. Maybe I'll see you guys." Matt turns to leave but kicks a tire before he goes. "Sweet fuckin' ride, bro."

"Sure is," says Brett, staring straight at me. "Ready to blow this taco stand?"

I barely know this guy, but I don't want to be at 7-Eleven all night.

"We're not strangers anymore," he says, as if he can read my thoughts. "You're Meri." He points to my chest, then to his. "I'm Brett."

Where will I be at 10:20? Here is only where things begin.

I unwrap another piece of Bit-O-Honey. "If I go with you," I present it like a challenge, "what about Charlie?" She and I have this pact that we won't split up unless we both agree to it. Boys don't make decisions for us.

I meet her eyes. *Do you want me to stay or go?*

Brett flips his chin toward Kenny. "Tiny'll take her wherever she wants. Right, dude?"

Kenny's face reddens. He slow-motion punches Charlie in the arm, really soft. "Up for that North Road party, Charles?"

Charlie plays it cool. She sips her Diet Coke, tips her head to the side, and does this lip-twisting thing she only does when she really wants something but is trying to make you think she doesn't.

Kenny shoves his hands into his windbreaker pockets.

"Sure," she says finally, as if just deciding. As if she hasn't been creaming her jeans for like ever at the thought of being alone with him. She turns to me. "You good?"

I'm not sure. My future's not predicted in a tide book. I don't know where I'll end up. Where will I be at 10:20? Maybe the North Road party. The candy in my mouth has grown soft; I take my sweet time chewing. "Think the Bug will be alright if I leave her here?" I ask Charlie.

"It'll be fine, babe," answers Brett.

He helps me up into his Bronco where those fuzzy blue seat covers make me feel as if I'm sitting on Cookie Monster's lap. A chain dangles from the rearview mirror, and on it hangs a silver Metallica bottle opener. It spins as we tear out of 7-Eleven.

Brett hits the Dairy Queen drive-thru first. "Want anything?"

"The food here's gross." That's the biggest lie, but I'm too nervous to eat. I'm alone in this Bronco with a guy I don't really know, fretting about the Bug—Dad would kill me if something happened to the first car he bought as a married man—and worrying Mom'll find out I'm not at Charlie's.

Part of me wishes we'd stayed together. I wonder if she and Kenny are on their way to the party or parked making out somewhere. Maybe they went on a walk on the beach or decided to go to the carnival.

Big yellow semitrucks rolled into town Wednesday night, and workers spent Thursday in the Peninsula Mall parking lot piecing together the Tilt-a-Whirl, the Hurricane, and the Zipper. That one I'll never ride because the cages spin so fast the g-forces can toss you right out, like what happened to this kid in Canada who got thrown and skewered by a flagpole. Charlie calls it the Shitter because she says the one time she rode, a kid crapped his pants. How do you see a kid crap his pants? "I smelled it," she said.

"What do we do now?" asks Brett, as if the DQ drive-thru counts as having just done something.

"Carnival?"

Brett pulls the Dilly Bar out of his mouth. "The carnival? You wanna hook up with a carny or something?"

I laugh. "Rides make me horny." I don't know why I said that.

He smiles and steers the Bronco toward Soldotna. The stereo is blasting, and we scream the words to "Sweet Child O' Mine" loud enough to drown out Axl Rose. We whiz past squat cars below us on K-Beach Road.

I am big and invincible. I can do anything.

When we get to town, everything seems smaller through the Bronco's window, unreal even. Maybe this is how Miss Soldotna feels waving from her Progress Days parade float at the kids scurrying for candy below her. Like she's not one of them anymore.

We pass the fake Swiss chalet that houses Moose Is Loose Bakery, where Mom used to work. Stupid names are everywhere here. Pizza Pete's. Bear Cache Jewelry. Pay & Save. These local businesses are quaint at best. Mostly embarrassing. I'm glad chain retailers have begun to replace them. If I ever get out of here, at least I'll know the stores where other people shop.

Half the town has come out for this rinky-dink carnival. The rides are ancient and the games—the kind where you throw balls into glass bottles or darts at balloons—are probably rigged.

Brett parks away from the crowd, but the ticket booth is in the center of everything, so we have to push through old people and moms in sweatpants dragging crying kids. Bedtime should've been hours ago, but it's June and daylight lasts forever this close to summer solstice. Without night, we all turn superhuman. Sleep is for those sorry mortals who live near the equator.

Brightly colored cages spin on a rotating track high above the parking lot. Kids scream from inside. The place smells like frying donuts and cigarettes. A scowling lady with wiry chin hair stares vacantly out at us when we get to the ticket booth window. She says each ride takes at least two tickets, so Brett buys us the pack of twenty. He grabs my hand, and I wonder if this counts as our first date.

He pulls me past the games toward the rides. "How about we start with the Zipper?"

I shake my head. "I won't ride that one."

"Sure you will."

I shake my head again.

"What? You scared?" He drapes his arm over my shoulder. His skin is surprisingly cold against my neck. "Nothing to fear. You're with Brett. Trust me."

I want to believe him. Ten minutes ago I was invincible.

The line for the Zipper is small, and at the end are two boys who look about thirteen. One is skinny with a black ball cap. The other is big and has on a hockey jersey. As we walk up, Skinny shoves something at Hockey Kid, who tries to grab it, misses, and a white thing falls to the asphalt. They both freeze and look up at Brett. They must think he's an adult.

Brett bends to swipe what has fallen. "Smokes? You sneaky little pricks. I'm gonna have to confiscate these. Better find your parents...."

The boys take off running. Brett pockets the cigarettes.

"Way to go, Dad," I say. "Planning to spank them next?"

"I only spank little girls," he says.

I arch my back and present my backside. He swats at me, but I pull away before he can hit me. The line moves forward. Kids shriek overhead as the ride lurches. My mouth goes dry. "I'm thirsty. How about you ride. I'll get a drink."

"After."

"I don't want to do this." I didn't mean to say it, but it just came out.

"You have to, Meri." He points to the sign at the entry. *No single riders.*

I can do this. Easy peasy.

In front of us, two girls step up into their green cage. Both are giggling, and one has a lump stuffed inside her coat, but the carny manning the ride doesn't notice or doesn't care. "Keep your arms and legs inside." He locks them in.

An empty red cage swings by, and a purple one clicks into place in front of me. Why, even when there's a line, are a few of the cages left empty? Maybe if you keep people waiting, they want to ride more. I'd happily keep waiting, but Brett pulls me behind him onto the narrow bench seat. He lays his hand on my bouncing knee to still it.

The carny closes the rickety mesh door. My stomach hurts, and my heart is speeding. I start to pray in my head. Please, God, if you just get me off here quick, before I puke or do something dumb, I will really try to be good. I straighten my legs and press my back against the cage, scooting my skirt down over my knees. We rise up slow. Easy peasy. Easy peasy. Easy peasy.

The speed increases until we tilt and our shoulders bump together. The cage flips around. My feet push hard against the floor, trying to right gravity. I let out a squeal as we spin faster.

Brett's smiling next to me. "You look amazing when you're terrified!"

My heart's pumping, but from excitement now, not terror. We zoom forward and down as our cage takes the first real plummet. My side pony blows by my ear. I hunch forward, gripping tight to the crossbar on my lap.

The ground flies at my face, but before the cage slams down, we swing around and back up. Faster. Faster. My hand slips, bangs against Brett's wrist. His fingers curve over mine, anchoring us to the bar. The red stone in his class ring makes me think of a buoy marking something important below. I push my shoulders back and lift my face to the wind.

Everybody's screaming. The girls in the cage above us—the green one—are hollering, "Omigod! Omigod!" I can't tell if they like it or not.

Another whip around, but this time the timing is different. I lose my center. Sky is everywhere and nowhere. I try to focus on the metal floor, the pale pink gum stuck in the corner next to my shoe, but sour spit invades my mouth. I've been seasick before. I know what comes next. I don't want Brett to see me like this. I close my eyes as the tide inside me rises.

"Stop the ride! Serious! Please." The girls above us are shouting what I'm thinking. "Stop the ride. Now!"

A howl—an otherworldly animal noise—ascends over the clatter. The sound terrifies even more than the shifting gravity. The wailing comes again, but shorter this time, a series of panicked staccato screams, punctuated by a final, choked yowl.

It hits my neck in a burst, a tiny wave crashing, a single squeeze of ketchup—warm and thick and dripping down my back. Rancid. I have to swallow hard to keep from gagging and catch a whiff of a salty, almost meaty smell. Like dog food?

"What the fuck?" Brett is next to me, nostrils flaring and eyes pinched.

I think the ride is slowing, but it's hard to tell. Speed and time have become as difficult to guess as the tide when you're in the middle of the ocean. Is it 10:20?

"Sparkle! Baby, are you okay?" one of the girls asks her friend, but then I hear whining and a tiny bark. The lump in the girl's coat.

Brett presses his face against the top of our cage. Or maybe it's the side. "You little skanks!" he yells out. But to me he says, "Don't worry, babe. I got an extra shirt in the Bronco."

I hold onto his arm as we sway. The Zipper creaks, and finally— click!—the cage opens. God, is this the best you could do? A metallic breeze chills the dampness on my neck and cheeks. I shiver.

Brett rubs my leg, and the pressure of his warm palm reminds me of my mom—how she used to massage cramps out of my calves in the middle of the night—and when he stands, I want to pull him back into the empty space next to me, but I don't have to because he turns and reaches for me.

"Let's go," he says, and I grab his hand.

You'd think getting drenched in dog barf would make for a terrible first date, but Brett's sweet about it. He leads me back to the Bronco, digs around in the backseat until he finds his ratty old Kenai High football sweatshirt, then waits like my personal guard outside the door while I change.

Concealed behind the Bronco's tinted windows, I tug his shirt over my head and inhale a delicious combo—wood smoke, the mint of icy-hot, and a little bit of engine oil. Brett Smell.

The Bug is all alone when we pull into the lot next to 7-Eleven, but she's totally fine. Brett leans across to hug me, not caring that there's crusty barf in my hair.

"Thanks," I say, my cheek against his.

Then, so fast I barely have a chance to pucker, the hug shifts and his lips find mine.

I want to linger in the moment, fully inhabit my body and revel in his lips pressing warmth against mine. But this holy temple reeks to high heaven. I can't let this be our first kiss.

I pull away, self-conscious. "I have to get back to Charlie's." I fumble clumsily with the Bronco door until it springs open. Cool air rushes in, helping to dilute the puke stench.

He grabs my wrist. "No, you don't."

"I do." I shake free and jump down. "I stink."

"*This* stinks." He reaches toward me again. "Just get back in."

"Hold on." I flash my best smile, run over to the Bug, scribble my name and phone number on a crumpled receipt, and race back.

The stereo is so loud when I return that the Bronco visibly throbs. I lean through the open passenger door, my elbows trembling against the seat each time the bass booms a mini earthquake. Brett is tapping his thumb on the steering wheel to the beat of "She's Crafty."

"I'm glad I went for the ride," I shout up at him. I almost add, *besides the puke part*, but don't.

He turns the volume down a notch.

"Thanks for the sweatshirt." I hand him my number, as if in exchange. "Call me?"

He takes the paper. "You're something else, you know?"

Is that good? I want to ask what he means but don't want to risk looking stupid, so instead, I smirk and slam the door. Before I've even walked back to the Bug, the Bronco's tires spit gravel, and Brett is roaring away.

Charlie isn't back by the time I show up at her house, but Mrs. Taylor is passed out in front of the television, an empty bottle of Chardonnay on the coffee table. I tiptoe up the stairs with my Jansport, take a quick shower, and pull a sleeping bag off the top shelf in the hall closet.

My body is exhausted, but my mind is still buzzing. Over and over I replay the night. He said I was hot. He said I looked amazing. He held my hand. He gave me his shirt. He kissed me. He said I was something else. Rewind. Until finally I fall asleep on Charlie's floor, cuddled up in Brett's sweatshirt.

6/16/90

Brett didn't call today. It's only been one day, but I bet he's not going to call me. Ever.

6/17/90

No call. During church I wrote Brett a stupid poem but threw it away. This afternoon I had a long talk with Ben about boys and how they suck. Ben raised his little ears and barked once, but I think it was because he heard Mama Kitty meowing at the door. Dad's gone, so I brought Mama Kitty and her kittens in the house. There's one spunky kitten I've named Calico Cali that I really want to keep.

6/18/90

No call. Alex broke my Madonna mix tape, which really pissed me off because I had to borrow Charlie's Like a Virgin to make that mix. Apparently I can't own anything with the word "virgin" in the title, even though I'm supposed to be one until I'm married. Had to go pick Dad up at the airport. He's got the flu, so they sent him home.

6/19/90

Carnival Ride

Clouds drift across the moon's blank face
The Earth revolves under my feet
Stuck upside down to the surface of this world
Tumbling in a circle through space

4
Miracle Beyond Loaves and Fishes

Haven't heard from Brett since the Barfing Incident. He's probably sitting around right now with his friends laughing it up, calling me Dog Barf Girl and reliving all the gory details. Pretty soon Tiny and Matt and Charlie and the whole town—even Joaquin—will be fake coughing "DB Girl" every time I come around.

I *knew* I'd regret getting into that stupid Bronco. It's hard to distinguish in any given moment between a gut instinct that should be heeded and a fear that should be conquered. When in doubt, I opt for conquer. Now I have to live with the consequences.

Charlie hasn't called, either, which is weird because we've either hung out or talked on the phone pretty much every day since school let out. Her being distant only further convinces me that my new nickname is spreading like wildfire. My entire senior year will be ruined. I'll be friendless, and my final yearbook will be filled with notes like, "Hey DB, have a great life. Stay away from dogs and carnivals. Ha ha!"

There's a slim possibility that Charlie's hanging out with Tiny—*Kenny*—and is too distracted to call. Saturday morning we both slept late, and I had to be home before noon so I could spend the rest of the day with my mom at a horrible craft bazaar. We barely got to talk, but I told Charlie about getting barfed on.

"My mouth is all swollen," she said. She spent most of Friday night making out with Kenny. "But he has the softest lips."

"Brett tried to kiss me, too," I said. "I wanted to kiss him back, but the puke stink stressed me out."

She said boys were oblivious to stuff like that. "Anyhow," she said, "they have super jacked up senses of smell. Like completely odor-impaired. That's why they can wear deck shoes all day with bare feet and not die when they take them off."

Charlie seemed to think the whole barfing incident was no big deal. "You should've totally sucked his face."

Barf be damned! Charlie's right. In retrospect, I should have seized the moment and kissed Brett until my lips were sore. Maybe fate will deliver another chance.

"Don't sit around waiting on him," Charlie advised me. "Boys are dumb. Call him, if you like him."

Regret, you cruel mistress. I won't pull away next time.

I intended to call Brett. Truly. I could pave the entire Cassiar Highway with my lofty intentions, but Sunday I had church, then potluck, then evening service, where Pastor Dan's message took forever—why is the loaves and fishes miracle in all four freaking gospels? The story's not that complex. Solving my problems is way harder than figuring out how to share a handful of bread and fish with a bunch of Jesus fans who could simply go get food somewhere else.

Plus, Jesus had like a dozen guys working for him. I've only got Charlie, and regardless of what she said, I am freaking out about being known as Dog Barf Girl for the rest of my life. I've analyzed the Barfing Incident and that night's details about five hundred times, focusing especially on the stupid things I said or did. Why did I call him Dad? Why did I say rides make me horny?

I can't call him. He probably wants nothing to do with me, and anyway, there's no Brett Hale listed in the phone book, so I dial Charlie's number and wait through eight rings. I'm ready to hang up and am composing a lecture in my mind about the benefits of an answering machine when her mom finally picks up.

"Sorry, Meri," she says, explaining their trip to the ER Sunday on account of Charlie's sore and swollen neck. "The doctor said it was her glands. He thinks it's mononucleosis. Good Lord, she's been sleeping so much, I'm betting that's it, but test results won't be back for a couple days. She's in bed right now."

Mono? Maybe she just has the flu like Dad. I bet she got sick from playing tonsil hockey with Kenny. "When can she go out in public again?"

"I'll let her know you called," Mrs. Taylor says.

God, I need a miracle.

I've reread old notes from Charlie, written two poems, played with the dog, petted the cat, watered Mom's garden, journaled about my boring life, and watched *Little House on the Prairie* reruns, but nothing helps my interminable days alone slide by any faster. I spent one entire afternoon in the yard practicing tricks—back walkovers, handsprings, round offs, and aerials—even though there's no point anymore. SoHi's gymnastics program lasted about as long as it took for the school board's kids to outgrow their Mary Lou Retton T-shirts.

Finally, I call Pam and beg her to give me more shifts at the mall. She's usually the coolest boss ever but says there aren't enough customers to justify my extra hours. According to Pam, "Nobody travels to Alaska in the summer to shop for clothes, and anyway, it's store policy to schedule managers and assistant managers first." I remind her that technically I'm a manager in training, so she agrees to add an evening shift and a glorious Shipment Day. I love when those boxes arrive and we unwrap the newest styles—floral pants, brocade vests, and acid-washed jean skirts—like messages from the outside world. These are the clothes I imagine everyone in the Lower 48 already wearing.

Unlike Charlie, Dad's recovery has been miraculous. He's already barking orders and assigning tasks. After I clean my room, per his directive, I decide to wash the Bug without waiting for him to nag me. He's only been home a few days, and I feel like doing something nice.

I drag the hose into the driveway and fill the bucket until bubbles spill over the edge. The big garage door gapes open, and inside, Dad is wedging an aluminum sheet into a vice. Most of his two weeks home from the North Slope he spends alone out in the garage doing his projects.

"Meri!" he barks.

Maybe he'll call me industrious for taking the initiative to wash my car. I scrub *industriously* over the chrome door handle. Nah, he wouldn't use that word. Maybe hardworking . . . or *responsible*. He loves that one.

"What?" I wipe invisible sweat from my forehead, anticipating his praise.

"Don't look in here while I'm welding!" With a gloved hand, Dad flips down his Darth Vader helmet, and his gray eyes and stubbly chin disappear behind the mask.

I drop the hose, plunge my hand into the bucket and flip him off. "Luuuuke, I am your father," I say as white sparks pop from his welding rod, crackle through the air, and vanish into the cement floor. The torch blackens the metal and melts the feed wire as he traces along the line where two aluminum sheets abut. He is shaping these metal scraps into some new useful thing—a vision hidden from me behind the dark window of his mask.

I can't look away.

When the bits of light disappear and he lifts the mask, his brows push together and he locks me in his gaze. Dad's eyes are storm clouds, ready to shoot lightning. "What did I just tell you? You want a spark to burn your eye out?"

I shrug and start again at the muddy orange passenger door.

He lays down the torch, his helmet, and his gloves on the workbench and closes the distance between us. "Meri, how many times have I told you?" He slides his clean hand along the Bug's curved rooftop, as if smoothing an animal's fur, and shoves a now grime-coated palm in my face.

"I haven't washed there yet," I say.

He grabs the sponge out of my hand, dunks it in the bucket, and as he draws soapy circles on the roof, gray water drips down over my clean windows. "See where that dirt goes? Wash the roof first and you won't have to wash the sides again."

He plops the sponge back into the pail and suds splash my clean fender. "Think, Meri." He taps his temple.

I imagine grabbing the sponge and throwing it at his retreating back. Or maybe his head, since then I would be starting at the top. I could leave the roof dirty if I wanted. I could burn my own eyes out. My car. My eyes.

Mom says he doesn't mean to pick on me. That he's trying to teach me stuff. She says it's how he shows he loves me. I'd rather he just tell me.

I break down and dial Charlie's number on Sunday after church.

"This is a matter of life or death."

"She's lost her voice, Meri." Mrs. T. makes a sipping sound. "Don't keep calling."

"Can you at least hold the phone up to her ear and..." *Click.*

To think I once called Mrs. Taylor the Cool Mom.

My own mom is far from cool, but she doesn't shut me down like that. At least not when I'm clearly in distress.

After Mrs. Taylor hangs up on me, Mom offers to play Scrabble because as a word lover—a *logophile*—I dominate that game. She's already tried cheering me up by making meatloaf, my favorite dinner when I was like ten. "You've been acting like a lost puppy all week," says Mom, finally exasperated. "Why don't you call Nadine Jackson's girl—Sharman—from church? I know she was in youth group with you. Doesn't she go to your school?"

Sharman from church has hated me since our youth group leader cast me as Mary in the Christmas play back in sixth grade—just because of my stupid name—and besides, my funk is about more than just Charlie's absence. Mom doesn't know about Brett or the DB Girl thing. She believed me when I described my fabricated Friday night watching *Overboard* with Charlie, and more than anything, her blind faith makes me want to come clean. Unloading everything would probably feel good. Maybe I should tell her the truth.

No. She'd freak.

The subject of boys—especially "fornicating" with boys—is on the list of topics I can't broach with Mom. She goes nuts with her judgey lectures and scare tactics and general weird-acting. She still holds her hands over my eyes during movie make-out scenes. I swear she found me and Alex in a cabbage patch. That would explain Mom's attitudes about sex as well as Alex's perpetual sauerkraut breath.

My mom's mantra: "Kissing should be saved for that special someone." I've never seen her kiss Dad, but apparently there are a lot of "special someones" on the pages of the romance novels she reads by the truckload, because all the covers feature half-naked people sucking face.

The only other person in the entire world I would consider dumping my problems on right now, aside from Charlie, is Grandma Buckley. But Mom and Dad have a strict rule about calling long distance. Don't do it.

I dial my grandma's Idaho number anyway. After a few rings the machine kicks on. "You know what to do," says recorded Grandma. I don't leave a message, but hearing her voice makes me feel a little better.

Alex is watching boring Sunday afternoon TV. Since I have nothing else to do, I flop down on the couch next to him. Dad's big recliner is empty, but nobody ever sits in it except Dad, even when he's on the Slope.

"Hey, loser," he says. "Why you so mopey these days?"

For a nanosecond, I consider answering him honestly. But Alex and I aren't as close anymore as we used to be. We spent tons of time together when we were younger—mainly because we didn't live within walking distance of anyone else. We'd sit for hours when we weren't fighting, playing Legos on the carpeted stairs to our basement. Alex was a laid-back little kid who could build ridiculous towers out of the interlocking blocks. My plastic-wrap windows were the coup de grâce.

All Alex cares about now is playing basketball at the rec center, eating bologna sandwiches, and working on his stupid snowmachine with his best friend, Ryan. I mean, sure, I have my own stuff, too—dance team, work, National Honor Society—but right now summer is a big fat snooze fest for both of us.

Instead of giving an answer, I ask, "How about you drag your lazy butt off this couch and hike up to Fuller Lakes with your favorite sister?" Fuller Lakes is my number-one hike of all time, and though I'd never admit it, I miss hanging out with my brother.

Alex clicks off the TV. I can't tell if he wants to spend time with me or is just sick of watching *The Price is Right.*

Hiking puts everything in perspective. It's slow, so you kind of settle into your body—into the repetition of stepping—and you have no choice but to notice the details around you.

Shades of violet and cobalt bloom along the trail. Alex sets the pace faster than I'd like. His legs have long ago outgrown mine. He's barely breaking a sweat as I scramble up the dirt trail behind him.

Soon the trees recede and the landscape opens. Fireweed, lupine, and geraniums mix their sugary-sweet smells with the wet-dog-and-dryer-sheet odor of bear grass around the lower lake.

"Smells like your nasty spandex." He whacks a stand of extra stinky grass with his walking stick.

"More like your mouth."

Higher up, blueberries speckle the mossy ground. They aren't quite ripe, but we hunt for handfuls and eat them anyway. Until we spot a bear on the next ridge over. He's a brown blob from this distance and is as focused on his berries as we are on ours. But I have no interest in chancing a meet up with my omnivorous friend. If we can see him, he can see us.

"Let's head," I say, pointing across the way.

Alex squints. "Really? Afraid of a widdo ol' bear?"

I kick dirt at him and dash off, making tracks back down to where spiky green brush and leafy alders shroud the trail.

Instead of running after me, Alex meanders behind, as if in no hurry. He catches up when I stop for a water break at a spot where a stream is barely visible through the trees. The trail is quiet, save for the sound of rippling water over stones—forest music.

Alex tips his head back, his Nalgene bottle in hand. He is mid-gulp when a deep, growling grunt mingles with the water sounds.

Something rustles in the bushes.

"Shit!" Alex whispers. He caps his bottle and takes off down the trail. I race after him, my blood booming harder in my ears than Brett's bass. Even my hands throb.

Halfway down we have to stop and catch our breath. We are bent over and huffing, but the trail behind us is clear. No bears or people or anything. My giggle starts small but builds quickly to hysterical laughter, like a spark in dry leaves, until we are both consumed by it.

"You're such a wimp," he says, grinning like a goofball.

"Why don't you check your pants," I say, hands on my hips. "Pretty sure you shat yourself up there."

The rest of the way down the mountain, Alex scream-sings "no bears here!" to the tune of "Where Is Thumbkin."

The hike has taken us several hours, so I have to speed to get us home in time to shower before evening church. Alex doesn't bother with a shower.

Right before we leave, the phone brings a miracle beyond limit-less loaves and fishes. I run to answer the ring and hear Brett's voice asking for me.

"This is Meri," I say into the receiver.

Dad gives me his stern look. "Make it short," he says.

I yank the antenna up on the portable phone, run into the bath-room, and lock the door.

"Who's this?" My palm is sweaty against the receiver. Breathe.

"Remember me?" he pauses. "I'm the guy who loaned you a sweatshirt and saved you from a horny carny."

"Oh right." I try to sound as if I haven't been waiting around all moony for him to call. "Guess that makes me the girl who got barfed on by a dog."

"Couldn't find your number," he says. "Had to get it from Tiny."

I'm so excited and relieved—he called me! I'm not DB Girl—that I have trouble being mad, even though he deserves it. He should apologize. Or at least work to get back into my good graces. "No biggie," I say. "I've been super busy, anyway."

He clears his throat. "Me too."

I switch the phone to the other ear. "Soooooo. I bet you're calling to get your shirt back."

"You keep it," he says. "Looked better on you than it did on me."

He's giving me his shirt! I make my voice flat. "Thanks."

"So hey," he says, "I'm dipnetting down at the mouth of the Kenai next Saturday. Wanna come?"

Fishing. Gah! I've done enough to last my lifetime but make myself say, "That sounds awesome."

The truth is I've never actually been dipnetting. I've only ever fished for salmon using a pole from the bank or riverboat. Dad says dragging spawning sockeye out of the water with a giant net isn't "sporting." He also thinks it's dangerous. He says every year people get killed. Their waders fill up with water, and they get sucked under by the current. Plus, he doesn't like "combat fishing," which is what he calls it when people are lined up elbow-to-elbow along the beach.

"So I'll pick you up Saturday around four?"

I'm not in the mood to deal with my parents on this. "I'll just meet you at 7-Eleven."

6/24/90

He called! I could barely focus during church. I wish I could get Charlie's advice about what to wear dipnetting. I have to look good but still rugged-like and not as if I'm trying too hard. Dad flew back this afternoon to finish his shift, so at least I can use the big mirror in my parents' room to choose my outfit.

6/25/90

Out of the blue today, Mom said I should be a teacher. I said I wanted to be a writer, and she was like, you should at least get a teaching degree so you have something to fall back on. I said imagine our education system if all the teachers were just falling back. Either you should really want to spend your life helping kids learn something or you should do something else.

6/26/90

Dad turned forty-six today. We'll celebrate when he gets home on Thursday. Last year I got him a cordless drill because he'd been complaining about the hassle of extension cords. He held that drill in his hands for a long time, inspecting it. He put on his glasses and read through the pamphlet twice. He wanted to know every single detail about that dumb drill and spent the whole weekend alone out in the garage testing it out. This year I bought him a flashlight.

June 27, 1990

Dear Grandma,

When are you flying up to visit? Mom is driving me
crazy. You know how she can be. She treats me like I'm
still twelve. Even Alex has more freedom than me, I'm serious. If I can vote and go to prison, I'm old enough to stay
out past eleven, right? I'm sure you let HER experience
life when she was my age. Whenever I bring that up she
says it was a different time. I don't know what she thinks
I'm going to do. Speaking of boys, I'm in desperate need of
your confidential advice. Can I come stay with you a few
weeks before school starts? Pleeeeeease? We could play
cribbage and listen to Patsy Cline and stay up all night
reading and drinking unsweetened iced tea. Maybe you
could take me to the University of Idaho campus since
you live so close. I'd love to go to college near you. If I
go, I mean. I'd be the first in our family! Pretty cool, huh?
Maybe I'll be a famous writer someday. Mom wants me
to do at least a year at Peninsula Community College, but
I'd rather not be in this town a second longer than I have
to. Save me G-ma!

Love you,

Merideth

5
Dipnetting Isn't a Spectator Sport

I tell Mom I'm going dipnetting with a group of kids from church.

"What kids?" she asks.

"Just like, um, Sharman...," after all, she was Mom's idea, "... and some other people—it's not a formal youth group thing. Just whoever can make it." This is only a half-lie. The half-truth part is that Brett's mom actually does go to our church, so he's *almost* a kid from church, even though she's never brought Brett with her and I didn't even know she had a son.

"*Please*, Mom." I make praying hands. "Charlie's still sick, and I need to get out!"

She sighs. "Just don't tell your dad. He worries about you. I know you think he doesn't care, but he does."

Dad decides at the last minute to take Alex fishing in Seward, so on Saturday they all get up at the butt crack of dawn, pack up the boat, and leave me in blessed solitude. I stay in bed until noon, reading and doing that other thing you can only do alone. Before I hop in the shower, I call Brett.

"Change of plans," I say. "Pick me up at home?" Might as well save gas money.

Brett parks the Bronco down at the beach, near the mouth of the Kenai River. Gray-and-white seagulls circle above us as he grabs the gear out of the back.

I shimmy into the hip waders Mom loaned me. They still smell fishy. These are the same old mossy green ones she wore when she used to take me and Alex down to the river. We'd stay out past midnight fishing for reds off the bank. Back when Dad worked on the Slope four weeks on, two weeks off. She was like a single mom then. Sometimes she'd take a few shifts at the bakery, but mostly she hung out with Alex and me.

She taught us how to cast the pole with a quick flick and then draw the tip along with the current, all while we held a finger gently on the line until we felt a nibble and pulled quick to set the hook. Eyes closed, I could tell the difference between the bump of a salmon and the drag of weeds beneath the water—just by the feel of that line.

"You actually gonna fish?" Brett wrinkles his nose as if the thought smells bad.

"Why wouldn't I?" Memories plunge me knee deep into rushing water, pole arcing above, me heaving with all my strength against a fighting salmon.

He shrugs and heads down a short, sandy trail to the beach. Tall grass grows in clumps on either side. I grab a wide green blade, pull the grass tight between my thumbs like Grandma Buckley taught me, and blow. The call, like a duck being strangled, whistles out my hands.

Brett whips around, pushing his brows together and narrowing his eyes at me the same way my dad does when he's irritated. I throw the spent grass and stomp it into the path.

The smell of rotting fish hits my nose as we wind around driftwood toward the water. Tiny and Matt are at the beach already setting up. I should have known. Matt's wearing his old SoHi hockey jersey, which is kind of pathetic. He grabs a beer out of the Styrofoam cooler and chucks it at us. "Think fast, Hale!"

Brett catches it, pops the top, and barely waits for the foam to stop flowing before he swills down half the can.

Tiny asks about Charlie. "Do you know if she's getting better?"

I ignore him. Charlie's still sick, and I don't feel like talking to Tiny about her. They aren't even a couple. She's not his business.

"You here to see how real men do it?" Matt asks. Though he seems to be asking this of my boobs.

"Real men? Where?" I look side to side then straight at his crotch and pretend my x-ray vision is revealing something very disappointingly teeny.

"You're lookin' at a real man, baby." He grabs himself. "Real big, that is."

To think, last year I would have given a kidney for a chance to hang with Matt Selanof.

"You can tell a real man," says Brett, "by the size of his net." He snaps the circle of aluminum to its ten-foot handle. "Witness my bigness." He holds the protracted net out at an angle from his pelvis, thrusts against the handle, and sends the net arcing into the air. Sunlight winks off the handle as it wobbles mid-flight and lands in the sand near my feet.

Brett downs the rest of the beer and crushes the can between his palms. "Let's do this."

The guys whoop and make bets about who's going to haul in the most fish. A thrill of excitement ripples through my body. This is the bond of predators—the way ancient hunters must have rallied to ambush a herd. My blood pulses with the desire to conquer.

I didn't bring my own net—we don't own a long-handled one—but I wade out into the water anyway. The sun heats my face, and the waves lap against my rubber boots. I want to go out farther, but already I'm starting to shiver. This is where the Kenai River and the ocean inlet converge, and both are very cold. "Isn't there some kind of limit?" I ask, knowing there is.

Brett shakes his head. "Fucking Fish and Game officers never check."

"I heard they handed out some pretty fat tickets last year," says Tiny, as if I need him to validate what I say.

"Shit, Tiny," Matt says. "Let's at least have her clip the tails. I'm not filleting these sons of bitches until I get home, and my dad'll kill me if Fish and Game slaps a ticket on my ass."

Technically, it's illegal to transport unmarked whole salmon because people could sell them—dipnetting is for personal use only.

But it's not my problem Matt doesn't want to clean his fish at the beach. I didn't come here to slice the corners off fish tails. The air here is fresh and alive, I'm already knee deep, and a salmon just nudged against my boot.

Brett sloshes over and puts his arm around me.

I shake my head, trying to keep my teeth from chattering as the sea smells assuage the rotting fish-carcass stench that dominates the beach.

"Please, babe?"

"I'm not your tail clipper," I say.

"How about we take turns?" He points up near the cooler to a leather sheath with an ivory handle sticking out. "You start, then we trade places."

I want to stay in the water, try my hand with Brett's net, but I sigh. "Fine."

"Just cut the points off the tails," says Matt like he's the authority. His dad is a bigtime commercial fisherman who I've heard pays his deckhands in cocaine. "Square 'em up, so they won't think we're trying to sell to the canneries."

"I doubt those fuckers will get off their asses long enough to pay a visit," says Brett. "My mom's new husband works for Fish and Game. He's the goddamn laziest piece of shit I've ever met."

Matt's already in up to his chest and leaning so that his net extends out farther than Tiny's or Brett's. I imagine his waders filling and dragging him under.

I kick the surf as if it's Matt's head. This is so bogus. Brett never said anything about bringing his boy posse. Asshole.

Tiny yells over at me as I slowly make my way out of the water. "Need help?"

I shake my head and tromp up the beach. "I got this."

Matt's the first to drag his net—tangled around four flopping salmon—up the beach. He leaves a swerving trail in the sand on his way to the cooler, where he bonks each salmon hard in the head with the fish whacker and lobs them into a pile near where I stand holding the knife.

I try slicing through the tails, but the knife is dull and the fish are slippery and this is bullshit. I manage to mangle the tails of Matt's fish just as Brett starts backing toward me. He dumps his net at my feet, and Kenny appears beside him with more salmon to add to the pile.

I'm cutting as fast as I can. My hands are numb with cold. They're acting like I'm their wife or mother, here to prepare the dinner instead of bringing it in.

"When's my turn?" I ask as Brett dumps another three fish at my feet. I almost slice my finger.

"Soon," he says.

Screw him. "I need a potty break." Brett doesn't get to give me permission to fish. I drop the knife so the blade hits Brett's boot and bounces onto the sand.

"What the hell? You trying to ruin my waders?" Brett yells.

"It slipped." The feel of my hand letting go of the grip and sending the knife zinging down toward Brett's boot is satisfying, but I need to take a walk before I really explode.

"I told you," says Matt. "Fucking *women*."

Seagulls scream as I make my way along the beach, away from Brett and the guys wading farther out past where I'm comfortable watching. Who cares. They're assholes anyway. Maybe they'll drown. I hate to admit Dad was right about something; I'm glad he never took us stupid dipnetting. Probably the only thing in the whole universe we can agree on.

A breeze blows salty against my cheek, and waves crash against the shore. I break into an awkward jog. Gravity feels stronger because of my heavy hip boots, but still I manage to gain distance.

Dipnetters line a narrow spit of sand extending like a tongue into the deeper water. They stand elbow-to-elbow with nets protracted. Below them, oblivious salmon hurl their bodies up the river. Years ago, these same fish swam out through the Kenai River's mouth, along the arm of the Cook Inlet, to leave and explore the vast mysteries of the Pacific Ocean. Sad that now the poor suckers might not make it back.

Two kids near me are pulling a blue plastic snow sled filled with sockeye up the beach toward makeshift tents where women sit around fires, ready to clean and gut. They cut me off, and I nearly trip over their sled and fall into a blond boy in a jean jacket who is kneeling on bleached driftwood, mechanically slicing through a pile of silvery fish. His fingers and the knife blade are bloody. He slides only the red filets into a white bucket. Everything else—the head, back, belly, tail—he flings onto the beach.

Hundreds of discarded salmon bodies litter the wet sand as if the ocean spit them out or the sky rained them down. I watch the gulls pick at the carcasses. The birds posture and fight for no reason—there's more than enough. So much usable meat left behind by people. Nobody takes the time to fully clean their fish because the river is teeming with more. I kick at one with my boot, and she wiggles against my toe. A few eggs still cling inside her.

Beyond the gray beach, the sea churns as if the inlet water is in a giant bowl being sloshed around. Whitecaps ripple its surface, and fishing boats on their way into harbor appear and disappear against green-gray waves.

Distant blue mountains tower around us like a great wall, holding us in. The biggest, Mount Redoubt, dominates the western horizon. A plume rises above her summit—a reminder. Six months ago I was in Ms. Tapia's fifth period Spanish listening to Charlie babble on about her lame mom-and-daughter Christmas break ski trip when out the window the sky turned from gray to brown to black. The parking lot lights blipped on, and we all pressed our noses against the glass, expecting the Four Horsemen of the Apocalypse to come riding out of the murky heavens.

Turns out Redoubt had erupted again, but unlike the barely noticed December eruptions, this time a giant ash cloud had blown over the peninsula and was blotting out the sun. January 8, 1990. The world went dark, and gray powder covered all the snow, trees, fields, houses—everything. They cancelled school for three days, and we had to wear masks to keep from breathing ash dust. But we were fine. Better than fine. Once you've lived through the end of the world, you think you can live through anything. You think God left you on this planet for a reason.

Across the inlet, the sun is following the jagged mountain peaks from left to right, the summer path that eventually makes a circle around the sky. Though I know it won't fully set, the sun lights the horizon on fire as it dips.

The wind has whipped into a frenzy, and already my ears hurt. A guy near me is wearing a red knit cap and I think, smart. He is bent over a bloodstained piece of plywood cleaning fish, and something is familiar about the way his arms move. I watch his wide shoulders flex and roll under his raggedy black tee, and as I get closer, I see the braid of black hair poking out from beneath the cap. Joaquin.

My ears no longer feel cold. Warmth spreads down my body, and my heartbeat quickens the way it does when I'm about to step out onto the floor at a gymnastics meet—after I raise my arms in salute of the judges and everything gets quiet. Once the music starts, each move I make becomes either a point or a deduction. What is possible turns into what is. But in that stepping-out moment, *anything* is still possible. I can't help staring at Joaquin, holding on to the space in time before he turns and notices me.

If I'm lucky, when Joaquin sees me, he'll flash me that rare smile of his. The one where his cheeks sort of bunch and his nose scrunches, so somehow he looks embarrassed and confident and sexy all at the same time. I love that smile.

I stand there grinning like an idiot. But it's okay. Because right after I imagine him smiling, it's as if I tapped him on the shoulder with my mind. His head jerks up, and his eyes meet mine, and everything I imagined actually happens.

His nose does that cute scrunchy thing, and his mouth widens enough for me to see an almost-undetectable little gap between his two front teeth. Then he says, "Hey," real cool-like.

"Hey," I say, my eyes resting on the dimple in his cheek. "Long time, no see."

From down the beach a man I think maybe is his dad yells something in Spanish. Joaquin drops his eyes and starts gutting again. A group of kids working this section of the beach are whistling and giggling in our direction, and I realize they are probably his siblings—his sister and three younger brothers.

I squat down next to him. "How's your summer going?"

He shrugs, not looking at me. He slices each fish behind the gills and down the belly then slides out the guts in an expert, practiced motion.

I want him to look up, to see in my face how happy I am to have found him here. He has no idea that I've been looking for him ever since our dance at Spring Fling. "You never called," I say. I mean to sound offhand, but it comes out like an accusation.

His brows push crinkles in his forehead. "Not really a phone guy."

I stand up and lean into one hip, blocking what's left of the sun and casting a long shadow over him. "What kind of guy are you?"

He stacks each salmon whole—head and all—in a big blue cooler lined with a trash bag. Nothing but the guts are left behind. "Busy."

"Ouch."

His eyes find mine. "I don't mean that in a dickish way." His face is honest and open, as if he has nothing to hide.

Not like me. I shift my focus to his left earlobe where a diamond stud is peeking out from beneath his hat. "How do you mean it?"

"Never mind."

"I mind," I say, hands on my hips. "What's the problem?"

He stops stacking and glances down the beach to where his dad is busy helping his brother untangle a net full of fish. "You and me... we're not...we're different."

"You're right," I say. "*I've* never done it before."

His head whips around. "¿Que?"

"Never dipnetted." I try to look offended. "What'd you think I meant?"

He gives me a long stare, like he's sizing me up, and fixates on my boots. "Chest waders are better." Dark baby curls have escaped from under his red hat and blow with each wind gust into his eyes.

He pulls the hat lower and tucks the strands back. "I could show you how. If you want."

There's nothing else I'd rather do. "I want."

Not ten feet away, his brothers have begun packing up gear. "Stay here a sec, yeah?" Joaquin heads toward the water to where his dad is taking apart the nets. The pieces clatter into a pile on the beach.

Joaquin's mom sounds like she is giving orders, but she's speaking so fast in Spanish that I can only make out a word or two. I don't think she notices me standing there, but suddenly she is looking straight at me. I'm embarrassed for being caught gawking and am about to turn away when she smiles, and I see a reflection of Joaquin in her face: same cheeks and nose. I know almost nothing about this woman, but I want her to like me. I smile back and wonder what my face is saying to her.

Joaquin returns with two black garbage bags, a knife, two unassembled nets, and two pairs of chest waders. "We'll use these."

Each member of Joaquin's family is loaded with a backpack and bungied-together bundles of gear. His dad is carrying the big blue cooler. "Where are they going?" I ask.

"Back to my house." He points up the hill at the road beyond the parking lot. "We live in the trailer court up there. The one right off the Spur. It's only like a fifteen-minute walk from here."

"Don't you need to go with them?"

"I thought you were tired of being a virgin."

It takes only a nanosecond for my head to catch up. "Who isn't?" As if music has started, I feel myself readying to perform. "How about we pop my dipnetting cherry."

The water's gotten rough, but the chest waders keep me dry and warmer than Mom's old hip boots. "Thanks for gearing me up, all proper-like," I say. "Although *my* boots," I point up the beach to Mom's waders, "have good juju. They're my mom's from when I was a kid." I tell him how we used to go down to the river and how she taught me to fish. "She used to be way more fun."

"Family is everything," he says. "I love to hate mine."

"Amen," I say.

The best thing about dipnetting is Joaquin's arms around my waist as he helps me hold the net steady. Second is being nearly submerged in the vastness of Cook Inlet with the water constantly pushing against you. You can't be complacent in the ocean.

The third best thing is the tug you feel on the aluminum handle when you know there's at least one salmon in your net. If not for the killing part—scooping a female full of eggs, the next generation of sockeye, out of the water before she's had a chance to lay those eggs— I'd count that feeling of catching as being what I love most about fishing. If I'm being perfectly honest, there is a high you get when you pull a fish out of the water with that stupid giant net. Makes you want to cry out like those dumb seagulls.

"Pull!" Joaquin yells when I try for the first time on my own.

"I am!" The salmon will lose this fight and knowing that makes lugging in the net more difficult.

"Harder!"

I finally drag myself out of the water. The fish flops around in the green netting and stares at me with an expressionless side-eye.

I am guilty, but so alive. The way I felt when I learned to fly-fish with Mom. Like the rush after the Mt. Redoubt apocalypse. I could take on the whole world.

"Now we clean," he says, grabbing the knife's rubber grip and kneeling beside our small pile of fish.

Joaquin, our salmon, the shore and waves—all look softer bathed in summertime's perpetual twilight. I yawn. The sky may be confused, but my body knows it's getting late. Down the beach a familiar shape lumbers our way. Shit! I totally lost track of time.

I wave, as if I'm glad Brett is joining us. "Hey, Brett! This is—"

Brett spits. "I know who he is." He and Joaquin are both from Kenai, except Joaquin's still in high school—a senior, like me.

Joaquin slices into a dead salmon's belly, sliding the entrails onto the beach. When he stands, blood drips from the knife blade.

"Waaaaa-keeeeeen Santos," Brett drawls. He hurls a beach rock against the surf.

Joaquin lifts his chin. "Hale."

"Didn't I see the rest of your clan head out?"

Joaquin takes a step forward. His boot leaves a wet imprint in the dark sand. "Since when's my family your business?" The knife hangs slack in his hand, point down.

Brett sneers. "Since you stayed past your welcome." He picks up another stone.

"Meri here wanted to try dipnetting." Joaquin's fingers tighten around the knife handle, and he plants himself between Brett and me.

Brett's eyes become slits, his focus darting from the knife to me. "Pretty long bathroom break," he says to me.

"Playing the role of tail cutter isn't exactly my idea of a good time." I fold my arms over the chest waders I'm borrowing from Joaquin. "What would you like me to do next? Wash slime off the fish whacker?"

"For your information, I thought we'd go to a movie."

"Wait," Joaquin steps back, "you're here with this guy?"

Brett grabs my hand. "That's right. And now she's leaving with this guy." He pulls and I trip in the waders, but he catches me before I fall.

Joaquin's eyes bore into me, but I can barely look at him. My eyes fix on the small mark—a boy version of a beauty mark—low on Joaquin's cheek near his jawline. He grabs our nets and starts pulling them apart, hard and fast.

"I need my waders," he says. Aluminum clatters as he throws the hollow parts into a pile on the beach.

"I'll get them back to you. I promise." I feel as gutted and empty as the salmon at my feet. "Keep my mom's in the meantime. As collateral." I yank my hand free from Brett's, slosh through the shallow breakers back over to Joaquin, and hug him.

His arms stay slack at his side, but his body presses into mine.

"Just make sure I get my waders," he says.

I whisper close to his ear, "Please call me this time," and recite the digits to my phone number. Twice. "*Please.*"

He turns and begins picking the disassembled pieces of net up off the beach.

Brett is already walking away, back toward the Bronco. Catching up to him wearing the oversized chest waders makes my legs ache and my lungs burn. But I do it.

We change out of our waders in total silence. He puts the gear in the back of the Bronco and doesn't say a word about the fact that I'm no longer wearing Mom's boots. In the car I try to talk Brett down. "Look, I'm sorry I didn't stay with you guys. I was just, you know, kinda bored."

"That guy's a shitbag, Meri." Brett keeps his eyes locked on the road. "He's the reason I bring my own gym towel."

What does that even mean? I want to defend Joaquin, but I stay quiet because maybe Brett knows something about Joaquin that I don't.

Brett takes me to the matinee showing of *Pretty Woman*. The film's been playing at the Orca Theater for like two months; this is my third time. I still love it. It's about a guy who hires a prostitute then falls in love with her. Julia Roberts plays the most gorgeous and prudish whore in the entire history of harlotry. She won't kiss any of her johns because it's too intimate. In the end, despite her checkered past, hunky Richard Gere falls for her. Because she's smart and bodacious. It's ridiculous. I don't even know why I like the movie.

It's raining when we get out of the theater, so Brett holds his coat over both of our heads as we run to the parking lot. He's back to being relaxed and cool. He says he's sorry for being such a jerk.

"I shouldn't have wandered off." Even as I say it, I hate myself. Why should I be sorry? And why am I using that pathetic voice I use with my parents when I'm in trouble? I sound like a contrite little child. The worst part is, I don't even mean what I'm saying. I had every right to leave, and he had no right to say what he did to Joaquin.

He finds my hand and gives a little squeeze. "Glad you came out with me today."

"Well, I do love *Pretty Woman*."

"Me too." He parks in my driveway and cuts the engine. Raindrops patter lightly on the roof.

Taken separately, Brett's features are attractive. Hazel eyes with reasonable lashes, a classic roman nose, and lips neither overly full nor thin. But sometimes the way they work together—eyes narrowing to slits, nose wrinkling, mouth twisting into a smirk—mar his looks. I never know what his face will do.

But now he breaks into a grin, "I especially love that piano scene."

"I heard she used a body double." That's what Alex told me.

"Probably she's too fat in real life," says Brett. "Or maybe she's got saggy tits."

I suck in my stomach and push my shoulders back. "I'd probably need a body double, too."

His eyes take in the whole of me and settle on my face. "I don't think so," he says.

The way Brett is looking at me—like Richard Gere when he wanted to kiss Julia Roberts—warms me all over and replaces any remaining tension from our beach fight with the now of his lips.

He leans closer. "I'd make love to you on a piano any day of the week."

Blood rushes to my cheeks, but out the corner of my eye, I see Alex in his yellow rain slicker walking out of the garage with Ben, our little poodle dog. Mom likes one of us to watch for owls while Ben does his business. I hope desperately Alex can't see through the Bronco's tinted windows. I push away.

"Sorry." I point to my brother and Ben. "Mom's already sending the patrol out after me." I open the door. "She thinks I went out with my church youth group."

"You're kidding, right?"

"My parents are weird." I flash Brett what I hope is my confident—maybe seductive?—smile and jump down. "Thanks, Sharman!" I yell then lower my voice. "Guess you'll have to take me out again."

He chews his cheek. "Raincheck, then?"

"If you don't lose my number this time."

7/2/90

Mom was pissed when I got in later than I'd said and didn't have her hip waders, but as long as I return her waders to their place in the garage before Dad notices they're missing, everything will be fine. Dad will never know I went dipnetting. Anyway, he was wrong. Dipnetting's amazing. He's never done it, so how would he know?

7/3/90

Midnight Ride

Windows down
The wind lifts our hair
like we're soaring.
We bounce over frost heaves,
glide down the Spur.
We are flightless birds
who can't accept the limits
of our wings.

Dad and Alex won't be back from camping until Saturday,
so Mom and I went to the Fourth parade by ourselves.
It sucked. Mainly loud fire engines and politicians in
convertible Corvettes. I lit a few sparklers when we got
home but Mom said they were scaring the dog, so I called
Charlie and (miracle!) her mom finally let me talk to her.
Charlie's voice was super hoarse. She wanted to know every
detail about dipnetting, especially the parts about Kenny,
so I told her the whole story, including how the guys
were being assholes and how Joaquin was the one who
taught me to dipnet and that he looked sooooo hot. She
remembered him from the dance last year and agreed he's
hot, but when I told her I couldn't decide who I like better,
she reminded me that Brett has his own car and then was
like, why do you even have to choose?

6
Not Solitaire

It's weird how you walk around with these big blank spots, not knowing jack about a thing, but having opinions as if you do, and then you go and actually do it—fill in the blank—and presto, you now know something even your parents don't. You've either waded chest-deep into fast-moving icy water, held the ten-foot aluminum handle, and pulled in a net full of flopping salmon—or you haven't.

I hate regret, but I hate stupidity more. Secrets are sometimes the only gateway to knowing. I sure as hell won't be telling Dad about dipnetting. Nor will I mention Joaquin, who called yesterday, but after only thirty seconds—the length of time it took for Joaquin to say, "Is Meri there?" and for me to nearly have a heart attack and answer, "This is Meri"—Mom picked up the phone in the kitchen and was all, *I need to make a call, get off the phone right now, blah blah blah, my calls are so much more important than anything that could possibly be happening in your life.* It was embarrassing, and I didn't even get directions to Joaquin's house.

But I do know his family lives somewhere in the trailer court off the Spur Highway. Anchor Court. I've gone with Mom and the church ladies to hand out clothes and canned food door-to-door. That was the real first time I saw Joaquin, not last year's Fairytale Moment. I was delivering stupid hand-me-downs and old cans of garbanzo beans to those neighborhoods the Church Canned Food Brigade deemed "less fortunate." It was the summer after my sophomore year. I watched him from our car while he played baseball in the overgrown field next to Anchor Court. He was tall—six feet at least—and from under his ball cap, black hair curled behind his ears and pulled into a braid that fell to the middle of his back.

The sun blazed overhead, making the day hotter than most. Joaquin was pitching to a younger boy I guessed was his brother. Each time he threw the ball over the pizza-box home plate, sweat shined off the muscles in his arm. He didn't look less fortunate.

After that, I knew he existed and that he was gorgeous. I just never thought I'd meet him. And I definitely never thought he'd be interested in me.

A giant anchor rusts alongside the Spur Highway. Above the anchor, a wooden sign reads, Anchor Court Mobile Home Park. I flick on my blinker and wrench the wheel to the left, nearly colliding with an on-coming car—a Ford Probe with racing stripes. My heart slams against my chest as if Matt's car just smashed into my Bug and crushed me. Adrenaline floods my arms and legs.

My hands are shaking, but I manage to pull over and park near a stack of old tires just beyond the anchor. I concentrate on trying to quell the panic I feel from almost dying. The recognition that Matt was the one behind the wheel and that he probably saw it was me turning into Anchor Court and will tell Brett isn't helping. Maybe Brett won't care. I'm still not sure how much or even if he likes me.

The first trailer is a light-blue single-wide. A piece of weathered paneling leans against the trailer's hitch, and on it, spray painted in red, are the words Slow! Children at Play. Next to the sign, a metal mailbox is held upright by a post stuck in a white bucket filled with cement. There's no name on the box, so I keep going.

I drive around the court's loop at stalker speed. Four trailers in, a kid about Alex's age hunches in front of a double-wide hosing off a giant blue cooler. I recognize the cooler, and when the kid lifts his head to give me the once-over, his face is a mini version of Joaquin's, except fuller and without the beauty mark on the lower part of his cheek or the tiny diamond stud in his left ear.

He waves with one hand but keeps spraying with the other.

"Hey," I say out the window before killing the engine. "Just bringing back your guys' chest waders." I get out and pop the trunk. The Bug looks as if it's yawning. "Tell your folks thanks for the loan," I say, offering the waders to Joaquin's brother.

"Oh. Right." He stops hosing and grabs the boots. "I'll go get yours." He disappears inside, then returns in a few minutes with Mom's boots. He holds out his hand. "I'm Noah, by the way."

"Nice to meet you, Noah." I shake his hand all formal, which makes him laugh.

Noah's cheek dimples just like his brother's. "Bet you wanna see Joaquin."

"Um." I look to the side. "Sure?"

"He's over at Mikey's trailer." He points over two trailers to a white single-wide with a brown stripe running along the side.

I shove my fists into the front pocket of my hooded Cornell University sweatshirt and am about to jump back in the Bug when Noah yells, "Hey!" He picks up the dripping sprayer nozzle and says, "Nice shirt."

We both smile. It's stupid. I found the shirt on a fifty-cent table garage sale-ing with Charlie. The cuffs are frayed, and I could never afford to go to Cornell, but wearing the shirt gives me something to fantasize about—the big-time Ivy League college in New York that graduated writers like Kurt Vonnegut and E. B. White. The more I wear it, the more I feel like the kind of person who could own a shirt like this.

"Look, my brother's..." Noah sighs. "Joaquin's not near as good lookin' or smooth with the ladies as, you know, yours truly." He makes a show of slicking back his hair Fonz-style. "But he likes you, and I'm pretty sure you like him, so go sort out your issues and whatever, but then *you* should call *him*."

I roll my eyes. "What's his phone number."

"Got a pen?"

I shake my head. "I'm an excellent memorizer."

He rattles off the number and tells me to park here and walk over. "Mikey will blow a gasket if somebody's in his spot."

When I knock, Joaquin answers, but he only opens the door a few inches.

"What," he says, oblivious to the effect his snug white T-shirt and jeans are having on me. No arguing the boy's in good shape.

I stare down at the worn wooden stairs, trying to seem contrite and also needing to distract myself from thinking carnal thoughts. "Can I come in?"

"Depends," he says, flicking the deadbolt back and forth. "Is your *boyfriend* gonna come busting down the door behind you?"

My head snaps up. "He's not my boyfriend. He invited me to go fishing, that's all."

"Yeah? Then why'd you need me to show you how?"

"Please," I say. "Just let me in."

He turns and walks into the shadowy room but leaves the door cracked behind him. I follow him to the very front part of the trailer to a small table. The space is bordered by tiny upper and lower cabinets and a few appliances, including a toaster oven, microwave, and an avocado-green refrigerator. The white Formica table is covered in lines of playing cards and a stack of loose papers. He flips over the papers before slouching into one of two metal folding chairs.

"What you got there?" I ask. The bare bulb overhead casts the kitchen in a creamy glow. I can't tell if it's lighter inside or outside.

He shrugs. "Solitaire. Some sketches."

I slide into the chair across from him. "Who's Mikey?"

He tips back in his creaky chair, balancing precariously on the back two legs. "My cousin."

"Where is he?" I try to turn over the stack of sketches on the table, but he slams his chair down onto four legs and swats my hand away.

"Anchorage." Joaquin crosses his arms. "Is this the part where you interrogate me?"

"No. It's the part where I get to know you."

"I like to be alone," he says.

I try to ignore the jab and turn my attention to the half-finished solitaire game arranged on the table in front of him. "Who's winning?"

"The other guy," he says, a slight smile relaxing his clenched jaw. "Never underestimate the deck."

"Good advice." I grab the remaining pile of cards. "Is it stacked?"

"Always."

Music floats from a boom box on the counter. "Journey?" I wonder if it's a coincidence that "Lights" is playing—the song from our first dance. I start singing along.

His tongue teases at a piece of bright-green gum. "That was just what was in the player."

The way he says it, I can tell it's not true. "I won't tell anyone you're a sappy Steve Perry fan," I joke, flipping the top card on the deck. "Are we playing or what?"

He leans forward so close I smell spearmint. "You know it's not solitaire if we're playing together."

I watch his mouth move, as mesmerized by the flick of his tongue as by the flames that lick the glass of our woodstove. "Then let's play Not Solitaire," I say. "How about I go back to interrogating?"

He crosses his arms again.

"Why did your family move here?" I ask.

He sits forward. "Why did *your* family move here?"

Now I'm the one crossing my arms.

"My turn." He snaps his gum and rolls it away into his cheek. "Why you waste your time with that pendejo?"

"We just met." I take up the card deck and concentrate on Joaquin's half-played game. "If you're talking about Brett, I mean." Would Brett be jealous if he knew I was here? Stupid thought since we aren't officially dating. I match a jack of hearts to a queen of spades. "I barely know him."

"You should keep it that way." His voice tightens. "He's a user."

I try not to sound shocked or prissy. "Like, drugs?"

"People." Joaquin moves an ace and flips the card below.

How would he know? True, Brett acted like a jealous dickwad at the beach, but a user? That can't be right. He paid for the carnival, the movie, food. He gave me his shirt. "Maybe you just don't know him," I say, scooting my chair around so we're side by side. I shift the row of queen through seven onto a newly exposed king.

"I thought *you* didn't know him."

"I know him enough. He's just a guy." I flip the three of hearts. "With a nice ride." I cringe at myself for using Matt's words. "Maybe you're jealous." I try turning over the next card in the deck, but a jolt of energy travels through my wrist when Joaquin stills my hand. I yank my arm away.

"Take it easy," he says. "You can use that three."

Sure enough. I hadn't noticed an open four of clubs. "Very keen... Joaquin." I laugh at my stupid rhyme.

"Weirdo."

"Is that you smooth-talking?" I want him to touch me again.

He chuckles. "No, that's me actually saying you're weird. You coulda just said, 'Nice catch.' Something normal."

The more nervous I get, the more heightened my language. A curse of my word junkie-ism. "I'm practicing up for the vocab section on the SAT." It's the best excuse I can think of. "I hear it's really hard."

"How hard?"

"Oh, it's hard. Freaking rock-hard, baby." I like where this game is going. I shift the stack of jack through three to a newly revealed queen. "You know that's called a double entendre?"

His forehead wrinkles.

"When you say a word that means something else—like something sexual. Like if you said, 'I'm about to win this solitaire game,' and I said, 'Wow, that's a big deal,' but I was looking at the bulge in your pants." My eyes drift down. He inches his chair closer to the table so I can't see below his waist. "That's a double entendre."

"So you're saying when I'm hard it's a big deal?"

"Something like that." I'm not sure if it's all the sex talk or the fact that I've been crushing on Joaquin since I first saw him—even more since dipnetting—or Steve Perry in the background now belting out "Separate Lives," but all I want to do is kiss him.

Joaquin focuses on the cards, evaluating them, waiting for me to flip the next one. His little-kid lashes swoosh up and down with each blink. His nose makes a perfect V at the tip, and his lips are just the right amount of pouty full, especially the bottom one that he's biting.

I hold what's left of the deck in my hand; the game can't continue unless I want it to. I wait until he gets impatient, and when he finally looks up, I do it. I plant one on him. No, it's not my finest kiss, but my mouth at least connects with his—for just a millisecond—before I back up and take a shaky breath.

"I still think you're weird." He smiles, then leans in and kisses me back. But better.

7
Anchored

Twilight filters through the window. Joaquin's shirt is off, and I am tracing the tiny white lines that jag like lightning across his bare shoulder.

"From working with my dad," he says, his shoulder flexing. "Fiberglass is heavy."

His cousin's couch is long but narrow. With two of us side by side, Joaquin has to wrap both arms around me and push his palm against the small of my back to keep me from rolling off. I'm not complaining.

We press closer together. The cushions beneath us smell vaguely of beer, and the khaki armrest near my head is dotted with hard, black cigarette burns. My Cornell sweatshirt is wadded behind Joaquin's head, and his hair falls in thick waves around his shoulder. This is the first time I've seen it unbound, and I decide I like it best this way. I wrap a curl of black hair around my ring finger and twirl in my own strawberry-blond strands.

I'm trying to imagine what our kids would look like when he flexes the arm I've been using as a pillow, shifts his body, and brings his face close. From this angle, his nose looks gigantic—I'm guessing mine does, too—and his lips are rubbing together as if smearing imaginary Chapstick.

I want him to kiss me again, but thanks to the zombie-mouth poster of the smoker with oral cancer my mom points out every time I go to the doctor, I'm having to work hard not to think about saliva and germs. Joaquin smokes sometimes, but his teeth are whiter than mine, and his lips aren't the least bit dry or peely. Screw the poster.

I close my eyes right as his lips touch mine. He presses slowly, but I feel the tiniest movements as his mouth connects with mine. All my surfaces tingle. I'm caught off guard, teetering between freak-out and total exhilaration, like riding the Zipper, but way better and less scary. My foot slips off the couch and thwacks the floor.

This wasn't how it was with Brett or Kyle or…my first French kiss flashes in my mind. The Buckley Family Reunion. My second cousin's pointy tongue shoving through my thirteen-year-old lips, pushing franticly against my teeth and cheeks and the roof of my mouth, as if trying to touch every inch of my oral landscape.

What's happening now is totally different. His tongue isn't forceful or squirmy or gross; it's smooth and tastes like spearmint—kinda awesome. But he must have swallowed his gum because I don't feel it.

He traces a line from my ear to my neck with his finger, kissing my lips lightly before beginning an unhurried tour along the side of my neck and back to my mouth. Joaquin kisses the way he dances, controlled and deliberate, waiting for you to follow, if you want. I'm trying to relax and learn his moves, to mirror the curve of his tongue with mine.

He runs the tip of his tongue along my bottom lip. My entire body throbs. Fornication is a serrated blade. Is this how the devil seduces you? Joaquin's hair coils around our faces like a dark tunnel. When does kissing stop and fornicating begin?

His fingers lift the lower edge of my shirt. I grab at the material. My body is a temple. He slides his open palm under the fabric and rubs my skin. My back arches as his hands curve over my bra and a little groan escapes. This feels every bit as good as kissing, and I want him to keep doing it, but a spring or something is sticking into my shoulder and an alarm is going off in my head.

Right now Mom's probably biting the inside of her cheek, watching the minutes click by on our stove clock. My eyes flick down to the watch on his wrist. I can't quite see the numbers, but it feels late, and there's this urgency, like the tide is going out and I'm about to be carried out to sea.

Mom expected me home by eleven, after the movie I never went to see with Sharman-from-church, and though my mom won't actually kill me, I don't like the truth any better: her waiting up for me in a circle of lamplight on our overstuffed sectional, reading her Harlequin romance to distract herself from the thought that I have crashed and am at this moment inhaling my final breaths as I bleed out in a ditch.

"My mom's going to kill me," I say, as he lifts my shirt higher.

He stares at my exposed belly. "Me vuelves loco, chica," he says. I wish I'd paid better attention in Ms. Tapia's Spanish class.

"You make me crazy."

I love that he can say it in two languages, but I doubt he means crazy about the real me, the loud, too-talkative, spazzy redhead people have called "dork" or "the Dictionary." More likely the summer-fling me. The physical me.

"You're so white," he whispers.

Even in the low light, the contrast between his hand and my near-albino stomach—my "halibut belly"—is glaring. I pull the shirt down. "Is that a bad thing?"

"Nah..." He pushes off the couch and stands up, but I pull him back down. Because just as scripture warned, my flesh most definitely lusteth. I shove my lips at him. My mouth collides with his nose and top lip; my bottom teeth clunk against his front teeth.

He stiffens. "Easy, killer." He helps our mouths meet, and his eager response to my kissing him gives me a rush. I pull my shirt up over my head. His hands move along my bare waist and up over my ribs. Through the thin fabric of my bra, his mouth touches my nipple. It hardens, and my flesh is on fire with lusteth-ing. All I want is more of me inside his mouth and more of him inside mine.

I reposition my head on his shoulder. My lashes and nose brush his neck where the skin is soft and sweet, like oranges and new sweat. I lick him. I can't help it.

"Whoa," he says. "Don't think you want to do that."

"I do." My lips touch his neck twice, so slow that my mouth stays on his skin long enough for me to breathe—in, out, in, out—with each kiss. I feel powerful. I bite his earlobe, tease at the diamond stud with my teeth.

"Come here, you," he says. His lips brush my forehead.

"Joaquin..." When I say his name it sounds breathy and whiny, like I'm that annoying kid at the grocery checkout begging for candy. What do I want? More than I should. I'm sick of Mom reminding me to save myself until I'm married. Virginity is overrated.

It takes all the willpower I can muster to grab his wrist and check the time. Almost midnight. "I really have to go." I don't mean it, but Joaquin untangles himself from me and finds his T-shirt on the floor.

When he reaches to help me up, I just sit there staring at his boots. He has the coolest black leather work boots, and he's wearing socks, which I love, because every other guy has Stinky Fungus Foot from going sockless in Vans or deck shoes.

My legs are straight out in front of me on the couch. The neon yellow laces in my Keds glow. When I point my feet to stretch my ankles, a kind of muscle-memory autopilot takes over, makes me grab my toes and fold against my knees into a pike position until my hamstrings strain and my back arches, catlike. I am fully in my body. A dancer. A gymnast. Moving in a practiced way. Not a girl on the verge of doing something new and unfamiliar.

The stretch hides my half-naked upper body. "I'll leave." I say into my knees.

"I don't want you to," He twists the diamond in his ear. "But your dad showing up with his shotgun would suck." He glances toward the door. "My cousin'll be back soon, anyway."

I stretch farther, flattening my chest against my legs, shortening the distance between my head and feet. His hand skates a shiver along the curve of my spine.

"That looks hard," he says.

I sit up. "*You* look hard."

"Double whatever," he says.

"Entendre." I let him look at me—at my overdeveloped, freckled shoulders and too-large-for-a-girl biceps and fair-skinned stomach—before I pull my T-shirt over my bra, sliding the material slowly over each breast, and then again with my Cornell sweatshirt.

Outside, the night is cool and breezy, but not dark—sort of half-light. The Kenai Beach is less than a mile away, and I can smell the inlet in the air. The damp, brackish scent of sea life. "Salty fecundity," I whisper.

"So weird," he says but flashes his signature smile, and I know he means something else, too. Something weird plus something good. *Double entendre.*

He hugs me before I get in, and I cling too long. Once I start the Bug, I roll down the window so we can kiss once more before I drive away. In the rearview, I watch him walk back toward his cousin's trailer. He turns around, pulls a hair tie from his pocket, smooths his hair back into a ponytail, and watches me drive away.

I roar past Anchor Court's rusty anchor and lurch out onto the Spur Highway. My own reflection flashes in my side mirror. There's an angry red zit the size of a dime about to explode on my forehead, probably a result of the extra hairspray. Thanks, Charlie's Finesse Super Hold, *for nothing.*

Cold rushes in through my open window, swirling and snarling my hair as I speed up, but I'm past caring. I don't feel sexy anymore, just guilty. I'm practicing what I'll say to Mom, talking to myself over the Bug's engine.

The night air stinks. Maybe what I smell are the decaying salmon carcasses left on the beach by dipnetters like Brett. I remember the look on his face when he found me on the beach with Joaquin.

Two boys. One summer.

I press hard on the pedal, and the Bug accelerates past seventy. I'm tempted to fill the tank and keep on driving all the way to Anchorage—just because I can—but I don't feel like leaving Mom on the couch all night on the verge of cardiac arrest. Plus, Dad would go berserk, and I cannot get grounded in the middle of summer. Against my will, I speed past the last gas station, take the turn onto Raspberry Road, and steer myself back home to the place I'm supposed to be.

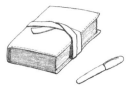

7/7/90

*Big fight with Mom over how I'm always coming home late.
I was like, it's not my fault you worry so much and by the
way, I'm almost eighteen. She said I still lived under her
roof, and that got me so mad I was like, is this how it's
going to be if I stay home next year and go to community
college? She almost started crying and said, "Maybe I
should stop caring about you." That's a direct quote. I
wanted to say her caring is more like CONTROLLING but
felt bad and was about to apologize when the phone rang.
It was Brett telling me how much he was missing me.
He wanted to know what I'd been up to and if I'd been
hanging out with other guys because he'd have to beat
them up if I had. I laughed, but I think he really likes me.
I don't know if Matt told him about seeing me at Anchor
Court, but just in case, I told Brett I'd gone there with my
church to drop off canned food. I instantly regretted saying
that. I'm going straight to hell.*

7/8/90

*Joaquin called. Yay! We have a DQ date for next weekend.
I'll have to sneak out somehow. Joaquin asked if Brett and
I were an item. I said I haven't seen him since dipnetting,
which is technically true because I haven't actually seen
him. Not yet.*

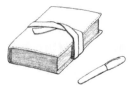

I told Mom I had to close at work today so I could meet
Brett for dinner at Garden of Italy. He calls it Garden
of Shitaly. When I got there he gave me this cute little
stuffed moose that was wearing a tuxedo. Brett was all,
"Mr. Moose will be your waiter tonight." He kept having Mr.
Moose fake kiss me and say things in his moose voice like,
"Brett's a stud and Meri's so hot."

7/11/90

Joaquin cancelled because his dad needed help with some
boat thing. I don't know. Fixing boats is his dad's job. I
wish Joaquin acted like he cared a little more. Maybe it's
like he said at the beach. We're just too different. He
doesn't fit into my world, and I don't fit into his. I mean,
I really like him, but I'm not sure he's into me. Maybe
there's a good reason Brett doesn't like him.

July 16, 1990

Dear Meri,

I'm so very sorry, but I won't be flying up to visit this year. I've not been feeling so well. Your Aunt Lily has really been fussing over me.

Don't worry, though. I've already fixed up a room for you to come down next summer, and if you decide to go to the University of Idaho, I would absolutely love for you to live with me while you're in college. You don't have to, of course, if you want to be with the other girls in the dorms, but please know my door is always open to you.

Merideth, you are going to do great things in life.

Love,

Grandma

8
Bluff

It's a rush sneaking around all clandestine and spy-like, but I don't want to have to keep lying to my parents every time a boy calls or wants to go out. I'm old enough to date, and my parents know it. Plus, the chances they'll approve of Brett are pretty good. He's clean-cut, has a solid job, lives with his church-going mom in a nice house, and even though he's a few years older, he looks like the kind of guy parents like mine imagine their daughter dating. I don't know how I know this, but I do. As much as I know they wouldn't approve so easily of Joaquin.

Last month, when Mom was on her way to join the ladies of the Canned Food Brigade on another "trailer mission," I distinctly recall her saying, "Those poor people need grace." The words echo sharply in my mind. As if "those people," the low-income families who live in Anchor Court, would be lucky to have our garbage sacks of old clothes and expired cans of green beans. Dad was helping her with the bags. "Be careful," he said.

I'm not sure what Joaquin and I are to each other, but certain secrets are better kept.

"I met a new friend," I say to Dad, who typically isn't interested in my social life. He nudges me, looks across the table at the corn bowl, and clears his throat. This is how he says "pass the corn" without actually having to talk to me.

On the weeks Dad is home, Mom insists we all sit down together at the table for dinner. Dad spends most of the agonizing forty-five or so minutes chastising Alex and me for etiquette infractions, including elbows on the table, chewing with our mouths open, and using our thumbs to push peas onto our spoon. Why they subject us to this torture is beyond me.

I stare down at the bowl of watery yellow kernels. "He's nice," I say.

Dad clears his throat again.

"He's kinda from church," I say, "and wants to pick me up on Saturday for, like, a movie-date thing."

Mom's reaction is predictable. When she hears "date," she says, "Why don't you just go out in a group?"

I want to tell her technically we've already been out three times, if you count the carnival, and I lived to tell about it. But in a surprising turn of events, it's Dad who turns to Mom and says, "Lydia, she's almost eighteen."

I'm still recovering from my shock when Mom says, "How is he *kinda* from church?"

Alex narrows his eyes. "What, is he like the janitor guy that comes and cleans on weekends?"

I chuck a piece of corn at him. "Shut up!"

Alex ducks, and the kernel lands behind him on the mildew-stained windowsill.

"Knock it off!" Dad clinks his silverware on his plate. "Meri, I thought I asked you to pass the corn."

"You know his mom." I say, finally picking up the bowl. "Irene. She usually sits ahead of us in church." A single blue flower is stamped on the outside of the dish, and I press my finger against it for luck. "His name is Brett."

Dad grunts, swirling the slotted spoon in the grayish corn water. "She has a son?"

Mom pushes the basket of Wonder Bread to the edge of my plate, but I shake my head. Bread and butter with every meal is Dad's thing, not mine. "Anyway," I say, "I told him he could come by on Saturday a little early and meet you. If you're around."

"So he's coming here to meet us." Mom's hands clasp together as if she's the mom in *The*-freaking-*Waltons*. "Well, good."

Easy peasy.

By Saturday morning I am freaking out. What if Brett acts like he does around his friends—all *fuck this* and *fuck that*? My parents will crap a loaf.

I call to remind him that if he messes this up, it'll make hanging out nearly impossible.

"I got this, babe," he says. "Leave it to Brett. Parents love me." His assurances do little to take the edge off.

"Can I have some TUMS or something?" I ask Mom.

Instead she makes me a bowl of cream of wheat. "Honestly, Merideth," she says feeling my forehead. "You might have a flu bug or something. You sure tonight's a good idea?"

Absolutely not. "I'm fine," I say.

Brett rings our custom doorbell at six thirty as Mom and I are finishing the dishes. Our house is invaded by the sound of General Lee's horn in *The Dukes of Hazzard*.

"I'll get it," I yell, racing after Alex, who already is running through the door from our living room to the arctic entry. He elbows me out of the way. I smack into the wall heater and bang my kneecap on the bench where we store all our winter gear. I ignore my throbbing knee and wrench free the red mitten peeking out from under the bench lid. I chuck it as hard as I can at his head, but the mitten barely grazes Alex's ear, as he flings open the outside door.

"We don't want any!" he says, slamming the door in Brett's face and then taking off laughing like a kid half his age.

"Moron!" I open the door.

Brett's standing there holding two roses.

"Hi there, handsome," I say, admiring his black button-down and tight jeans. I've got on a black skirt and a thin, creamy rayon top that just came into Jay Jacobs last week—I splurged. We'll look good out together.

"Looking fine, Miss Miller." His eyes move up and down the length of me. "Sure like that shirt," he says, as if he can see through the gauzy fabric.

Dad steps into the entryway, and Brett reaches his hand out all confident and manly. "Hello, Mr. Miller."

"You must be Brett." Dad shakes his hand, and suddenly I'm trapped in a sitcom.

Turns out I let myself get strung out for no reason. Brett's a total gentleman. He brought a rose for Mom, too, so she's practically swooning within the first thirty seconds. Then he tells a story about once when the phone company truck's hydraulic bucket got stuck and Brett was stranded up a pole for hours. Dad laughs when Brett describes having to pee from forty feet up. I think the anecdote's just a way for Brett to brag about his lineman job, but I kind of like Parent Brett. He's sweet and polite. I hardly recognize him as the same guy.

"We're off to see *Pretty Woman*," he says lightly, then elbows my dad. "I bet you both know who picked that one."

My parents nod-and-smile us out the door.

A light rain is beginning to fall. I duck my head and run to the Bronco. The drops ting-ting on the roof as we're driving away.

"We're not watching that dumb movie again," says Brett. He says Matt's parents are halibut fishing in Homer for the weekend, so Matt's throwing a house party. "He's celebrating his new job in the aviation industry."

I can't believe Matt actually made it as a pilot. "What airline?"

"Glacier," says Brett. "And it's gonna be a rager."

"Will I know anyone?" I haven't been to many parties. Only a handful with Charlie, and usually it's a bunch of kids my age drinking rum-spiked cola in the woods.

Brett's voice gets all soft and slow. "You'll be fine, babe."

Matt's parents live way the freak out in Sterling, off Robinson Loop Road. Rain beats hard against the windows as we drive. Brett keeps replaying Pink Floyd's "Comfortably Numb."

Matt's driveway is already crammed with cars when we show up. Brett parks super far away along the narrow shoulder of Robinson Loop because he doesn't want some wasted jackass dinging his precious Bronco, so we have to hike half a mile through pelting rain. I stupidly wore black pumps because I stupidly thought we were going to the movies. By the time we make our way down Matt's endless driveway, I'm soaked, my feet are throbbing, and my shoes are hosed.

Matt's parents' place is monstrous—more hunting lodge than house. His dad runs a massive commercial fishing operation, and his mom's a bigwig with the Kenaitze tribe, so they're pretty loaded. The covered porch is as big as our living room. Aluminum pipes dangle on fishing line from the eaves. Homemade wind chimes. My dad once made me a set, and I finally buried the dumb things in our backyard because the sound creeped me out.

Rain slaps against my face, and the pipes start chiming. I bump into a long-haired guy in a trench coat leaning against a giant log pillar smoking. His face is blank; his pupils are black holes. He blows smoke in my face, and my nose burns with the aroma of something earthy and pungent.

"Sorry," I say as I rush up the stairs and hurry through the lavish double doors behind Brett.

"Hale!" Matt appears next to Brett the second we step inside. The music is loud—a dance mix with lots of bass and synthesizer—and a few people next to the stereo system are rubbing up against each other. Dirty dancing. They're obviously wasted, and it's only a little after eight. Matt grabs Brett by the shoulders. "Been drinkin' all day, dude. What took ya so long?"

Everyone here looks older than high school. A couple making out in the den on a red velvet couch look sort of familiar, but I can't see their features clearly.

"Keg's in the kitchen, bro," says Matt.

Brett tugs at my hand. Along the way people shout, "Yo! Hale's here!"

My palm feels warm in his. I am the girl he chose to bring.

We weave through the crowd. Brett stops to small talk with a group clustered near a glass coffee table. I don't know anyone, so I watch and listen and keep hold of Brett's hand. A few faces I recognize—people who've lived here forever and stayed around after they graduated. One girl used to be on the dance team in high school; now she's a checker at Pay & Save. I think she's engaged to this older guy who works on the Slope. Maybe. I don't see him here.

There's nothing really amazing about this party. People are mostly standing around talking and drinking. But then, what else is there to do after high school? You go to some lame job every weekday, watch television, or go to house parties on weekends; and if you're lucky, someone's there with you so you're not alone in your tiny, boring life.

I shiver. That won't be me. That *can't* be me.

"Let's roll," says Brett, tugging again on my hand.

Maybe something interesting will happen tonight. Anything's possible. Beats doing squat at home or driving aimlessly around or hiding with Charlie in the woods while she gets her buzz on with a bottle of Malibu Rum.

At least this is new.

The keg is sitting on the floor in the kitchen. Guys cluster in front but make room for Brett. "Thirsty?" He hands me a *real* glass—a heavy amber goblet—half-full of beer.

I can't believe Matt's letting people use his parents' fancy glasses. Mine would lose their minds. Thinking about Mom and Dad makes my stomach clench, turns the moment dangerous. I reach for the glass and take a sip. Bitter liquid bubbles in my mouth like Alka-Seltzer. I force it down, but my face betrays me.

"Not a beer girl?" laughs Brett.

Matt elbows me. "Maybe tequila?"

I didn't even know Matt was behind me.

"This way," he says.

We walk by open sliding glass doors leading out to a deck where a few people are smoking and then into the dining room. A game's being played on a huge oak table.

"Beer pong?" asks Brett. He lets go of my hand.

Matt grins. "Shot pong."

Two blond girls sidle up next to Matt and Brett, laughing. They glance at me then give each other a look. I know what that look means. *Out of her league.* Charlie and I have used it on freshman girls flirting with upperclassmen. The girls lean over the table and let their low-cut shirts give the guys a show. I wish Charlie was here.

"Who wants a turn?" Another hockey guy—a senior from last year—has a Ping-Pong ball in his hand. Lee Johnson. He's cute and sporty. Boring, but nice. We were in geometry together. "Meri! You wanna go?"

The blond girls glare. I didn't expect Lee to recognize me, but I'm glad he does. Those girls can suck it. "Um, what do I do?"

"Just stand here." He motions me over to the table where ten filled Dixie cups are arranged in a triangle like bowling pins. "Bounce the ball into one of those cups."

When I squeeze in front of him, Lee presses against my backside, and I bump the table. The Dixies slosh. Lee snakes his arm along mine, as if positioning a rifle. I don't need him to steady me. "I think I got this, Lee," I say.

He lets go, but doesn't move away. His chest is hot against my back. Somewhere a microwave dings, and I catch a whiff of burnt popcorn.

"Hey, buddy," Brett is now standing beside us. "Give the lady some room."

Lee flicks a Ping-Pong ball Brett's way. "I'm just showing her how to play."

"I said step off." Brett shoves Lee's shoulder, and the blond girls laugh shrilly.

I bounce my white ball on the table. It lands on the rims of two side-by-side cups, teeters then topples into one. Lee grabs the cup, throws the ball at one of the girls, and brings me the shot. What he lifts to my mouth smells like cinnamon.

"Goldschläger, baby," he says.

"Step the fuck off!" Brett lunges between us. The blonds both scream. Lee's body shoves against mine, and clear liquid splashes onto my new rayon blouse.

"Not the shots!" yells Matt, diving for the table. Like an opening umbrella, he throws out his arms and arcs his body over the jiggling Dixies.

"Get off my girl," says Brett to Lee, who is leaning on me to regain his balance.

My girl?

"Shit! You asshole," says Lee, just as Brett slams him against the counter.

Lee winces. "What the fuck is your problem?" The front of his shirt is wet, and he's holding his elbow.

"You're the problem." Brett's lips curl back from his teeth, exposing yellowed incisors slightly higher and longer than the rest. Reminds me of a feral cat. I've never seen him lose his cool like this. Even on the beach with Joaquin, he seemed in control. I don't know this Brett.

"Keep your hands to yourself next time, prick." Brett grabs my wrist and pulls me away. "Let's get the fuck out of here, Meri." He doesn't slow down when I say my feet hurt, just drags me the hundred miles back to where we parked.

In the Bronco I kick off my shredded pumps and rub my cold blistery toes.

"Take it off, baby," says Brett hitting the gas hard enough the tires screech. He looks like a hungry cat.

"Foot fetish?" I crack, though I'm pissed he's acting like nothing happened. As if he didn't just almost beat the crap out of Lee. And ruin my shoes.

Robinson Loop is mostly deserted. We pass a lone pair of headlights heading in the direction of Matt's party, and I'm grateful when we're turning onto the Sterling Highway in the direction of town. I lean against the cool of the window. "Are you taking me home?"

Dark grey clouds swirl above, making the sky so overcast that half the orange streetlights have blinked on. They illuminate the cab and Brett in brief bursts. I try to read his face as he veers right at the Soldotna Y, toward home.

"It's fine if you want to head back to Matt's party," I say. "After you drop me off, I mean."

"Babe, being with you is what I want." He rubs my thigh. "Just you and me."

The Bronco doesn't slow as we near Raspberry Road. I wonder if Mom is already sitting in her spot on the couch, waiting up. I wonder if she'll stay there until I get home and if she'll smell the boozy cinnamon on my shirt. Part of me wishes we'd turn off, but we speed right by and into Kenai.

Brett parks on the bluff overlooking the beach, cuts the engine, and switches off the headlights. He leaves the heat on and the music playing—Pink Floyd on repeat—and we sit awhile listening again to "Comfortably Numb," both of us staring out at the dark water.

There's enough light to see bright edges flash off the waves, which means the sea is choppy. If I were in a boat right now, that kind of rough would hang me over the side and have me retching my guts out. I wonder what the salmon do when the water's all pissed like that. Probably just swim deeper, let the breakers punch the shore. Sometimes I wish that I could just swim deeper and wait out the stuff I don't want to have to deal with.

Tonight the beach is only a tiny sliver. High tide. If I had a chart book, I'd know the exact moment the inlet will crawl to its apex, give up, and slump back down.

Brett swivels to face me. "How many boyfriends have you had?"

The question catches me off guard and is edged with irritation. I don't want to answer. Like a salmon, I feel myself swimming down, as Pink Floyd encourages me to recede.

"How many," he repeats, "before me?"

I shrug. "Enough," I say, because the answer is not none, but almost. Kyle was one, for sure. I've hung out with a few other guys. My mind drifts to Joaquin. "Why?"

"Just curious." He leans his face close to mine. "You're so beautiful, babe."

Nobody except maybe my mom and grandma has ever said I was beautiful. To hear Brett say it makes me think maybe I am something rare and special, at least to him. Warmth washes over me, his words loosening the knot in my belly.

We've parked along the jagged cliff edge not far from where the Kenai Believers Church clings to the crumbling land. I don't even have to squint to see its neon cross shining like a lighthouse beacon. Dumb cross. I imagine Brett's mom sitting in the pew ahead of us, her small head bent forward, probably praying for her son. "Does your mom know we're hanging out?"

Brett is staring out his own window at a few scrubby alders. "My mom doesn't know a single thing about me."

His answer stabs a familiar hurt. How can these people who brought us into the world become so disconnected from us? I lay my hand over his. "Hey."

He turns back and our eyes meet and there's a jolt in me, like wires connecting. Like *we're* connecting. I say, "My parents don't have a clue what's going on with me, either."

Brett reaches out, touches my hair, and gently tucks a few loose strands behind my right ear. The ear that's now pulsing with every heartbeat.

I hold very still, willing this moment to stretch on, hoping it can if I keep talking. "They don't know anything about my life...what I care about or dream about doing..." My mind conjures the image of future me sitting with a book in my lap on a manicured green campus by brick buildings covered in ivy. Am I a Cornell student? A writer? A literature professor?

Brett's hand drops. His lip curls above his snaggly canine, and he laughs the big, pushy laugh of a person making fun. Before I can react, his expression goes serious. "So who do you dream about doing?"

I push him away. Screw you, asshole. "Your dad."

He laughs again like an explosion splitting our connection. "You're bad," he says, bending forward to close the distance between us.

I lean away until my head thuds against the cold glass of the window.

He repositions himself in his seat. "What are you afraid of?"

I won't tell him what scares me most. Leaving my family, my home. Going away, alone, without a single friend. Not being strong enough or smart enough. Not knowing who I am. Instead, I start counting out common fears on my fingers, "One, clowns. Two, nuclear war. Three, elevators. Four, getting pregnant." I stick up my thumb. "And five, never getting out of this shithole." Aside from the clowns one, these all are genuinely true for me, especially elevators. Nothing about getting into a closed metal box and being hauled into the air by a pulley and a few cables sounds like a good idea to me.

"I'm here." He leans in again, and his lips find mine, but harder than I expect. His tongue forces my mouth open. He kisses like my cousin, only this is worse because Brett's mouth reeks of beer.

"Wait," I say, my head bowing as I dig in my denim bag. I hand him a silver stick of Big Red and unwrap one for myself. Before the gum has even softened in my mouth, he's bent forward again, sucking at my neck.

"I want you just with me," he says. He pushes my black skirt up around my waist so it looks like a belt.

I want him to slow down, but I don't want him thinking I'm young and stupid. I'm almost eighteen. I know what I'm doing.

"I'll treat you better than anyone," he whispers. "Let me show you."

His hand slides up my thigh and between my legs. A cold finger touches me through my panties then around and under. Until he is touching inside me, and I want him to stop.

He moans. "You feel good."

I wriggle away, beginning to tremble. When did I stop feeling safe? "My mom is waiting up for me," I say, keeping my voice as steady as I can. "My parents expect me home like now."

"Can't you be a little late?" He grabs my hand, and shoves my palm onto the crotch of his pants.

I shake my head. "To them this is our first date, and they're kinda crazy conservative. My dad likes guns."

"Well," he sits back and crosses his arms, "thanks a lot for the blue balls."

I feel young. And stupid.

We drive back to my house in silence, but before I get out, he pulls me to him and kisses my cheek. "I'll call you."

Mom is still up reading when I walk in the door.

"Night, Mom." I hurry past, hoping to avoid her hammering me with questions or sniffing my shirt.

"How was the movie?" she asks.

I turn, smiling too big, and give her the thumbs up.

In my room, I try to sleep but feel like crap, so I get up and work on my half-done college applications. Chances are slim that the overwhelming slew of details will come together, but still, pissing away the option of going to college by not even applying is pathetic, like giving up.

Autopilot kicks in. These applications aren't going to finish themselves, as Dad would say. I suddenly feel determined. Name. Address. Phone Number. My most personal information turned impersonal. I finish three. Easy peasy.

Completing the applications releases some kind of accomplishment endorphins. Wired, I move on to the Alaska State Student Loan application and ask for twenty grand—who knows how I'll pay it back. In my savings I have $2,451.86, all I've managed to scrape together my entire life, and that total even includes the bonds Grandma Buckley gave me when I was born.

The last thing left to fill out is the form to take the SAT. My scores will be sent separate from the applications to my choice schools. I've put off this dumb entrance exam so long that I'll probably have to drive to Anchorage in late fall to take it to ensure my scores arrive at the colleges before admission deadlines.

I'm just finishing when Mom—who I didn't even know was still up—knocks softly. She pushes the door open a crack. Her hair is smushed up on one side, so I'm guessing she fell asleep on the couch.

She tugs my old Care Bears quilt tighter around her shoulders. "You still awake?"

"Barely," I say. I can tell she wants to ask about my night.

Instead she says, "I forgot. Charlie called. She's not contagious anymore."

I want to tell Mom everything, but my heart refuses language, and even if I could speak my troubles, I'm not sure she could hear them. I switch off my lamp. "Thanks, Mom."

She says goodnight and swish-swishes in my blanket cape down the hall.

7/27/90

Matt's party sucked, but at least I finally finished applying to Cornell (pipe dream), the University of Idaho, and Peninsula Community College (just in case). I wish Joaquin would call. Mom has been on the phone every day with Aunt Lily. So annoying. If I find out Joaquin's been trying to call this whole time but keeps getting the busy signal, I will be so pissed. My aunt is perfectly capable of living her life without Mom always butting in and trying to take care of everything.

7/28/90

Our garden's pea plants are loaded this year. They need to be picked. Peas left too long lose sweetness and outgrow the pods. Their once-round sides flatten against each other and push against the pod's thin green skin. But peas never burst out. Run your thumbnail along the dark seam and it splits. The half-shells fall away, but even then, the fat peas stay tucked in close. Deformed and overripe. Stuck up in there. Usually at least one is stunted, no bigger than a sesame. That one's smallness gives the others room. But it's not their fault. Being big feels good. I understand why peas stay.

7/29/90

Tonight I asked Dad if he'd check over my financial aid paperwork. He stared at the TV like he didn't hear me. After like an entire minute of me wanting to scream, he crossed his feet at his ankles and said maybe after the show. Mom eventually did it.

Brett wanted me to go out, but I told him I had to work in the morning. He wanted to know why work tomorrow meant I couldn't go out tonight. I feel like he's trying to control me. Just like my parents. But maybe I'm being too sensitive. I wish I could have stayed over at Charlie's so we could talk and hang out, but she was going out with Kenny. Oh well, I snuck one of Mom's romance novels and had a lovely night with Lord Wendell Darrington, Duke of Cavingshire.

9
Secret Spot

My morning shift at Jay Jacobs is especially grueling thanks to a mob of cranky ladies shopping for swimsuits. The changing area reeks of coconut and self-loathing. I empty their fitting rooms as quickly as possible to avoid a queue, but each is a new disaster. Plastic sanitary liners are stuck to the mirrors. Bikini tops and bottoms are scattered on the floor or looped by their strings from the hooks. I am exhausted even before I begin rehanging.

My tiredness is partly due to the fact that I haven't been sleeping well since Matt's party. I can't stop analyzing, replaying words I'd like to revise, and regretting tiny moments when I could have done one thing but did another. Did I send the wrong signals? Is that why Brett got so pushy?

I don't know what I'm doing right now, with Brett or Joaquin. I never had a boyfriend until I switched to public school—never held hands or kissed a boy except on a dare once (just on the cheek) and that time my cousin accosted me.

Eighth grade was my first year in public school. I met Kyle and had my first orgasm. *Phone sex*—at least, I think that's what you'd call what Kyle and I used to do, alone in our own bedrooms, receivers pressed to ears.

The first time he'd only asked me to describe what stuff looked like, like my boobs. How big was that round pinkish part around my nipple? What did it feel like when my nipples got hard? Could I make my own nipples hard? Would they get hard if I imagined Kyle's mouth sucking them even with his braces? Stuff like that.

Yeah, I was super freaked out the first time but pretended like it was no big deal, because I didn't want him—or anyone—to think I was a prude. Kyle was my first real boyfriend, and I was new to public school. Maybe this sort of thing was normal, the kind of thing regular boys did with regular girls. I figured Kyle must have liked me, because why else?

I had worried that my dad might randomly pick up the phone and listen without me knowing. Or worse, somebody might open my door. But the risk was worth it. Kyle was so into me.

The next time we talked, Kyle wanted me to describe what I saw when I pulled down my underwear. I'd never really looked too closely at those parts of myself before. I mean *really* looked at my body. Kyle wasn't that interested in the hairy outside part so I had to fish around in my makeup bag for my round compact so I could use the tiny mirror to help me see. I angled the glass just so, but the film of peach face powder made it hard to see. I remember my fingers were cold and shaking a little. When he told me to touch myself I actually dropped the mirror.

"What do you mean?" I asked.

His voice got all soft and drawn out, like the way my brother Alex talks to our dog when he's trying to calm him down. "You know, babe." He told me to put my hand between my thighs to warm it up then slip my finger down—real soft, like it was him—and move it around that one spot, slow. I didn't like doing it at first. It had to be all kinds of wrong. I just wanted to talk. I just wanted Kyle to like me.

I didn't want him to think I was prissy, but I didn't want him to think I was slutty, either. I mean, I have morals. It's not like Kyle and I ever did anything in real life. We made out a little after school a few times, and once he put his hand up my shirt over my bra. But mainly it was the phone stuff.

After a while—maybe a month or so of us going out and "talking" a few times a week—I started to relax. My body began to respond to him—I mean, to *me*—and not freak every time I touched myself. My heart would start beating fast, like I was supposed to run somewhere or do something, like I wanted something—but I was too afraid and nervous to get it. So I would breathe and stop and just tell Kyle that I had to go.

Then one day, I didn't stop or breathe or go, and it happened. For the first time. I could hear Kyle breathing hard into the phone, but my eyes were closed, and I wasn't really thinking about him anymore, just feeling my body tighten and tighten and tighten until I thought I couldn't take another breath. I heard myself whimper.

Kyle's voice sounded very far away. "Meri? You good?"

Yes, good. My whole body had grown chewy, like that magical nougat filling in candy bars—but in bursts, back and forth between the chewy feeling and hot little squeezes, like pulses of bliss—until finally I let out my breath, and then every part of me, even the toe that's next to my big toe that shouldn't be longer but is, relaxed.

I opened my eyes slowly. "Yeah?" The phone was lying on the bed about a foot away. I pulled it close to my ear.

"Did you go?" he said.

I didn't answer.

"Did you?"

Suddenly I felt weird—like maybe I should feel bad about it. "I guess so. Did *you*?"

"Maybe," he said, but I was pretty sure he'd been having them for a while. He was always saying dumb things like, "Oh, that feels nice, Meri," and making awful grunting noises, which made we wish my dinosaur of a phone had a mute button. I waited for him to say more, maybe that he really liked me or thanks or...I don't know...good job?

"I gotta go," said Kyle. "See ya in science tomorrow, 'kay?"

"Sure," I said. "Hey, Kyle?" It was stupid, but I felt like some part of what just happened was still a mystery. I needed someone to explain it or at least tell me that it was going to be okay. That I was okay.

"What?"

"Nothing. See you." I heard him hang up.

The last time we talked on the phone, it started out like usual. I snuggled under my covers, receiver to my ear, waiting for him to shut his door and get back on the line because I wanted to feel that chewy nougat feeling, and I didn't know if I could do it without Kyle's words prompting me to think this and try that.

But I wasn't even sure I liked Kyle anymore. We met back in eighth-grade choir when he was still kinda short and hadn't yet sung his amazing version of "Can't Help Falling in Love" at the all-school assembly. I kept waiting for him to open up and show me his true inner self. Maybe sing a song for me or something. I thought there'd be more to him, actually. I thought he'd be like a cross between George Michael, my favorite singer, and maybe David in the Bible when he was super hot for Bathsheba.

Kyle was nothing like those guys. Mostly he reeked of boy sweat, and when we weren't on the phone, all he ever wanted to do was make out or try to get me to go to all-nighters with his Mountain Dew–guzzling friends. They were all obsessed with the game of Risk. I never went, and Kyle never sang to me—not even one note.

When he got back on the line, I said, "Um, I know this is awful timing, but I gotta go. My mom just called me to dinner."

"At seven?"

Kyle was suddenly just a boring guy with a good voice, and I was in the middle of a brilliant realization: I didn't need him. I could have Phone Time all by myself.

"Yeah, we're, uh, eating late. My dad just got home." A complete lie, but I didn't care. I was already touching myself, which I would have thought was totally disgusting the year before.

"Sure. I get it," he said. "Parents are the worst. No worries." He said it fast, like he wanted me to think he didn't care. Maybe he didn't.

"I'll see you tomorrow," I managed to say, maybe even a little sexy-like. I barely heard him hang up because I was rubbing myself in the way I found felt the best and was imagining this other boy at school, Darren, the smart-and-quiet-but-still-hot guy, kissing me and telling me how pretty I was when the phone receiver, which I never hung up, started making this horrible loud beeping noise. I didn't want to stop what I was doing because I was so close to chewy nougat, but suddenly I heard another sound that nearly made my heart stop.

"Meri? Can I borrow a pen?"

I yanked my hand up.

Alex was shoving at my door. "Hey," he said, his one eyeball squinting through the space he'd pushed open. "Whatcha doing?" The wooden chair wasn't holding the way I'd imagined it would.

My heart beat louder in my ears than the damn phone.

"Let me in, Meri!" His shoulder made a soft thudding as he rammed his small body against the door. "Why can't I get iiiiin?" He pressed his head through the widened space.

"Piss off," I said, trying to act sleepy and not mortified, which was probably making me resemble a deranged, half-naked pothead.

"If you don't open up, I'm gonna get Mom." He waited two seconds. "Moooooom!"

"Shut your piehole." I set the beeping receiver in its cradle on my way to the door. "I was just hanging up the phone, buttlick."

"Why isn't your door opening anyway?" He was still pushing against it.

"Um, my chair's in front of it. I had to move it to…find an earring I dropped. It was a stud. Really tiny." I pinched a millimeter of air between my thumb and index finger trying to emphasize how small my made-up earring was while my other hand pulled at the thin white tee barely covering my butt. I had just started sleeping in T-shirts and was suddenly aware how much shorter they were than my old nightgowns. "But I found it. The earring, I mean. So don't worry. You won't step on it or anything."

"That's a real relief." Alex didn't give a damn about my made-up earring. The minute I unwedged the chair, he nearly fell into my room. His eyes moved from me to my bed to my phone and back. His sheltered kid brain was shuffling information as if flipping through the color panels on a Rubik's cube, trying to fit the right parts together to solve the puzzle.

"Well?" I said.

He held out his open palm as if he wanted me to give him five. "A pen?"

"Oh, right." I dug around in my desk drawer. "Here."

He grabbed it. "Your room's a big fat mess, you pig."

I punched him, but only half as hard as I could.

"Ow!" He rubbed his arm and pretended to stab at me with the pen then sat down in my desk chair. "Why so violent? Kyle piss you off?" Alex never liked Kyle.

"No," I said. "You did."

"Why? Because I asked you for a pen?"

"Did I say you could sit in my room?" I flopped onto my bed and pulled the blanket up to cover my half-naked body. "And by the way, you better not let Mom hear you say 'piss.' She'll wash your mouth out with soap."

"Nah. She only does that when you say the Lord's name in vain."

"Whatever. Get out."

He got up then turned and looked at me hard and determined, like maybe he solved the Rubik's cube. "Kyle's an idiot," he said. "You can do better."

I broke up with Kyle the next day. Mom and Dad never even knew I'd had a boyfriend.

After the morning swimsuit rush, Jay Jacobs empties and by noon is deader than church on Super Bowl Sunday. When I finish cleaning out the fitting rooms and rehanging the swimwear, I ask Pam if I can leave early.

She eyes me suspiciously. "You look terrible," she says. "Better not be partying." She gives me a lecture about the dangers of alcohol and the company's zero-tolerance policy before agreeing to let me go. I use one very clean dressing room to change into sweatpants, an old tee, and Brett's sweatshirt.

I told Mom I was going to visit Charlie after my shift, and I will visit her, but I need a little time to sort out my boy problems, and there's a certain place I go when I'm in need of serious introspection.

On the drive to Kenai, my bloodshot eyes keep blinking back at me in the rearview. When I pass 7-Eleven, I think about the night I met Brett—less than two months ago. Back then, the idea that I could be with such a mature and confident guy seemed like a dream. That whole night I thought I was the luckiest girl in the world, even after I got puked on by that poor dog. The day at the beach was awful, but maybe Brett was just showing off for his friends, because later at the movies, he was great again. And I loved the way he was at our Garden of Italy date. So sweet.

But I'm still not sure who he is for real. When he showed up at my house to take me to Matt's party, he worked my parents so easily. That was impressive—him acting responsible and respectful. But it was a total performance. Not the real Brett.

I know for sure the angry guy he was at the beach and Matt's party isn't who I want to be dating. There are versions of Brett that I like, but are they even genuine? When is he pretending with me?

I wonder who Brett is when I'm not around. I don't think we're an official a couple, even though he called me his girl. I pull at the sleeve of Brett's football sweatshirt and bring it to my nose. I can't tell if it still smells like him or just an old shirt.

I pass Anchor Court and catch a glimpse of Joaquin's cousin's trailer. I want to stop to see Joaquin, but I'm in no condition to see anyone, especially a person I really want to like me. Besides, he's probably gone anyway, working with his dad or playing ball with Noah or some other thing. Haven't heard from him since he cancelled on me, so maybe he's not into me anymore.

I turn left off the Spur Highway, pass the baseball fields and an apartment complex, and drive until the road dead-ends at a waist-high rock wall. I park the Bug and walk toward a narrow opening in the wall. When I step through, a cool breeze with the scent of salt and seaweed lifts my hair. I can hear distant waves but can't yet see the inlet.

I follow the winding path, flanked on both sides by tall beach grasses. Their yellowing stalks hiss and swirl around me. I pop the head off a stem, scrape the seeds free with my fingernail, and sprinkle them like tiny coins along the pathway.

In minutes I am standing in a clearing on a hillside not far from my church overlooking where the mouth of the Kenai River mixes into the Cook Inlet. There's a weathered wooden bench near the cliff edge. Beyond the bench, steep stairs cut into the hillside and continue down to the beach.

I slump onto the bench and run my hand over the initials I carved there last year. My two Ms look like twin birds in flight. Charlie and I always planned to get out of here together. Just us. She doesn't need Kenny, and I don't need Brett. Or Joaquin. Stupid boys only pull us down, anchor us to this place. Neither of us needs that. I kick at the hard dirt until my sneakers rub two trenches. Why is everything in life so freaking difficult?

I step up onto the bench, causing my already ripped sweatpants to tear a little at the inseam. Gaining two feet of perspective is worth the rip and the risk of breaking my neck. The bench slabs are grayed and peeling but seem sturdy enough.

Below, the blue-green inlet rolls relentlessly toward me, waves foaming as they bite the dark sand. The Aleutian Range rises up beyond the sea, the Chigmit Mountains bordering the inlet. I locate Mount Redoubt and Mount Iliamna. Their sapphire peaks, like the ones you see on Alaskan postcards, are tipped in white.

Silvery clouds congregate in the sky, doing their darnedest to dim the late afternoon sun. My mind drifts with the clouds back to the day Joaquin taught me to dipnet. From where I'm standing, I can see the exact spot on the beach where we waded into the waves.

I want to linger in the moments when I'm in the water with Joaquin, but the memory is overshadowed by Brett's angry outburst. Should I be flattered that Brett was jealous? He acted the same way at Matt's party when I was with Lee.

I hug my arms around my middle and again inhale the faded smells of his sweatshirt. He said, "I'll treat you better than anyone." Did he mean he'd treat me better than anyone has treated me before or that he'd treat me better than *he's* treated anyone before? I wonder about the other girls he's dated. Maybe Brett's been hurt by a girl. Or maybe by his stepdad, who sounds like a real dick. My mom is overprotective and my dad is distant, but I know my parents love me.

Gulls screech overhead, probably arguing over food. One wings off alone and dives, retrieving something in her yellow beak before flying away. Smart bird. Like that gull, I should focus on my goals—on figuring out how to get out of Soldotna—not overanalyzing Brett. I can't fix this guy's issues. Anger bubbles in my chest, but mostly at myself. I push his sweatshirt up over my head and toss it into the grass. Swish.

I raise my arms as if might grow wings. The breeze blows my T-shirt so the sleeves flap. I close my eyes and scream into the wind. All my confusion and frustration raises my voice and empties my lungs. I yell again, with more oomph, until I've screamed myself out of air and it's quiet again, save for the wind and waves.

"Hush...hush," says the ocean in my ears, like a comfort. "Rush... rush." Like a calling. My future is as distant and mysterious as the faraway ocean. But if salmon can find their way out there, I can, too.

I'm so wrapped up in my moment that when fingers slide between mine, I nearly vault off the bench and am left teetering with the force of my own retracted arm.

Hands grab my thighs to steady me. "Easy, killer," says a familiar voice.

When I look down, Joaquin is smiling up at me. That dimple of his is my kryptonite. "You're invading my secret spot," I say, wishing I could crawl under the bench. I hate that he probably heard me screaming like an idiot and that I'm wearing ratty sweats and a stained tee. I want him to only ever see the put-together me.

"Nothing's secret in Kenai," he says, reaching so our fingers can thread together. He tugs at my arm, but I tug back. He leaps onto the bench as if it is only six inches high and stands firmly beside me.

"I was blowing off steam," I say, trying not to look at him.

"I'm glad I heard you," he says, as if he truly means it. His eyes on me are so intense. Unless he's blind, he's taking in the whole of my disgusting state and isn't turning away.

"I'm not feeling so hot today," I say. "I totally won't be mad if you keep on walking. We can hang out later, you know. If you want."

"Now is good with me," he says, looking out at the horizon.

We stand together, not saying anything for what feels like infinity. I'm certain it's the longest I've ever stood in silence beside another human being, and the effect is weirdly calming. The full force of my tiredness descends, and I sag against him.

He holds my weight and wraps an arm around me. I don't let go of his hand so my arm is kind of awkward, but I don't care. The evening has grown cool, and Joaquin is warm. All that was wrong when I arrived suddenly seems set right again.

"I'm supposed to be visiting my friend, Charlie," I say. "She's sick."

"You should probably go then," he says.

"In a minute." How is it that every time I'm with him, I don't want to leave?

Charlie's nesting like a baby bird amidst three pillows and a rainbow quilt, watching TV, when I get there. A dozen or so wadded pink tissues are assembled in a line along the arm of the couch, and there's a humidifier humming on the end table. It's blasting a steady stream of water vapor at her face. The room smells thick and stale.

"Hey, sickie," I say, trying not to breathe too deep. "You still alive?"

"Barely." She hits pause on the remote, and the video cassette clicks to a halt. Robin Williams freezes on the screen. He's standing atop two school desks in his white shirt, tie, and slacks, playing the role of the idealistic teacher, Mr. Keating. "There by the grace of antibiotics and NyQuil go I." Charlie's pupils are big and black.

"And *Dead Poets Society*, apparently."

"Carpe diem, dude," she says.

I step over empty Fritos bags, discarded shoes, and a mound of books on my way to the couch. "What's with all the books?"

"Aren't we taking the SAT next month?" she asks as she scootches over.

I've barely studied, and I didn't turn in the forms in time to take the test next month. I've been distracted by my boy issues. But I don't want to fess up to Charlie about my complete lack of focus or that I won't be taking them on the same day as her, so I nod and change the subject. "Where's your mom?"

"She's been taking extra shifts at the recovery clinic." Charlie shrugs. "Lots of needy alcoholics in this town." She pushes play again on the remote.

I sit and watch *Dead Poets Society* with her, remembering the first time we saw it last year at Orca Theater. We were so wired when we walked out, yelling "carpe diem!" all over the place and daring each other to do stupid stuff in the name of seizing the day. Charlie begged her mom to buy the video the second it was available, and we watched it twice that day.

Today Mr. Keating's speeches sound as fanatical as Pastor Dan's sermons. I reach over and press pause. "I'm sorry you're sick," I say, because I feel bad that Charlie's been miserable and alone. I want to tell her everything that's been going on with me. I give her a little side hug. "I've missed you."

"Is this the part where we make out?" She giggles.

She drives me nuts when she turns everything into a joke. Makes it impossible for me to tell her anything. I need my best friend right now, not a sarcastic asshole. I push myself off her couch, but she grabs the edge of my tee.

"I'm only kidding, MerMer," she says. "C'mon. You know I love you."

My sweatpants tear a little more as I flop down. "There's a ton I've been wanting to tell you."

"Speak," she says. "And it better be juicy. Kenny came over yesterday when my mom was gone, and let's just say, stuff happened." She wiggles her tongue.

"Gross." Her teaser deflates me. I don't feel like competing with her sexual exploits. "You're lucky your mom trusts you. Mine is annoying the crap out of me."

"Yeah?" she says, staring at her front door. "At least your mom is around."

"She's *always* around."

Charlie acts like she doesn't hear me. "Your mom is so nice.

Remember that time in eighth grade when we went as scary cats to the Halloween dance and your mom helped us with our costumes?"

Charlie defending my mother is actually more annoying than my mother herself. "You mean that time we looked so weird nobody would dance with us?"

"Your mom was with us all day," says Charlie sleepily. "She was so great. Like there was no other place she wanted to be." She lays her head on a pillow. "I wanna be a mom like that someday."

The last thing I want to talk about is being a mom. I press play on the remote and sit with Charlie a while longer until she finally falls asleep.

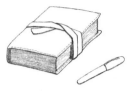

8/8/90

Dad spent his last night at home glued to the boob tube. He loves family shows where perfect fathers like that dad on Growing Pains joke around with their kids and solve everyone's problems. I'm in the same room, and he doesn't even acknowledge me. Sometimes he eats in his dumb recliner, which Mom hates because he gets food stains on his undershirts. But she says television's better than the bottle.

8/9/90

I took Dad to the airport then swung by Anchor Court to see if Joaquin was around but got nervous because I didn't call first. I've never actually met his Mom and Dad. So I left. Brett called when I got home, but I said I couldn't talk. He called back an hour later. I feel like the more I cold shoulder him, the more he wants to be with me.

8/10/90

Aunt Lily called crying tonight. Mom put her hand over the receiver and mouthed "drama queen" and I laughed, but then Mom started crying, too. Grandma Buckley's in the hospital. I've never seen my mom lose it. After she hung up, she climbed into bed and wouldn't get out, so I had to make dinner. I actually wish Dad was here. When I brought her a plate—a loaded baked potato, her favorite—she shook her head. Said she wasn't hungry. I said, "You have to eat," but she said, "I need my mom," and rolled away from me. I saved the potato in the refrigerator. Just in case.

Mom bought tickets for the two of us to fly to Grandma's, but I can only stay a week. Pam wasn't happy about me taking the time off work, but I told her my mom needs my help and this might be the last time I get to see my grandma before she dies. I hope that's not true. I wonder how sick she really is. We leave on Aug. 23, the day Dad gets home. I'm excited to fly. Alex is mad that he can't come but Mom said there'd be nothing for him to do. I said at least he gets to hang out a bunch with Ryan. They'll probably play basketball the whole time and talk about snowmachines. Whatever boys do.

August 23, 1990

Dear Joaquin,

I'm writing you from an airplane. This is only the second time in my whole life I've ever flown, and I wish the windows were bigger because I like looking down at tiny trees and stuff.

We're bouncing all over the place right now, so it's kinda hard to write. Turbulence, they said. I'm scared we'll end up at the bottom of the Pacific. I actually checked the cockpit on the way in to make sure Matt Selanof wasn't our pilot! Ha!

It's so cool that we're going outside, but I wish we were going somewhere exciting, like NYC. I'm going to Idaho with my mom to take care of my grandma. She's really sick. Not sure if Noah told you.

Welp, I was hoping we could go out or something when I get back. I'll be gone a week and a day. Please write back and tell me what's new.

Your favorite weird girl,

Meri

10
Outside

We're still asleep in Grandma's guest room, me on the floor and Mom and Aunt Lily sharing the double bed, when the hospital calls to say Grandma Buckley's getting prepped for emergency surgery. They say she has a brain tumor. Aunt Lily starts crying and hyperventilating, so Mom has her breathe into a paper bag.

"We'll get through this, Lil," Mom says, rubbing Aunt Lily's back. "I need you to stay strong with me."

"Grandma will be fine," I say lamely.

Aunt Lily glares at me.

"Why don't you stay here, Mer," Mom says, biting the inside of her cheek. "Hold down the fort."

"The fort's not going anywhere," I say. "I want to see Grandma."

"Hospitals are full of germs and sick people," counters Mom. "No sense exposing you."

"But I'm healthy, so who cares?"

"I've worked in a hospital," says Mom seriously, "where all kinds of super-viruses fester in little nooks and crannies that don't get cleaned—strains that resist antibiotics and lodge in your brain and cause cell death. You're still young. Let's not risk it."

The whole scenario seems unlikely, but the thought of getting a virus in my brain...

"Anyway," she says, "your grandma'll be all hopped up on pain meds, so she probably won't even know who's there."

I don't want to, but I stay behind to tidy Grandma's house.

The shower soothes away my anger at having to stay and my worries about a brain virus. Why do I let Mom get inside my head like that? It's ironic that she hates horror movies because the woman can take even your teeniest worries and freak the shit out of you by putting said worries on steroids, listing all the horrible crap that will happen if you do *x*, *y*, or *z*.

For example, smoking pot—even just once—will poison your eggs and get you addicted to drugs. Then you'll get knocked up, have a brain-damaged baby who's missing an arm or a leg—most likely an arm *and* a leg—and you'll name him something unfortunate, like Chet, and then you're trapped for the rest of your life, a drug-addict mom with poor limbless Chet.

For premarital sex, the anecdote is similar to the drug one, only more immediate and shameful. You'll get pregnant and catch diseases, like chlamydia and syphilis, probably go mad like Henry VIII, your sex organs will rot, and no one will ever marry you. You'll be alone *forever*. It's your choice. "Just say no, Meri."

I dry myself off and pull flannel boxer shorts and the white tee I got from Kyle in junior high from my suitcase. Plenty of people have had sex and lived to tell about it. "Just do it," I say to no one in particular.

I start gathering up the old newspapers and magazines strewn about on the living room floor anyway. I arrange them all in a neat stack on the coffee table.

I already miss home. And Charlie. When I called to tell her about Grandma and that I had to fly down with Mom to help out, it made me feel better when Charlie said, "Your grandma's rad! She has to get better because I want her to meet Kenny and give me her opinion."

Every summer except this one, Grandma Buckley has flown to Alaska to visit us, and she always takes Charlie and me out for ice cream sundaes. Our Girl Summit she calls it and says we can talk about anything—but mainly she gives us sketchy advice about boys. Charlie's favorite Grandma Buckley quote is "Nobody buys a cow without tasting the milk first."

Charlie promised to write me a letter ASAP so I'd get mail at

Grandma's. Before I hung up, Charlie said, "Make sure to call Brett. He told Kenny he *really* likes you."

I did call Brett, but he seemed mad about me leaving and told me to hurry back.

At the last second I dialed Joaquin's number, but he was out with his dad on some boat repair job, so Noah gave me their mailing address.

Grandma's house is small and dusty inside. I can't actually see dust, but I lug the vacuum out anyway and push the ancient appliance around the living room. The thing is so huge and loud, operating it should require a heavy equipment license. I detach the hose part and start sucking spider webs out of the corners.

Balled up on Grandma's floral couch is a tea-colored afghan that's basically a bunch of doilies all hooked together. How do you fold that shit? I shake it out and hang it over the back of the sofa.

Under the couch cushions, I find a green knitting needle, a blank postcard with a photo of the Grand Canyon, and a tiny pearl earring set in silver filigree. I recognize the earring as Grandma's—I've seen her wearing the set many times. I want this piece of her, so I jab the earring in the extra hole in my left ear that Mom doesn't know I got six months ago and secure it with its gold back. The Grand Canyon I hide in my pocket, and I toss the needle in the knitting basket.

I haven't seen a mailman yet. Out Grandma's front window in the park across the street—East Park or East City Park or something like that—tents are being set up, and a bunch of weird-looking hippie people are mulling around them. It looks like a fair, only with no animals or dust or cowboy hats.

Grandma's AC is purring, and though the air feels cool inside, the hummingbird thermometer on her window says seventy-six. Mom said the temperature will climb to ninety-five degrees by afternoon, so unless I want to get sunburned and heatstroke, I should stay indoors. What does ninety-five even feel like? The hottest day I can remember in Soldotna was eighty degrees.

I slip my bare feet into my Keds and open the door. Sunlight blasts my eyes and warmth washes over my skin as if I just stepped into a bath. I blink and wish I'd brought sunglasses. Kneeling, I check under the porch mat to make sure the key is in the hidden place where Mom said it would be in case of an emergency, and yes, a brass key is duct-taped to the black underside. I lock my grandma's door and take the cement stairs two at a time.

Across the street, open tents line grassy rows and tables are set up next to food stalls. Music from an acoustic guitar and a voice like a missionary singing worship songs floats my direction. I don't recognize the lyrics, but maybe it's a Christian event. Mom and Aunt Lily probably won't be back from the ICU until dinnertime or later.

I cross the street and enter the park. At the nearest booth, a girl about my age is trying on scarves. She sizes up her reflection in a hand mirror hanging on a string from a tentpole. The girl seems exotic, tanned, with long, honey-brown hair worn loose except for a few tiny braids woven with red ribbons.

Her camisole is a mini version of one of Mom's slips—the kind with the adjustable satin straps that Mom wears under her church dresses—only this girl is braless and the cami has been cut so her waist is bare. A black tattoo curls around her belly button and below, a jangly metal belt. A gauzy skirt sits low on her hips and swirls around her legs, and her leather sandals look like something I once wore when I played Mary the mother of Jesus in the church Christmas play. I can't decide if the whole ensemble is some new fashion or if this girl doesn't care what's in style.

I meander closer. She's carrying a denim satchel covered in pins and patches, mostly flowers and band names, a few I recognize. One pin stands out—a metal "U of I." She must be a university student.

Beside me, a woman holding a plate of little paper cups offers me a sample of something that resembles rice.

"Tabbouleh," she smiles and points to a food booth across the aisle. The woman is dark and angular. A red scarf covers her black hair and gold bobbles hang from her ears.

"Thanks." I don't want to be rude, so I empty the cup like a shot in my mouth. The flavors are strong and mostly unfamiliar, though I recognize garlic and lemon. I can't decide if the tab-whatever is good or just weird.

The exotic girl with the honey hair floats from booth to booth, and I follow. Whenever I get close, I smell her, musty and sweet. Not a fragrance I'd buy for myself, but I want to know what it is, so I pretend to be fascinated by the same silver ring she's admiring—a band engraved with alternating moons and stars—and when I'm close enough I say, "I like your perfume."

She turns, and for a second her eyes narrow like she's trying to remember something. "Oh! You mean the patchouli?"

I have no idea what she just said, but I nod.

"I'm Brita." She holds out her hand, and I shake it.

She turns back to the ring. "Mind if I buy this? Or were you going to get it?"

"No. But it's pretty."

She pulls the band from the velvet display holder and offers to pay the man eight dollars.

"That one's ten," he says.

She flashes him a smile. "Nine?" Her teeth are inhumanly white, and I wonder if this girl is some kind of magical woodland fairy. The man's eyes are glassy, and he stares at her cami as he extends his open palm.

"Nine," he repeats.

She pays, slips the ring on her middle finger and ducks out of the shaded booth.

I follow her back into the bright, hot sun. "Do you know the way to the university campus?" I ask.

"Just down the hill." She keeps walking but turns and gives me the once over. "Where you from?"

"Alaska." We're almost out of the park.

Her eyes light up. "How cold is it there?"

I hurry after her onto the sidewalk and follow her down the hill. "Really cold in the winter, but not bad in the summer."

"Igloos?"

I can't tell if she's being sarcastic. "No."

"Didn't think so," she says but looks disappointed.

I want to keep us talking, so I add, "Lots of moose, though."

She's moving surprisingly fast in those Jesus sandals. "Never seen a moose."

"Where you going?" I ask as we near town.

She stops. "I thought you wanted to see the campus?"

As we stroll through Moscow, Brita explains that she's a second-year geology major and that the local soil was blown here by wind and is called loess. She interrupts herself now and then to point out notable bars and restaurants, and the food co-op, which I think is basically the grocery store.

"I actually had a hard time," she says, "adjusting to this place after Phoenix. All these fields and rolling hills. It's like another planet. I hated it at first, but now I'm used to it."

"I've never lived outside of Alaska," I confide. I don't even know this girl, but she seems nice.

"I'd never been out of Arizona, either, except for, like, a few vacations. Everything felt all weird when I first got here. But the people are cool. If you come you should totally live in the dorms. That helped me a ton because I lucked out and my roommate's like the sister I never had—my actual sister's a primo bitch." She laughs. "Now I go back to Phoenix and I'm like, who are these freaks?"

"Don't you miss home?"

"You kidding?" she huffs. "That place is soulless. I get more than enough family in Phoenix when I go back for Christmas."

The sky overhead is completely clear. The blue is deep and heavy with heat. No clouds to offer shade, and there aren't enough trees along the sidewalk to keep my arms from prickling and turning pink.

"This is technically where campus starts." She points at a squat building with a glass front. "That's the SUB—the Student Union Building—but I'm on my way up to the Admin. It's worth seeing. The campus here is so pretty with all the brick buildings and ivy."

My mind flashes to the image of myself under a tree with a book in my lap on a campus like this one, surrounded by brick buildings covered in ivy.

"Barely feels like we're in Idaho, right?" she says. "Almost like an East Coast campus." This girl is far more talkative than I expected her to be, but I'm glad, because I can't seem to form my thoughts into words.

We turn and head uphill to a wide concrete path lined with enormous trees. I'm relieved for the shade, but I'm so thirsty. The incline feels harder than it should. I'm sweaty and dizzy and losing track of which direction we're going.

"This is called the Hello Walk," she says. "I've been told one of the presidents who lived near Greek Row would say hello to everyone he walked by on the way to the Admin, but I've never seen the university president, and I actually think that story's a crock of shit."

Branches with giant leaves arch over our heads into a dense canopy that nearly blocks the sun. Beyond the trees, the scene feels unreal, like a photo in a book or the pictures I've seen of Cornell University. Open paths wind through the neatly trimmed green lawns toward soaring brick buildings covered in ivy. I had no idea the campus would be so stately and stunning—or so *hot*.

Our path opens to what looks like a columned brick castle. I cup my hand over my eyes to block the sun while I tilt my head back and stare up at the gothic-looking clock tower.

I can't bring the tower into focus. I blink. I shake my head. I'm broiling. There's a buzzing in my ears. Blink, blink. The sky drips down around me. The trees and bricks blur. Green to red to green. Go, stop, go. Blink. The buzzing is louder.

I blink and blink and blink, but my eyes won't open.

Am I dead? I smell fresh-cut grass and above me glimpse a girl who could be an angel, except she's tanner than conventional angels. Her eyes are as blue as the sky behind her face.

"Drink this," says the angel. She brings a clear plastic bottle to my lips.

The water is warm, but tastes amazing. I want to gulp and gulp—I've never been so thirsty—but she tips the bottle away. "Slow up or you'll barf."

She lowers my head, and the sun materializes beside her face. Hot light blasts my eyes. I roll to the side, and blades of grass tickle my nose.

"You fainted or something," she says, and I remember at once that her name is Brita and we met at the park and I am in Idaho because my grandma has cancer.

A wave of nausea rises when I try to sit, convincing me to lie awhile in the grass.

"You epileptic?" asks Brita.

"No. Why? Did I have a seizure?"

She shakes her head and looks disappointed again, like when I said we don't live in igloos.

A few people are watching us, lurking, as if to make sure I don't need real medical attention. My whole face is hot, but I'm not sure if it's from sunburn or embarrassment. "I gotta get back to my grandma's."

"Come inside the Admin a minute," says Brita. "It's cooler."

I don't have the energy to argue. She helps me up, and I shuffle across the circle drive to the shaded stone stairs. The hall is cool when we step inside.

"Wait here and I'll walk you back to the park." She leads me to a bench and clomps off in her Jesus shoes.

After a few minutes of sitting, I feel good enough to cross the hall to a porcelain drinking fountain, and as I'm carefully sipping more water, I feel a hand on my arm. A girl wearing flannel shorts that look similar to mine says, "Hey, I'm new here. Do you know how to get to the UCC?"

I smile and shake my head.

Brita returns with a granola bar, and I drink a bit more from the fountain before we head back. The sun doesn't feel as intense on the walk home, but I'm still overheated and exhausted by the time we get to the park. The fair is still going on, but I'm not interested in exploring the booths. I thank Brita for showing me around.

"No problem," she says. "Maybe I'll see you on campus next year."

Mom and Aunt Lily don't get home until well after dinnertime. Aunt Lily doesn't even say hi to me, just goes straight to bed. Mom notices my sunburn, but she barely makes an effort to bawl me out.

"I told you not to go out in the heat," she says.

"How's Grandma?"

"They opened her head up," says Mom. "They took out some of the tumor, but the cancer's a weed with roots going every which way."

"So what now? Radiation? Chemo?"

"Nothing," she says. "We pray for a miracle."

August 24, 1990

Sweet Meri Ann,

When are you coming back? You totally missed the SAT test today. I kicked its ass. You're going to have to take yours in Anchorage. Speaking of Anchortown, the boat show's this weekend. I wish you were here cuz it's our LAST WEEKEND BEFORE SCHOOL. Your driverly skills are required. My mom and her newest boy toy are for sure going to overnight in Anchorage, so you could have stayed at my house. I have no idea why they're even going. Boy toy can't even afford a house let alone a boat and anyway, darling Mumsie hates fishing. (So do I.) What's going on with your gramma? Guess what? Kenny and I have been hanging out a TON! Don't you love me anymore? Write back soon!

This island sucks. Get me off.

The Professor

8/24/90

I met a girl named Brita, got a raging sunburn, and cleaned Grandma's house (it wasn't that dirty). The University of Idaho campus is nice. So are the people. I can see myself going there.

8/25/90

Today I stayed inside all day (away from the sun) trying to read this stupid book while Mom and Aunt Lily were at the hospital. I'm pissed Mom keeps coming up with stupid reasons for me not to go. I miss home, which is dumb because we haven't even been here three full days. I know there's no way my letter could have already arrived in Alaska and been read by Joaquin, who could then write and return another letter, but I can't help watching out the window for Grandma's mailman.

8/26/90

Mom and Aunt Lily brought Grandma home in the Buick. She can't really walk, and she's all swelled up. Her silver hair's matted on one side, and on the other, her head is shaved and divided in half by a dark scab that curves above her ear and ends just before her temple. She's mainly been sleeping. I hope I get to have a good talk with her before I have to leave.

Got Charlie's letter today. It's not my problem she doesn't have a car, but at least she wrote me. The first day of school was today. Brett called once. He told me he missed me then wanted to know what I was wearing.

8/28/90

Joaquin hasn't written me back or called—not once—even though I gave him the number. Maybe he can't afford long distance. It's probably for the best. Grandma sleeps in bursts—a half hour here, an hour there. I wouldn't want her woken up by a constantly ringing phone.

11
When Being Alive Is
Just Being Not-Yet-Dead

Even though there are tumors in Grandma's brain, her mind is still sharp. I guess the cancer focused more on the task of killing her body than stealing her sensibility, because when I empty her urine bag she whispers, "Thank you, honey." When I wash off her backside, "Oh, thank you dear, I don't want to smell like an old person." When I ask if she wants me to bring her fresh drinking water, "Please, sweetheart," or, "That would be lovely."

Her dogged civility somehow makes her dying worse.

The hospice people gave us a special bed for her that she can raise and lower with a button. We take shifts watching her sleep, bringing her water when her mouth is dry, and sometimes pudding. Mostly she sleeps.

Tonight the curtains are drawn and a lamp erases the darkness in a circle around us. Mom, Aunt Lily, and I crowd around and each rub a bloated arm or leg to get the fluid out. This hurts her, so we concentrate on being our most gentle, keep our heads down, and avoid looking at each other. When I glance up, tears leak out the corners of Grandma's half-closed eyes, as if all of what we are feeling has pooled inside her and her swollen body can't hold it.

While Mom sleeps a few hours after dinner, Aunt Lily and I stay up late watching the rise and fall of Grandma's chest and read on separate islands—me in the rocker and her in the armchair.

Aunt Lily's reading a cancer book. I've been trying to make sense of the dusty copy of William Faulkner's *As I Lay Dying* I found on Grandma's bookshelf.

When I opened the novel to the first page, folded long like a bookmark was a school essay I sent Grandma in fifth grade about my great aunt's funeral. I thought maybe Grandma left the book here just for me. I was ready to read something profound, but so far the thing is mostly gibberish.

I keep slogging through, hoping for deep thoughts about death, but the only character who makes any sense to me is Dewey Dell. I skim to her parts until I get sleepier, and when I can no longer follow what's going on, I stash the novel in my backpack and find a few old comic books in the garage to read instead.

Days and nights blend. When she's asleep, I watch Grandma's heartbeat shimmer in the waxy hollow of her neck. During the night I read the comics to stay awake or write letters and stuff in my journal. In bubble letters I draw Meri Hale next to Meri Santos and try to decide which sounds better. I like both names better than boring Meri Miller.

From my chair, I angle my head so that the line between the thin blue blankets covering Grandma and the air just above her intersects at the bedrail. If the blankets lift above then fall below the bedrail, I know she's still breathing.

Once, I couldn't see the rise and fall, and the seconds ticktocked by until I ran over and woke her.

"Oh!" she said. "I'm still here."

I couldn't tell if she was relieved or disappointed.

She smiled her old-self smile. "Sorry I can't die a little faster."

We all hate when she says this. She could recover. Or at least could live a while longer. Grandma says she's ready, but death isn't in a hurry. I wonder if she has some idea when it will happen, like a premonition. If she does, she doesn't tell us about it. I don't want her to die.

I'm doing a shift tonight with Aunt Lily, but she's already snoring softly in her chair. We're all pretty exhausted from the weird hours.

I tiptoe over to Grandma's bedside. She's been sleeping propped up, and her head lolls to one side. She almost doesn't look like herself with her puffy face and her mouth half-open. Her breathing is consistent, but there's a gurgle that shouldn't be there and each inhale sounds too sharp.

I'm surprised when suddenly she stirs and her eyes flutter open. I smile down, slightly guilty for watching her like a creeper while she was asleep. I grab her water cup by the bedside and bring the red straw to her mouth.

She takes a sip, her eyes still unfocused. "Is someone crying?" she asks me.

"Aunt Lily's snoring," I say, setting down the cup and repositioning her pillows.

"Gordon used to rattle the windows some nights," she says, chuckling. She sits up and clears her throat. "That man could snore with the best of them."

Grandpa Gordon died in a plane crash when I was a little kid, but I've heard countless stories about him. He looms larger-than-life in my made-up memories. "How did you know he was the one?" I've asked this many times before, and she always tells me something different—his fancy Ford pickup or his blueish eyes that looked like tiny planet earths or Greta, his prize-winning cow.

Tonight she squeezes my hand. I hadn't even realized I was holding onto her. "You know by the way you feel about yourself when you're with them," she says, her eyes brighter than I've seen them in days. "With your Grandpa Gordon, I was less uptight—more fun. I liked myself better around him."

I wish I could have known the two of them together. Mom says they fought sometimes, but she always knew they loved each other. I'm not so sure with my own parents. "I want to choose someone I can be in love with my whole life," I say.

"Love," she says. "That's quite a word." She coughs, and I help her take another sip of water. I don't want to wake Aunt Lily, or she'll come take over. I want to take care of Grandma on my own.

When she's settled again, I pull up her blanket. "What's the secret to love?" I ask.

Grandma thinks a minute. "When it starts, love is blank as snow. Anything feels possible. You can barely get enough of that other person. You want to know all there is to know about them."

I nod and think of Joaquin.

"But for some people, the more they're together, the more set in their ways they get. They tramp that blank snow down walking the same boring tracks over and over."

Sounds like my parents.

"Pretty soon they've worn trails only to the places in that other person they go most often. There's still tons of new snow in there. They could go millions of new ways. Discover a hidden snow cave. Build a snowman. Anything. But they don't. They keep walking the same paths, like a bad habit." She pauses to take a raspy breath. "Love is not doing that."

I don't say anything because I'm thinking about what she's said. Trying to puzzle out the meaning.

"Love is letting every day be new." She tilts her head. "Get it?"

"Get what?" asks Aunt Lily, finally roused.

Before I'm ready, I have to say goodbye and fly back to start school. Mom drives me to the airport in the Buick. I don't want to leave.

On the plane, I try not to think about my grandma or the fact that I'm alone. The stewardess brings me playing cards, refills my clear plastic cup, and makes jokes, but all her niceness bugs me. I don't need her to take care of me. I sip my soda to keep from saying something mean. I should be thrilled to be flying on a plane by myself, but instead I just feel lonely.

When the plane lands, Dad and Alex meet me at my gate. Alex runs up and gives me a big hug. Dad takes my backpack and carries it to the luggage area. "How was your flight?" He doesn't really want to know.

I miss Mom already.

Mrs. Porter's 5th Grade Class Writing Assignment

My Worst Fear

by Meri Miller

Mr. Gage died cleaning his horse's hoof. An aneurysm is when a blood vein explodes in your head but I'm not sure if it comes out your ear like in a movie. I didn't get to check his ears because I couldn't go to his funeral.

They said Great Aunt Dee died from cancer that went to her brain. Her funeral day was very sunny. The church was so bright I saw dust on the windowsills. When I saw Aunt Dee in her casket she was made up fancy and didn't really look dead like she was sleeping or if she got knocked out on her way to church. I should have shook her to make sure or put a mirror over her mouth like they do in movies to see if breath was coming out, but I didn't have a mirror.

If Aunt Dee was still alive, she got trapped in the ground and is probably dead now. Being trapped like that is my worst fear. I wish I could dig her up and check, just to be sure.

Dearest Wilbur,

I'm so glad you're back, MerMer. I totally
wanted to kiss you on the lips when I saw you in
senior hall this morning. But I didn't want Kenny
to get jealous. He wrote me this super perverted
note and bitched me out about saying Matt was
cute, which I did like a hundred years ago. I wrote
him a totally vulgar one back and called his ex a
flaming twat. Tell the Kenmeister if you see him I
want his bone. Psych! Don't say a word. Bring my
hairspray tomorrow you lousy slut. PLEASE!!! It's
Finesse and the bottle's ALMOST FULL. See you
at lunch. Remember National Honor Society meets
today!

Your Truest Friend,

Charlotte

8/31/90

I missed the first four days of school when I was in Idaho, and because I wasn't officially registered for some reason, I almost got kicked off the dance team. Dad came in today and straightened it all out. That was the one time since I got back he hasn't been a complete train wreck. The first couple nights he took Alex and me out for dinner. He tried asking questions about school and our friends. Today he made cheese sandwiches and burnt them. We ate in silence, and he made me clean up after. He said I needed to start making dinner, which is totally bogus. Alex is just as capable of heating soup and making toast as I am.

9/1/90

Dad made Alex and I take the kitties to the mall today and give them away. I begged to keep my Calico Cali, but Dad said winter would freeze her or if she survived until spring, she'd be wild, hiding and peeing in the hay. The cutest kittens got taken right away, including Cali, but there were two left over, and Dad shot them in the woods. He said they didn't suffer and dying now is better. We still have Mama Kitty. Next week I'll take her to the vet to get her fixed.

9/3/90

The sales were insane because everyone was off from school and at the mall shopping. Except me, who was there working my butt off on a holiday that's supposed to celebrate workers, not remind them how terrible work can be. Labor Day is the worst. Also, I'm still bummed about the kitties. At least I got out of making dinner tonight.

9/4/90

School was a blur. I'm behind in every class, and Charlie doesn't want to study with me because she spends every second with Kenny. Dance team tryouts were after school, and the audition piece was the whole routine we'll perform at Homecoming, so my brain was fried at the end. Tonight, after two straight hours of make-up homework, Joaquin called out of the blue to tell me he got my letter. I was like, great! Why didn't you call sooner? He said he'd been working a lot. Whatever. Charlie said Brett's been asking Kenny about me. I don't know what's going on with Brett or if we're a thing or what. Every day at school I have to watch Kenny go gaga over Charlie, and yes, I'll admit it. I wish somebody was going gaga over me.

12
Lessons in Politics and Trade

Through the window of sixth period, I see Dad's bright-green Chevy LUV with its matching camper top pull into the parking lot. I watch him creep up to the side door. Tomorrow Dad flies back to the North Slope, so today he drove me to school so he could pick me up and we could swing by the grocery store on the way home. I don't know why I'm in charge of acquiring supplies. Alex gets to ride the bus home, oblivious as usual. I hope nobody sees me get into the Lime-o-sine.

When the bell rings, I grab my pack from my locker, shove in my homework, and say my goodbyes to Charlie and Kenny, who barely notice because they're being all flirty and gross by the senior lockers. Dance team practice starts tomorrow, and I can hardly wait to have someplace I have to be after school. Dad hates when anyone makes him wait, so I barrel out of the commons as quick as I can.

"Hey, Dad," I say as I jump in. The cab smells oily and vaguely like wet animal fur. Southwestern-style seat covers scratch at the backs of my arms. My Jansport pack sits like a child on my lap, and I hide behind it as we drive out.

Dad keeps his eyes on the road, hands at ten and two. His green British Petroleum hat sits high on his head. "Mom won't be back for a while," he says. "Your grandma's not getting any better, so I'll need you to help out more."

I nod. Outside, the trees are almost bare. Haphazard piles of moldering leaves are all that's left of fall, my favorite season. It came and went without me.

Dad turns up the volume on the radio so he can hear *Trader Time*, the local radio show where people call in and try to sell their junk or get other people to sell them junk they want. DJ Jack helps an old man describe his posthole digger. "It's a manual kinda digger, right, sir?"

The old man either doesn't hear or understand. "Huh?"

DJ Jack tries again. "You turn it by hand?"

"Of course you turn it."

DJ Jack doesn't want his listeners to be confused. "This isn't one a those tractor implements, is it?"

"What?" The old man sounds offended now. "I already said so. This ain't no tractor jobby-do. This is all elbow grease. I had this digger since fifty-nine and replaced the handle just this spring. It'll last a guy fifty more years."

I hate *Trader Time*.

"Dad?"

DJ Jack repeats the old man's phone number. A commercial for Peninsula Plumbing comes on. "It's your doody..."

"Dad!" I say it louder. I can't listen to *Trader Time* for a second longer.

The muscles in his jaw tighten, but he turns down the volume.

I'm thinking, trying to come up with something fast to keep us talking and *Trader Time* off. The last class of the day was Government. Three branches of our government: legislative, judicial, and executive...a dictatorship versus a democracy...the right to vote. "Do you vote?"

"What?"

"Vote. You know, in elections. Do you vote every election?"

"Of course I vote! Boys *died* for that right. Better believe I vote." He reaches for the radio knob. "What kind of a question is that, anyway?"

"Just talking about it today in Government."

His hand drops to his knee. "Listen up. Voting is a privilege—a *responsibility*. You remember that."

"Uh-huh."

"The Electoral College is a sham—that's for damn sure." The hand on his knee balls into a fist. "But people who don't vote shouldn't call themselves Americans."

I know he served in the Air Force, but why all the passion about voting?

Dad shifts in his seat; his head grazes the cab ceiling. "Alaska is still part of the fifty states, and unless we manage to secede from the union in the next few months, come eighteen, you will cast a vote."

"Right. Of course." Had I been giving off a voter apathy vibe?

"Good girl."

The silence that follows is as unbearable as *Trader Time*. The Chevy's engine starts to annoy me, buzzing like a room full of people. I might as well be alone. Dad is back to driving at ten and two. At least before he had been talking to me.

I make my voice soft, as if he is a deer. "Dad?"

"Huh?" He turns.

"What political party are you?"

He grabs for the volume knob and turns. "None of your business."

Trader Time is over.

9/6/90

Dad flew back to the Slope. I'm glad and not glad. It's weird how in a single month, my parents have gone from needing to know my every move to leaving Alex and I to fend for ourselves like wild animals. Mom doesn't like it, but what can she do? She's thousands of miles away. At least I made the dance team. Yay, me. My tumbling skills have always guaranteed me a spot. Also I was voted secretary of the Spanish Club, not that anyone cares.

9/9/90

Alex and I didn't go to church today. When Mom called to check on us, I told her it was because I had too much homework, which is basically true, but mostly I didn't want to go.

9/11/90

Brett surprised me and stopped by the school today. Actually he came to pick up Kenny, but when Charlie and I walked up he was all, I was hoping I'd see you. He said he liked the spandex pants I was wearing for dance practice and asked if I'd wear them to the movies with him Saturday. Even though I'm annoyed he didn't call or anything while I was gone, I said I'd go. Dad's not home, so I guess I'm in charge.

9/15/90

Saw *Young Guns II* with Brett. Boring movie, but Brett
held my hand. Our palms got sweaty, so halfway through
we stopped. There were only like four other people in the
theater because it was a matinee. Brett wanted to go drive
around after, but I said I couldn't. I didn't feel like it and
also didn't want to get home too late because it's just
Alex and I now and neither of us likes to be home alone at
night. He's never actually said that. I just know.

9/17/90

Homecoming is this weekend. The dance team performs
at the game, and I know the routine, so I'm sure that will
go fine. More importantly, this will be my last high school
homecoming dance ever in my life. I asked Brett if he'd
consider going with me, and he was like, Not my scene,
babe. I'll probably just go with Charlie.

13
Bones For Flying

Two booths over, Charlie and Kenny are attempting to swallow each other's faces. If I wasn't so grossed out by the idea of their sex juice on my backseat, I'd suggest they go out to the Bug. Nobody in Dairy Queen wants to see what they're doing.

I pull at the cheap pink formal I bought on clearance last year and wore to homecoming because Mom wasn't here to make something better or take pictures or ask when I'd be home. Charlie said she'd be my date so I didn't have to go alone, but after we danced for five seconds, it became the Charlie and Kenny show. I've spent all evening playing the role of chaperone and chauffeur. Out of desperation, I called Joaquin from the payphone at SoHi and begged him to meet me here. I should have just asked him to go with me in the first place, but it felt wrong to ask him after I had already asked Brett.

Across the table, Joaquin half smiles. He's not a big talker, but I like the challenge.

"Tell me something weird about you," I say, pleased to finally be interacting with someone who seems interested in being with me.

Joaquin stretches and pops his back, as if warming up for a sporting event. He's likely buying time, deciding what or how much to tell me, but knowing he's putting thought into his answer makes me warm all over.

"Something weird, huh?" Joaquin folds his arms over his chest. "Isn't me sitting here in my sweats with you over there all dolled up weird enough?"

Kenny was giving Joaquin shit earlier about his "nice pants." I think Kenny's being a dick because of Brett, and Charlie's started to give me shit, too. "Where's he from, anyway?" she asked when we were up at the counter ordering food.

"Here," I said. "Same as you."

I'm tired of everyone judging Joaquin without knowing him. He's one of the most genuine people I've ever met. He's a great big brother. He worries about his family and work just like anyone else. He's never done anything to Brett or Kenny, and I'm annoyed at Charlie especially for not giving him more of a chance.

"I want to know stuff about you," I say, pulling a pack of SweeTARTS from my sequined clutch and tearing the wrapper from the disc-shaped candies. When I have a little pile collected on the table, I start stacking them in columns, organizing them according to color. I think back to the first time I saw Joaquin, before I knew him. All I saw was something I wanted. Maybe I'm as bad as Charlie and Kenny.

He pushes up the sleeves of his sweatshirt but still doesn't say anything.

I pop an orange candy into my mouth. "How about I go first. My thing is that I refuse to eat pink and blue SweeTARTS. They're gross. So I either have to throw them away—which I hate doing—or I have to find somebody to pawn them off on." I shove the pink and blue columns to his side of the table.

"That's just wasteful." Joaquin grabs a handful of blues and crunches down. "They all taste the same to me."

I shrug. "Now you."

He leans forward and swallows solemnly, as if he's on the verge of revealing a horrible secret. "First swear you won't laugh or tell a single soul." He holds out his pinky.

I loop my baby finger around his. "Pinky swear." My stomach tightens. What if he plays with dolls or sells drugs or tortures baby kittens?

Our pinkies are locked together, but instead of releasing after we shake, the rest of his fingers close around mine so that we're holding hands. He grins. "I collect wishbones."

"No, you don't." Wishbones? I did not see that coming. I squeeze his hand just to make sure it's really holding mine.

He nods. "I started in junior high. For luck, mainly, but also because bones are cool." He's dimpling out, and his face is all lit up in the cutest of ways. His brown eyes are blinking fast, framed by the longest black lashes. He looks more like Noah right now. "They're called furcula, or little forks. I have jars and jars full."

I look down at our hands, intertwined. His palm is warm but not sweaty. Rough and calloused and kind of abrasive but in a good way, like if our palms rubbed together, they might spark. Like he is iron and I am oxygen, and together we ignite. I force myself to concentrate on speaking. "Where do you get them? The bones, I mean."

"From, like, turkeys and chickens. After, you know." With his free hand he pantomimes eating a chicken leg.

"That's sorta gross." I'm mildly horrified and majorly intrigued. Mostly, I just want to keep holding his hand.

"Nah. Wishbones are wicked cool," he says. "Not only for the wish-making part. They're an important bone. Like a strut between a bird's shoulders. They're supposed to help it fly." He clicks his tongue and shakes his head. "No help, though, to the turkeys or chickens."

"Ironic," I say.

"Life," he says, letting go of my hand. "Not everything makes sense." He reaches into the pocket of his sweatpants and pulls out his keys. Tangled in the key ring is a slightly yellowed wishbone. "Try your luck?"

He pinches one end between his thumb and index finger, and I grab onto the longer length. The bone is smooth, and for the moment, Joaquin and I are connected by this luck maker.

"If I win," he says, "you go with me to my homecoming. It's in two weeks."

My heart flip-flops like a salmon out of water, and I feel equally starved for air. I pull hard, with the force of a person unconcerned with fate. There's no way for me to lose.

The wishbone breaks, gifting Joaquin with the biggest piece. "I win," he says, looking genuinely pleased with himself. "You never said what you wanted."

"Same as you," I say. "Guess we're both *wieners*."

He groans. "Weirdo."

From their make-out booth Charlie yells, "Meri, remember my hairspray from summer?"

"No," I say. There are so many other things I want Charlie to care about.

"Do I have to tattoo the word 'hairspray' on your freckled face?"

I roll my eyes. "Indisputably, I need a face tattoo."

"*Indisputably*, you need to get laid."

I feel my cheeks burn and stare daggers at Charlie, but she's oblivious.

When I call to tell her about Kenai's homecoming, Mom doesn't say no outright. She says, "I think one homecoming's enough, don't you?"

"I went with *Charlie*." I say, "Maybe I'm a lesbian."

"You're not," she says, "and formal dresses are expensive."

"Joaquin goes to Kenai," I say. "I can wear the same dress I wore to the SoHi homecoming."

She pauses. "What kind of a name is *Wah-keen*?"

"A good one," I say. "Joaquin is a good person." I don't mention that she's met his family on one or more of her forays with the church ladies to Anchor Court or that Joaquin's mom serves us pizza every time we go to Pizza Pete's. I don't think either would help my cause. But I'm also pissed that she doesn't trust my choices.

"Mer," she says, "we've given you a lot of freedoms already this year. Aren't you already seeing that Brett boy?"

As if she's being so generous. She's not even here. How would she know? "I'm not *seeing* anyone," I say. "We went to a movie. So what?"

I hate how easily she bought Brett's fake-out routine. He was obviously acting with his yes-sir-home-by-eleven and no-drinking-ma'am-I've-got-a-day-job bullshit. How could my parents not see that? "Nobody's married here, and anyway, we still haven't established my sexual orientation."

"Grow up, Merideth," Mom says. "Dad and Alex need your help while I'm gone."

How completely unfair. Though I can hear in her tone that she's made up her mind, I don't let up. "Alex is a big boy. He can figure it out." I need one of Joaquin's lucky wishbones right now.

"No." Mom's voice is firm. "You're not going."

I growl. "Great. The hottest guy on the peninsula asks me out, and I have to say no?"

"Your grandma, *my mom*, is very, very sick—probably *dying*—and all you can think about is boys and dances?"

I hate being reminded about Grandma. "How is she?"

"She has good days and bad days," says Mom. "She wrote you a letter today. I'll send it soon."

I wish I was there. But I was sent home. To get on with my life as a high school senior, which is exactly what I'm trying to do. "It's just one dance."

"I said no," Mom says, but now she's on a roll. "How do you think Grandma would feel if she knew that right now her own granddaughter was unwilling to put aside selfishness long enough to help her family?" This is classic Mom, brandishing her guilt shotgun and firing at will. "Do you want me to have to tell her that?"

I hang up and stomp upstairs to my room before she can launch into one of her patented lectures, like "I'm Your Mother and I Know What's Best for You" or "Dating Tips from When I Was a Teen." The latter can be summarized: find a nice guy from church who has a good job and looks and acts and talks exactly like you. Because a guy like *that* would never hurt you. Because what is familiar is probably safer.

The longer I consider these "truths," the less they resemble truth.

September 23, 1990

Dear Meri,

Thank you for coming down this summer and helping when I had to go to the hospital. I'm better now than I was, but the chemo makes me so tired. I wish I wasn't sick, but God never promises us a tomorrow. He just gives us the gift of today. Never forget that. I hope you are getting along alright up there on your own. Having your mom gone so long must be very difficult for you, but please know how much she's helping. This won't last forever, and I'm grateful to you for letting me borrow her.

I wish I was going to be there to see the amazing things you will do and watch you figure it all out. The world is a great big place, Merideth, but you are a great big person. Bigger and bolder than even you know. Don't be afraid. Explore! Your mom worries after you, but don't let that stop you from going after what you want. I promise she will keep loving you.

Whatever happens, I am so very proud of you and love you more than you can know. Live each day like it's a gift for you to open.

All my love,

Grandma Buckley

P.S. My advice about boys is to find one who brings out the best version of you.

These weeks without Mom have started to blend. I go to school, dance practice, and home, where I end up making mac 'n' cheese or heating up canned ravioli for everybody, then I clean up, do my homework, sleep, and repeat. Once in a while Charlie calls to tell me how great Kenny is or bitch about him if they're in a fight. Brett's been calling a lot. It's nice to feel like someone wants to be with me. Joaquin's been giving me the silent treatment since I had to cancel as his homecoming date.

9/28/90

Big shocker! Dad let me meet Brett in town for dinner. Dad's liked Brett ever since they bonded over the peeing-from-a-telephone-pole story. Charlie and Kenny joined us at Pizza Pete's. I could only stay out until eight, but just leaving the house and doing something fun with friends was heavenly. It sounds pathetic, but I've been SOOOO lonely. Especially now that Charlie spends all her time with Kenny. At least if I'm with Brett I get to see her once in a while. I miss Joaquin, but this is just easier.

14
Better Than Eternal Suffering

I'm at the kitchen table trying to help Alex with his homework—an essay on the Civil War—when he slams his pencil down.

"Leave me alone!"

I take a breath. "I'm doing the best I can here." We're both tired of the new routine, but I don't have the energy to put up with his crap. I'm dealing with my own. Dad will be home in two days, and I'm not yet sure if that will improve things or make the situation worse.

His eyes narrow. "Stop acting like you're Mom. You're not."

I push my chair back, and the metal feet scrape across the linoleum. "Screw you, dickwad."

"Screw you, too!" He flips me off. "Just go do whatever it is you do while I'm stuck here by myself. Or with Dad." He kicks the table leg. "Which is worse than being alone."

"It's not my fault Grandma's dying." I feel close to tears. "Go hang out with Ryan if you're lonely. Stop acting like a baby."

"Stop being a bitch."

My stomach tenses. Alex has never called me a bitch. I sprint to the stairs before he can see my face—I can't hold the tears in any longer.

Behind me, Alex is saying, "I'm sorry, I'm sorry, I'm sorry," but I don't stop. I take the stairs two at a time, run down the hall, and slam my bedroom door.

The house settles into complete quiet, as if it's empty. Because it is. The two people who should be here refereeing have bigger things to do. Even God has left us to attend to other emergencies. I sit cross-legged on my bed and hit the top of my clock radio. Billy Joel's voice drifts out, a song about being a poor piano man. Oh boohoo, Billy.

Brett will probably call again tonight. We don't have much to talk about, but it's just nice to have someone calling me. Nobody else seems to care. Joaquin still hasn't called, and other than surface-level chitchat at school, Charlie's been distant. We used to call each other every day. We were, as Mom said, "connected at the hip." She used to hang out after school and do her homework while I was at practice and after we'd go get drive-thru and I'd take her home. Guess Kenny's been giving her rides.

I dial Charlie's number.

"Hello?" Charlie sounds distracted, but I'm so relieved to hear her voice that I almost whoop into the receiver.

"Hey, Charles. I've missed you."

"Contrary Meri." She crunches on something—probably a gross Frito. "Did I not just see you, like, two hours ago en la escuela?"

"Yeah, but I mean, we barely got to talk." Next to my bed is a picture of Charlie and me in eighth grade at the Halloween Dance dressed up in our horrible cat costumes. I'd do anything right now to go back there.

"Omigod! Did I tell you Kenny bought me a necklace? I know you know we're going out now, but after school today—for no reason—he gave me this really cute sterling silver C on a chain. I'm so gonna wear it tomorrow."

Jealousy pricks at me, but I try to sound excited. "Wow! That's awesome."

"I know. Omigod, he is so amazing. Don't you think? Whenever he sees me he sticks out his lower lip, you know, like a little kid. So cute. It means he wants a kiss."

"Cute," I say, wondering if when I die I'll be damned to hell and it will be a continuous loop of this conversation.

"Yeah," she says. "He's so adorable."

Why am I getting so irritated? I should be happy that Charlie's obsessed with Kenny and he's obsessed with her. But where does that leave me? I want to dive through the phone and shake her back into being *my* Charlie. "How does Kenny feel about you going to college with me next year? Is *he* planning to go somewhere?"

"He's gonna stay here and work," she says. "Which is a totally smart idea. Don't you think?"

Automatic dishwashers were a smart idea. The escalator was a smart idea. This is more like the zeppelin. "I guess. But isn't that what student loans are for?"

"Who wants all that debt?" The question hangs between us, and before I can respond to all that it implies about her future plans, she says, "Oh sorry. My mom needs the phone. Can we talk tomorrow?"

"Sure," I say. Our whole exchange was making me want to vomit anyway.

"Later, slut," she says, and as I'm about to hang up I hear her tinny voice shouting at me through the receiver, "Oh wait! Bring that hairspray I left at your house forever ago!"

After school on Friday, I drive to the mall and inhale a chocolate chip cookie at I Love Cookies before I have to clock in at Jay Jacobs. I'm on shift tonight with Pam. I straighten the rounder of high-waisted jeans while Pam, who is Seventh-day Adventist, complains about how she's not allowed to eat halibut.

"Bottom fish are unclean," she says. "But sometimes I sneak bites of other people's fish and chips—mainly just the crusty parts." She stops organizing the clothes and looks up. "You don't think that's a big deal, do you?"

I shrug. "I don't see how a bite of fish is worth God's attention, but I'm not Seventh-day Adventist."

Pam's perfectly polished fingers smooth the pleats on a pair of Z. Cavaricci's. "What are you?"

"A Believer." I pull a rumpled purple jumper off a hanger, shake out the wrinkles and rehang it. "I don't know. Our church is nondenominational, but my mom says we're basically Baptists."

"Oh boy," Pam's pencil-drawn eyebrows lift. "Real Bible-thumpers, huh? Fire and brimstone and all that?"

I sigh. "I guess." A part of me actually likes the idea of hell. Any God who is willing to go through the trouble of tracking every sin, listening to countless apologies, and damning people to everlasting torment must really care about them.

"We don't believe in hell," she says smugly.

I start refolding a stack of sweaters. "What happens to the bad people?"

"They get destroyed," she says. "Painless and quick."

"I guess that's better than eternal suffering."

There's a rustle and the screeching of hangers on a rounder behind me. "What's better than eternal suffering?" asks a deep voice.

I look up and see Brett. Damn him. "We don't carry men's clothes, sir."

"Maybe I'm buying something for my girlfriend."

Pam perks up. "I can help you with that," she says. Pam's never met Brett. "Describe your girl. What's she like?"

"Gorgeous. About yay high." He holds his hand below his chin.

I roll my eyes. We're almost the same height.

"Nice, um..." His hands make an hourglass in the air. "Red hair and a whole lotta sass."

I hit him and finally Pam gets it.

"Pam," I say, "This is Brett Hale. My *friend*."

"Her boyfriend," he corrects me.

September 29, 1990

My dear Merideth,

I'm at your grandma's house and it's the middle of the night. Aunt Lily and Grandma are asleep. It is a hard thing, you know, to watch a person slowly go from larger-than-life to very small. To lose your own mother is terrible beyond words. Someday you'll understand. (But not too soon, God willing.)

All week little memories from my childhood have been popping into my mind...learning to swim in Lake Pend Oreille, being baptized by Grandpa Gordon, and going with your Aunt Lily to that horrible turkey farm. What loud and stinky little monsters (I mean the turkeys). We sure were scared! I remember my first dance at the Grange Hall when your grandma stayed up all night to finish sewing my blue dress.

I don't know how long Mom will hang on....The doctor says it could be one month or six or even a year. Some days she's so with it, and others she's barely conscious. I feel like I'm losing both of you at the same time. I guess life is about letting go. At least Mom will be in heaven, so that gives me comfort.

I have been praying ever so hard for you. Alex says boys call at all hours and you've been going out with them. I have ALWAYS stressed, both from a Christian and a medical standpoint, that intercourse (sex) is improper and a sin outside of marriage (and with more than one partner). You're almost eighteen, so I know I no longer have much right to be your conscience, but do you feel that AIDS won't happen to you? Pregnancy?

Did I give you too much free "thinking time" and freedom to do as you please without enough grounding in what God would have for you? I thought you were spiritually strong. You have always said that you asked God to come into your life. Was that just for my benefit? Please read I Corinthians 5, 6, and 7. Especially chapter 6, verses 9 and 10.

Remember that even though I don't always approve what you are doing, I still love you. You are my first born and so beautiful. You have always made me proud of you, but I believe Satan is having a field day with you right now. Don't be tempted. I pray that you will stay strong. God loves you even more than I do, so when you make bad choices He hurts even more than I do.

I know you think you want to leave Alaska for college, but consider the University of Alaska in Anchorage. Maybe even the Bible college up there. You'd only be a couple hours away. My offer still stands: if you go to the Peninsula Community College, you'll get to live rent-free at home!

I miss you. Well, it is 11:30 p.m. and I'll need to start my shift with Mom bright and early, so I better try to sleep. Remember this letter is written in love. XOXO

Your loving mother

P.S. Please remember that you must set a good example for your brother and take care of him. Just like I do with Aunt Lily.

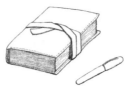

A letter from Mom came today. I'm so sick of her trying to guilt me and control me. I know she loves me, but her love makes it hard to breathe. Plus, I can't believe that God is sitting around crying over all my choices. He's got more important things to do, and my choices aren't even that bad. I'm starting to believe different things than my parents, and unlearning what they've taught me my whole life is like slowly peeling off my fingernails.

10/3/90

I can't count the number of times Dad has ordered me to bring him tea. Zillions. Never a please or thank you. You'd think he fathered me solely for fetching. Today I climbed the stairs to the kitchen, as usual, only this time I avoided the rug's worn places and stuffed my toes in those fluffy spaces where feet rarely touch—like a game. Two minutes later Dad's yelling, "Where's my tea!" so I hurried and poured and steeped except this time, when I stirred in the cream, I spit in the cup. Instantly I felt awful! Dad sat in his easy chair with his back to the stairwell, totally trusting me. I would have remade the tea, except he yelled AGAIN, so down the stairs I went, delivering spitty tea to my dad, who would never spit in my cup.

10/4/90

Today in our stupid Ethics in Government class, Charlie wanted to know if Brett and I had done the deed. I know it's because she has with Kenny and she wanted to compare notes. But I wasn't in the mood so I pretended not to hear her and concentrated on Kahlil Gibran's The Prophet long enough to read some shit about love and wings unfolding a sacred fire until she hit me in the head with a paper wad. When I looked up she started making out with the back of her hand. She's been super annoying. All she ever says is Kenny's so fine.

10/5/90

So this is bizarro. Today while I was at practice Joaquin left a message with Alex to have me call him. Maybe I still have a chance with him? Alex said he sounded like a decent guy on the phone, but what does a decent guy sound like? Maybe I should feel guilty about dating Brett, but I don't. At least SOMEBODY wants to be my boyfriend.

15
If I Leave Immediately

The Bronco rumbles into the school parking lot, and the entire dance team looks up from where we're stretching next to the track. Brett doesn't cut the engine, and the Bronco's idle is loud enough to draw attention to itself. A couple of the girls stop stretching. They toss casual glances toward the Bronco and hit the sexier poses from our drill routine, but the mirror-tint windows make seeing inside the cab impossible.

I bounce to my feet and wipe dirt and dead grass from the back of my itty-bitty skirt. I usually hate freezing my ass off on the days we practice on the field, but today I'm glad we're outside. With every roar of Brett's engine, the stigma of me being that weird girl from Christian school slides farther away.

"Later, Kitties," I say, though technically, we're the Soldotna High Mountain Lion Dance Team—that's a mouthful, so everybody calls us the SoHi Kitty Kats. They make a big deal out of saying goodbye—obviously they want to ask me questions—but before they have the chance, I grab my backpack and jog past Coach Berryman. "Gotta jet, Miss B.," I say. "My boyfriend's here."

My "boyfriend" Brett has volunteered to pick me up from practice because the Bug started belching blue smoke the night after Dad left for the Slope. I'm still stuck riding the school bus back and forth with Alex on days I don't have practice, but being back in the Cheesewagon with the underclassman isn't as bad as I thought. It's nostalgic, even. I miss being young like that, with years ahead of me to figure out life.

Brett revs it a few times as I sprint across the lot. Before I've reached the passenger side, he pushes the door open from the inside and stretches out his hand, but I can't quite reach it. Instead, I grab the side of the cab to step up onto the running board. My skirt rides up, and Brett slaps my thigh.

The other girls are still watching; I can feel their eyes on my back, so I toss my hair, launch my body inside the cab, and slam the door behind me. I lean over and kiss Brett sweetly.

"Hey, babe." His fingers slip under my uniform top, and he moves in for a lip-lock, but I turn and throw my pack into the back seat.

"Let's go!" I say, my voice full of an enthusiasm I don't feel. We still haven't left the parking lot, and I don't want the girls or Coach Berryman to wonder what's going on behind the tinted windows. I don't want to be seen as a prude, but the other extreme is just as bad.

Brett shoves the Bronco in gear, and we pull away. The school and the field disappear in the rearview.

"So," I say. "Where we going?"

"I'm taking us to dinner."

I wait, but he doesn't say more. "Where?"

"You'll see."

The clock in the dash reads 4:26 p.m. "Who eats dinner at four thirty?"

He looks over and smiles wide enough for me to see his snaggly left canine. "Early's better. Mooseburgers, two for five dollars."

I'm suspicious. "Is this some kind of a barbecue?"

"Sorta." He inhales loud and slow. "Uh, how was dance practice?"

Brett couldn't give two shits about practice or anything else high school. He's obviously trying to distract me. He refuses to go with me to my senior prom this spring because he "did that already" and says I should just go with my girlfriends. But who wants to go to their senior prom without a date? I don't.

"School was fine." I cross my arms and slouch back against my seat, knowing there's something he doesn't want to tell me.

"C'mon, babe, why ya gotta be like that?" His palm slides up under my skirt. He laughs as I scoot away.

We get into town, and Brett doesn't stop at either of the two Soldotna restaurants that could possibly be serving mooseburgers. All that's left along the main street are a couple seedy bars, and then you're heading out of town.

Maybe we're going on a picnic. A surprise date with Charlie and Kenny. There's nothing on the seat behind me except my backpack, but they could be bringing the food. I hope so because I feel better when Brett and I are hanging out with them, not just by ourselves. Less pressure to make out and whatever.

I act as if sex isn't a big deal, but I'm actually scared shitless to do it. Brett's moving faster than a guy my own age probably would, which stresses me out, but the fact that he clearly wants to at least confirms he likes me.

Brett slows the Bronco as we near one of the bars, Benny's. He turns into the back parking lot.

"What are we doing?" I can't be seen in Benny's. I'm still only seventeen.

"We're eating," says Brett, shutting off the ignition.

"Hello?" I point to the dance team uniform I'm still wearing. "There's no way I'm going in there."

"Fine," he says. "You can stay here and wait for me to eat my burgers."

He must be kidding. "I could get in real trouble, Brett. Seriously, let's just go somewhere else." I've never set foot in a bar before.

"No way. I can get two burgers for five bucks here. Best deal in town." He opens the driver-side door and hops down.

"Please?" I hate that I'm reduced to begging.

"Relax, Meri. You'll be fine." He adjusts his ball cap and looks at his reflection in the side mirror. "You don't have to drink anything, just come in and eat. Act older. Put on some lipstick." The car door slams.

Brett swaggers toward Benny's. His light-wash Levi's 501s are tight on his legs but somehow look droopy from behind. The jeans are supposed to fit snuggly over the ass—that's the whole point—but Brett's butt is flat; his thick middle pushes them down well below his waist, where they heroically fight the law of gravity, a law that is as unforgiving as the one against minors in a bar.

I roll my window down and shout for Brett to come back, but he ignores me and keeps walking toward the entrance. When he gets there, he doesn't look back, just jerks the handle and disappears inside. I hear a few lines from a country music song—I think George Strait's "Ace in the Hole"—before the heavy door slams shut.

I stare at the door to Benny's, a large wooden monstrosity with six mahogany panels. Each is carved with various Asian-looking scenes—mostly dragons and traditional pagoda-style buildings. The bar used to be a Chinese restaurant called the Emperor's Palace. I went there once after a choir concert when I was in junior high. Back when I was dating Kyle.

Kyle and junior high seem like a thousand years ago, as passé as the Chinese restaurant. I crawl into the Bronco's backseat where the window tint is the darkest, wiggle out of my uniform, and slip on the old gymnastics tee, Cornell sweatshirt, and jeans that I pull from my backpack.

I don't want to be here in the back of the Bronco getting ready to walk into a bar, but I don't want Brett to get mad, so I finish changing, wad my dance uniform into my Jansport, and head toward Benny's hulking door.

When I pull it open, a haze of cigarette smoke hits my nose, and I quell the urge to cough, as the door bumps against my butt and knocks me inside. I scan the room for Brett, squinting. My eyes take a second to adjust to the dimness.

Brett has somehow vanished, but my English teacher, Mr. Banyon, is sitting at a square black table whispering something into the ear of the assistant swim coach, Ms. Tuttle. *Married* Banyon doesn't see me standing there, but Ms. Tuttle does. I'm not sure who's more shocked, her or me, but since neither of us would want the other to tell, I bank on getting a free pass if I leave immediately.

Brett materializes out of the smoke just as I turn and bolt out that massive door like a panicked Scooby Doo, as fast as my legs will skedaddle. He must have caught the look on my face right before I whipped around, because he meets me in the parking lot less than a minute later carrying his stupid burgers in a white paper napkin.

My heart's still racing. I lean against Benny's and try to slow my pulse, my head hiding the sign that reads: No Minors Allowed. Shit. I could get in all kinds of trouble—kicked off the dance team or suspended.

"You look freaked." Brett shoves a burger in his mouth as mayonnaise drips out the side of his napkin.

"My English teacher and the swim coach were in there," I say. "I'm dead."

He finishes wolfing down the burgers, wads the napkin and throws it on the ground next to an armless Teenage Mutant Ninja Turtle.

"Just take me home," I say, on the verge of tears.

He shakes his head. "Nah, let's go back to my place." By "his place" he means his *parents'* house.

16
The Super Big Bad Thing

Lying in Brett's king-sized waterbed, I wonder if this is going to be one of those life moments you always remember because you want to hold onto it forever or because as much as you try, you can't forget it. You're never sure until the moment is over.

"You've got the hottest tits, babe." Brett moves his hand in squeezy circles over the tiny gymnast's head on my purple 1986 state championship T-shirt. I arch back, like the Julia Roberts body double in the sex-on-the-piano scene with Richard Gere in *Pretty Woman*, as Brett makes slurping sounds against my neck. His warm mouth feels okay, but I worry his sucking will leave marks. Under the covers, I feel his knee bend up and his toe wiggle at my waist, pushing my underwear down. His fingers work at the back clasp of my matching pink bra.

After a minute of fumbling, he says, "You should get one a those front kind." As if it's my fault he can't work a hook and eye, and I wonder, on whose front-clasping bra has he honed his unfastening expertise? Brett grows impatient and shoves one barely B-sized cup up to my shoulder. He stares at the lonely, exposed nipple hardening in the air.

When I peek down, my chest seems flatter—especially with me lying on my back. This isn't how I imagined it with Richard Gere. My still-fastened bra is cutting into me, so I reach behind quickly and, with a twist, release the stretched elastic.

"Much better," he says.

Part of me wants to yank my shirt back down, but Brett's slack jaw and his trance-like eyes so focused on me cause another part to want to keep the moment going. What I feel isn't exactly desire, but something equally strong. A kind of power. Brett has nothing else on his mind except me. I slowly pull my shirt over my head.

"Brett." I try to make his name sound like a moan—sexy.

He bites down on my nipple, and I nearly pee myself. I don't want to admit he was hurting me or that I'm about to wet his water bed. Maybe I could claim it was a leak. I lift my head off the pillow and gently press my palm against his forehead to unsuck his mouth. His lips are shiny, and his large, black pupils are glassy like salmon eyes.

"I know you like it when I do this," he says.

I had revealed once, after he begged me to describe what turned me on, that I liked the idea of a man's mouth on my breast. But not like this. "Yeah, I like it...." I glance at his closed door—the hollow kind, painted black, with a taped-on poster of a bikini girl riding a grizzly bear. "Won't your parents be home soon?"

The door may as well be a sheet hanging between us and the rest of the house. I can hear every creak and rustle, and in my mind Brett's mom could be throwing open that black door and seeing me naked in her son's bed any second. I imagine her disgusted face. Would she call my parents?

"First off, the stepfucker is never home," he says. "Second, Mom knows that if I'm gonna live here, my room's off limits." He rolls one leg over me. His thigh is thick and heavy. "Anyway, who cares about them? We can do whatever we want."

I'm nearly eighteen. An adult. In another century, I'd probably have already pushed out three babies. But this isn't the olden days. This is me in 1990. This is the Super Big Bad Thing. What if I get pregnant or contract HIV or worse? What if I'm damned to hell for all eternity? All seem equally probable and improbable.

"C'mon Merideth. We've waited. I love you...."

This is the first time he's said it, and despite a tiny alarm going off in my head, hearing him say "I love you" in his throaty boy voice makes me feel warm and gushy.

I'd never heard of it, but Brett said today is Sweetest Day, which is the day people everywhere declare their love for each other and make gallant, memorable gestures. I like the idea.

"Let's make today even sweeter," Brett says, reaching down to find my hand. I think he's going to lace his fingers in mine. Instead he pulls my palm over onto the bulge in his boxers. I touch him quickly and retreat, my fingertips sliding lightly over the flannel and functionless button above his open fly.

"Don't be a tease, Meri." He grabs my hand again and rubs himself roughly with it until his body starts shaking. "God, I want to be inside you."

I roll away. "Wait."

He pulls up the covers and scoots closer. His fingers are now cold and clammy. They crawl blindly up my inner thigh. I resist the impulse to clamp my legs together. I know where he's going. He'd done it before when we were making out in his Bronco. Said he was getting me ready, so it wouldn't hurt when we finally did. But I didn't want his cold fingers jammed inside me.

The house creaks a loud warning, and I bolt upright, pushing his leg off me. I listen for his mother's footfalls, my heart racing, as I wait for the click of his opening door.

"Chill already." Brett leans toward his nightstand. My folded Guess jeans fall from the bed to the floor. He hits the top of his clock radio, and a scratchy version of Def Leppard's "Pour Some Sugar on Me" shrieks out.

"Better?" On his side, he props himself up on one elbow, half-singing along.

My teeth grind together. Sometimes I just want to be done. I get sick of holding on so tight. Sick of not knowing a thing. Sick of worrying and protecting and dodging and resisting.

He gives my shoulder a little shake. "Loosen up."

"I *am* loose." I hate all that it implies, but I've already built too much momentum. It's like in gymnastics, when you first throw a trick. You commit a hundred percent. You can't back out. You get through that first time, and afterwards you fix your mistakes.

Brett moves on top of me as I lay on my back making self-conscious breathing noises. Tiny white stalactites cover his ceiling, twinkling like constellations. In the center, a circular light fixture stares down, a milky full moon. Even with the light off, I can see a tiny, dark body silhouetted on the other side of the glass. A dead fly.

Brett touches me between my legs. "Relax, babe."

I focus on that fly. Easy peasy.

Air bubbles gurgle in Brett's waterbed beneath us. His sheets reek of Calvin Klein's Obsession for Men mixed with his own body smells. I lean my head back and breathe through my mouth.

This is no big deal. Animals do it every day.

I close my eyes and pretend we're in the fancy hotel room from the *Pretty Woman* scene where Julia Roberts finally breaks her no-kissing rule with Richard Gere. Right before she tells him she loves him. I want to raise my hand and ask when the condom part is supposed to happen—they never show that in movie sex scenes, but Brett is already sliding his parts along my parts, his knees coaxing my thighs wider. The waterbed sloshes and tips as if we're in a raft about to capsize. Brett shifts his weight to stay above me. His forehead is damp with perspiration. A lot happens in real sex that you don't see in shows.

MC Hammer plays on the clock radio, and Brett's body begins gyrating. Slow at first and then faster, almost in time with "You Can't Touch This," and that strikes me as ironic.

It's as if I'm watching this happen to another person. Heat becomes pressure—not horrible like when you straddle the balance beam, but definitely no Julia Roberts pleasure fest—and well before the song is over, he groans and collapses on top of me. The whole Super Big Bad Thing couldn't have lasted more than a few forgettable, unforgettable moments.

"I love you, I love you." He says it like *thank you.*

My belly is warm and sticky between us. Brett reaches down and grabs his boxers off the floor, rolls back, and wipes himself. He grins and points to a spot above his belly button. "You've got something right here." He chucks the wadded flannel at me, and I mop off my stomach. When I throw them back, he ally-oops the soiled mess into a laundry basket filled with dirty clothes. Probably waiting for his mom to wash.

I reach for my championship tee, wedged between the bed frame and the rubber waterbag. The shirt is warm, as if I had never taken it off.

"You want a little Brett cuddle?" He pats the pillow next to him. Tiny flecks, innumerable as stars, dot the dark expanse of his pillowcase.

My mom said we shed thousands of skin cells every minute. House dust is mostly old skin cells. If I thought about it that way, Brett was already in me a long time ago. We probably inhale and swallow and get bits of each other in our eyes and mouths every day.

As he waits for me to snuggle up next to him, Brett's eyes drift closed. Without a hat, his hair clumps in sweaty sections, and beneath the thinning hair, his scalp surfaces smooth and white like the belly of a beluga. I follow the line of his jaw as it rounds and thickens near his neck and compare his stout middle to Joaquin's hard, muscled torso. I think about fornication and diseases and pregnancy. I should be overcome with guilt right now, but as I watch Brett's chest rise and fall, what I mostly feel is disappointed.

10/14/90

So the Super Big Bad Thing was bad but not like fires-of-hell bad. Just mediocre. Like not worth the hype. Like Young Guns II bad. Maybe I doomed it by calling it super bad in the first place. I still prayed that God would forgive me and felt guilty sitting in church today.

10/15/90

Brett calls a lot now. Like a lot. I feel bad because sometimes he says I love you, but I just say you, too. I don't love him, but I should, right? If you make love with someone, you should actually love them.

10/18/90

Charlie and I hung out after school today. I skipped dance team, and we went to the mall and both got cookies. It was nice. We just hung out. She told me this funny story about Kenny having to help his uncle who's a plumber unclog a toilet that had an actual frog blocking the pipe. The poor frog was trapped in poop, but was still alive when it came out, so they let it outside. I said it's probably going to freeze. I wanted to tell Charlie about Brett, so I started telling her about the bar, and she wigged out about Mr. Banyon and Ms. Tuttle, and then somehow we got on the topic of Halloween.

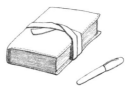

10/19/90

It's been two weeks since Joaquin left that message with Alex. Tonight I finally called him back. He asked me how I was and what was new and all the normal stuff. I felt guilty because of course I couldn't tell him about the Super Big Bad Thing or that I'm officially Brett's girlfriend. I kept saying fine and nothing. Then he had to go because his sister needed to use the phone.

10/20/90

Sweetest Day was actually today. Brett totally lied. On the bright side, I aced my statistics test. I called to tell Mom, but she said it wasn't a good time and that she was helping Aunt Lily change Grandma's gown. I wanted to know if Grandma was better or worse or what, but Mom said she'd talk with me later. I feel like she doesn't even care what's happening here at home. I shouldn't be so selfish, but all this stuff is happening with me and Mom's completely oblivious. Just writing that makes me feel guilty. I love Grandma and am glad Mom is there to help her. I wish I was there, too.

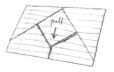

Merista

So awesome that you snuck into a bar! I can't
believe it took you so long to tell me about that.
Wonder if Mr. Banyon and Ms. Tuttle are getting it on? Right now I'm stuck in Chem with a
bunch of morons who don't give a shit about the
periodic table of fucking elements. What did I do
to get here?? Oh yeah, I didn't take AP with you
BECAUSE I'M AN IDIOT. I miss Kenny. A lot.
Surprising, huh? He's still recovering from his near
death experience. An appendix is a ticking time
bomb!! I heard his was HUGE when they took it
out. You know what they say about the size of
a man's appen-dicks...well, believe it. The dude is
hung like a horse. Ha ha! Let's partay this weekend, kay? Almost Halloween! I'm going as a sexy
fairy.

Smell ya later,

Charlie the Angel

10/31/90

Since Mom's not here, I had to come up with a costume
by myself. I cut off some overalls, put my hair in two
braids, and went as Pippi Longstocking. I looked ridiculous.
Charlie went as Tinkerbell, and Kenny was Captain Hook.
Charlie said she wished she had a bunch of little kids so
she could dress them all up as Lost Boys. Barf. They both
went to the stupid Halloween dance. I told Dad I was going
but bugged out to drown my sorrows in icy delights at DQ.
Right as I was walking in, I thought I saw Joaquin leaving
which I don't think it really was, but I ducked behind the
dumpster, just in case. I can't face him after what I did
with Brett. I don't even want to tell Charlie about it.

11/1/90

I got to talk to Grandma Buckley today. I told her about
my costume, and she said Pippi was perfect for me. Her
voice was whispery and that was weird because she's
usually a loud person on the phone. I asked if she was
getting better, and she said better than what? I said,
you know. She said she wasn't dead, so that's good. Mom
grabbed the phone right then and said Grandma needed to
rest, but I was pissed because we weren't done talking. I
was like, rest for what? I'm still mad about it. If a person's
dying, what's the point of resting?

11/2/90

I crammed as much as I could using the old SAT prep test
I got from the counselor's office. Tomorrow I'm driving to
Anchorage to take the test. I'm so nervous. What if I don't
score high enough to get accepted into any college?

17
This Is Worse

The Bug started this morning, thank the good Lord. The vinyl seat was so cold it shocked me conscious. Switching on the heat does absolutely nothing except move the freezing air faster toward my face, which at least is keeping me awake. I went to bed super early last night, but four a.m. still feels like four a.m.

The starless sky is dark when I get on the road, and before I even hit Soldotna, the beams of my headlights reflect off big white flakes falling outside. If I wasn't driving to Anchorage to take the stupid SAT, I'd turn around.

I slow to thirty-five through the tiny town of Sterling. I'm near Matt's parents' house, where Brett took me after telling my parents we were going to *Pretty Woman*. It's hypocritical, but I hate that he lied to them. I'm the only one who gets to do that.

Brett acted like an idiot at that party, almost starting a fight with Lee. Why did I keep dating him after that?

I cross Moose River Bridge and look down at the water rushing below the streetlights. Here the river is swift—kids go inner tubing in the summer, and nearly every year someone drowns. Humans do risky things all the time, for the thrill of it or out of curiosity or because it's just what people do. The stakes in life are high, if you're actually living.

I've been taking my chances with Brett, ignoring the danger signs. My mind replays for the zillionth time what happened in Brett's bedroom. What if I'm pregnant? I could never marry him. I could never spend my life with a person like him. Even though I'm lonely and he's so into me—physically, at least—I feel like the stakes are too high. Being stuck with Brett and trapped in this town for the rest of my life would be a kind of drowning. I pin my eyes to the road where snow is beginning to stick to the pavement.

Barely November and already the third snowfall of the season. These first few times are always special. Fall abandons us, strips the peninsula down to its most bleak, but fresh snow covers all that. Blank with possibility and waiting to be made into anything: a man, a fort, a sledding hill. I love new snow though would rather not be driving in it.

On the way out of Sterling, I pass Sadler's Home Center, where when I was twelve my parents bought me a daybed with a trundle hiding underneath for friends. I wonder what kind of bed my college dorm will have. Will I end up in college? If so, where? After being with Brett, I've become even more certain that I don't want to stay and go to community college.

Soon the highway straightens out into the flats, where scrubby trees and a sort of mossy swamp area stretch out as far as I can see, until the road inclines and the engine gets louder as the Bug struggles up the grade. I sing radio duets to keep from nodding off until even the golden oldies fuzz out. In the rumbling white noise, I toggle between obsessing over the SAT and worrying that when Mom gets home she'll sense I'm no longer a virgin.

Mountains rise to my left, immense and confident and clearly too cool to notice me. There are countless places I could pull off and start hiking. But today I can't hike away or look for blueberries or take my chances on meeting a brown bear. I'm tempting fate in a different way, choosing a path that could take me farther than I've ever been, beyond the ridge where the trees don't grow. I pass Fuller Lakes, where I went with Alex. "This is like the only part I would miss about Alaska," Alex said to me as we stood above the tree line, gazing out at distant peaks, dirty white glaciers, and the forests dotted with lakes. The view was stunning, but there is so much more I will miss.

A bald eagle eyes me from his perch high in a spruce tree near the road. He alights, swirling overhead, but I've lost sight of him by the time I reach the Seward Y. Left takes you north to Anchorage and right takes you east to Seward. Beyond Seward is only water. Beyond Anchorage is Fairbanks or Canada and, after a week of driving, the rest of America.

I turn left and head up through the alpine pass where, during the winter, the snow gets piled so high on both sides of the road that it's like you're driving through a cave. People bring snowmachines up here and ride around. Usually someone gets killed. I've heard that in other places people say "snowmobile" or even "Skidoo," which is actually a specific brand of snowmachine like Kawasaki or Arctic Cat. I have an Arctic Cat but almost never ride anymore.

There aren't many rest stops along the highway, so the pass out-houses are popular, but I keep on going. I don't want to be late and I'm hungry. I speed past Portage, where the glacier used to almost touch the road but has receded so far that now you have to take a boat to view it. I'm almost to Girdwood, closest town to Alaska's semi-famous ski resort Alyeska. Girdwood is just a bar, gas station, and quickie mart, but I stop for a bag of Cheetos and sixteen ounces of lukewarm coffee. I'll have to pee for sure when I get to Anchorage.

The last leg of the trip has me hugging cliffs, their sides sheared by engineers' explosives. There is just enough space for the two-lane highway. Beyond the flimsy guardrail are the dangerous waters of Turnagain Arm. As a child I had nightmares about my parents acci-dentally launching our car into the churning sea. I take the curves so slow, a line of cars collects behind me.

At 6:15 a.m., I relax a little as I pass Potter's Marsh, the grassy bird mecca that serves as my final landmark before Anchorage. I fol-low my handwritten directions into the city along mostly deserted side streets to the testing center near the University of Alaska.

I make it in plenty of time, but my stomach hurts as I walk through the center doors. I regret eating that family-sized bag of Cheetos and hope the nausea I'm feeling is nerves and nothing else. Dear God, please let this not be morning sickness.

These past months I've made terrible decisions. It's ironic, really. I'm hardly speaking to the person I wish I was dating and had sex with the guy I no longer really like, which only intensifies my desire to go to college out of state but also may have damned me here forever.

I check in, and a woman seats me and a bunch of other kids at our own kiosks. Each kiosk has a computer screen and an attached keyboard with one of those weird rubbery plastic covers over the keys. Mine's yellowed and disgusting.

Even if I'm not pregnant, I've done almost nothing to prepare for this exam, a requirement for actually getting into an out-of-state school. Except for taking the practice test. Well, that and almost thirteen years of school.

The woman talks us through how the test works, and we each answer a few practice questions that pop up on the screen. Then the real test begins.

The math is an expected challenge, but the verbal section is tougher than I anticipated. Especially the analogy part. *Mendacious is to veracity as pusillanimous is to what?* Who knows. I'm grateful for multiple choice.

Questions keep popping up on the screen. This test is worse than Brett sex. At least that was quicker. A fluorescent tube in the light fixture above me is about to go out and flickers something fierce. I glance up, give that bulb my evil eye, as if hating on it will make it stop. I whiz through the analytical section, and the screen goes blank. I am so relieved when "Test Complete" flashes up with the message that I will receive my results in the mail. Easy peasy.

I can choose three schools that the testing company will mail my results to for free, so I have my scores sent to the University of Idaho, Cornell, and the University of Alaska. That last one is for my mom. It's weird that she's two thousand miles away in Idaho and my dad's a thousand miles away in Prudhoe Bay. I could do anything I want right now.

I consider stopping at the Dimond Center Mall so I can lust over the clothes at the Benetton store. Last fall Mom and I went shopping there, and she totally splurged on this dark green sweatshirt with rainbow letters that spelled Benetton. I wanted the thing so bad. After she bought it for me, we barely had enough cash left for the gas to get us home, but all of last year I loved that shirt and its rainbow letters.

My stomach starts grumbling, and I realize this morning's Cheetos probably aren't enough to keep me going for the drive home. All I can think to do is go to this burger joint called Boolie's that we always eat at when we come to Anchorage. My dad knows the owner, an old guy named Jim Boolie. I've been there enough times that it's easy for me to find, but somehow the place isn't like I remember. I sit alone in a red booth while the jukebox plays Elvis songs; I leave before finishing my burger.

After that, I drive around Anchorage for an hour but can think of nothing I want to do. I don't know anyone in the city, and after almost running over a passed-out drunk downtown, I head south toward home.

I'm exhausted and starving when I pull into my driveway around seven, though I can't help smiling at the familiar red aluminum siding and white shuttered windows. Home.

Well, not home exactly. The house is dark and empty without my family here. Everyone except me has another place to be—Mom is with Grandma, Dad is working, and Alex is at Ryan's. Even the dog is staying at a friend's.

I turn on the television just to hear human voices and switch on the lights in every room. My stomach is threatening to eat itself, so I make two pieces of honey toast that I eat with impunity on the couch because no one is here to tell me to go to the table.

Nothing on the boob tube is worth watching, but there's no way I could fall asleep. My nerves are still buzzing with the stress of the day. I'm relieved when the phone rings.

"Hello," I say, hoping it's Charlie, or even Mom.

"Let's go tubbing!" Brett's voice yells from the receiver. "I know a lady who works at Tubs N Fun."

I am so over Brett, and I especially don't want to go tubbing with him at that gross place. "Soak and poke? Serious?" But I don't want to stay home alone, either, and maybe it wouldn't be so bad if I could convince Charlie to go, too. She's always up for a wild night—the crazier the better—so I doubt she'd say no. It could even be fun. Better, at least, than staying home by myself.

"'Course I'm serious." He already sounds half-lit. "My treat."

Twenty minutes later I'm climbing into the Bronco's fuzzy passenger seat. Brett acts like he's some kind of high roller and this whole thing is a special surprise for me. "Meri and Brett. Gonna be livin' large at Tubs N Fun."

I groan. "Shit. I left my swimsuit on the table."

"You don't need one," he says, rubbing my leg. I'm already having second thoughts. I should have just gone over to Charlie's.

"Let's do something else," I say. "Public Jacuzzis creep me out."

He wrinkles his forehead as he nearly clips a mailbox. "What's not to like? Tubs. And fun."

"People get infections there," I say, because that's what I've heard. I've never actually been.

"Some rotten-crotch girl started that rumor," he says. "Course she would *say* a tub's where she got it." He smiles over at me and accidentally steers too close to the edge of the road. "Oh, crap!" He overcorrects, and we fishtail on the icy pavement. "That's why there's chlorine."

I fasten my seatbelt. Drunk Brett is not only getting on my nerves, but his driving is also making me anxious.

"It'll be fun, babe." He reaches over and shakes my shoulder. "I'll buy coolers."

I don't even like wine coolers. "Great. Charlie loves coolers. And I'm only going if Charlie comes."

Brett blows his breath out slow like my dad does sometimes. "I thought we could go alone. For once."

"I promised Charlie we'd hang out tonight." Truth: I just called Charlie and begged her to come out tonight. "Kenny's still recovering from his popped appendix. I can't just *abandon* her."

He stares ahead at the road as we bounce over ice ruts and potholes on our way to Kenai. Tiny white flakes have begun to swirl around us. "Fine. Charlie can come with." He shrugs. "Nothing wrong with a little two-on-one action."

I ignore that last part. "Swing by now. She's on our way, and she said she'd be ready whenever we got there."

"Shit. Okay, boss."

Brett's hands tense into fists on the wheel, but we both sit quiet as we pull into Charlie's driveway. Through the big window in her living room, I can see her looking out. She's got her brown bomber jacket on, like she's been sitting there a while.

In less than thirty seconds, Charlie dashes out her front door. Her Keds leave tracks in the fresh snow, and as she runs, she holds her denim bag over her head so the flakes don't ruin the blond bang she's sprayed into a perfect arch over her forehead.

"Hey, beeotch," she says as she gets in. "Took you long enough."

I blow her a kiss. "Love you, too." I lean my seat forward and smush myself against the dash so she can squeeze into the back.

"Hi Charles." Brett checks his side mirror and backs out. "Sorry to hear about Tiny's untiny appendix."

"That's not his only enlarged organ." Charlie pulls a pink compact and lipstick from her denim bag. She smears on a coat of frosted peach, and her lips disappear into her face.

Brett smiles into the rearview. "You up for a once-in-a-lifetime exotic spa experience?"

"Oooooh!" Charlie claps her hands. "Naughty." She glances my way and scrunches her face into a scared mime impression. I nod in agreement.

We swing by 7-Eleven first. I buy two Big Gulps—a Pepsi for me and a Diet Coke for Charlie—and a pack of SweeTARTS. I make little piles of the blues and pinks on the dash and try to off-load them on Brett and Charlie. Brett shoves a handful of blues in his mouth and says he's good with free candy.

The liquor store is the final stop before Tubs N Fun. Charlie puts her order in for Purple Passion and some Malibu Rum—the one in the white bottle—to add to her Diet Coke. Brett makes her pony up fifteen bucks. I don't ask for anything, but he brings me a four-pack of Bartles & Jaymes anyway. While Brett buys the alcohol, I freak out to Charlie about not having a swimsuit or extra underwear.

"There's no way I'm getting in the hot tub naked!"

Charlie shrugs. "How different is a bikini from your bra and panties?"

"I don't want to have to wear wet underwear!"

"Then don't wear any," she says.

Maybe I can just put my feet in.

18
Tubs N Fun

Charlie and I hang back near the door while Brett negotiates with the woman behind the counter. "Hey, beautiful," he says to her. She has frosted hair, an animal print zipper shirt, and a plastic nametag that says Debbie. Brett cups his hand near his mouth and waves her in for a secret. Without hesitating, she leans across the counter, her fake knockers bulging.

I look around for Charlie for moral support, but she's over by the plastic fichus, sucking rum-spiked cola through the Big Gulp's green straw. Behind the counter on the wall is a poster of Fiji and a digital clock, 7:45 p.m. Charlie doesn't have to be home until eleven. I cannot spend the next three hours here. Everyone knows this is where teens come to have sex and pedophiles bring underage girls.

After Brett stops flirting with Fake Boob Lady, he saunters over with a key. "We have the room for two hours. If anyone asks, you're my sister and Charlie's our cousin."

Charlie raises her cup of rum and Coke. "Cheers, cuz."

Brett looks at her like she's mental. "Just follow me and don't do anything stupid."

He leads us back out to the parking lot, opens the back of the Bronco, and unzips a black Nike duffle. Charlie tops off her Big Gulp with more rum and hands the white bottle to Brett, who wraps it and the Purple Passions in a dirty T-shirt. He eases the bundle into the duffle. The coolers he jams into stained gym socks that have probably been lying in the back of the Bronco for weeks—I can't believe he expects me to drink out of those bottles now—and packs cans of Miller into the remaining open spaces.

He slings the bag over his shoulder. "Ready?"

We follow Brett back into Tubs N Fun and stop when we get to the door marked Four. The number's just a sticker like you'd use on garage sale signs, and the bottom corner has peeled up a little. Brett jams the key into the chintzy brass knob and jiggles until it turns.

"Ladies first," he says as he opens the door. Enough light filters in from the hall that I can make out a set of wooden stairs several feet ahead of me. Charlie and I bump shoulders on the way in. We bust out laughing. It feels good hanging out like we used to.

Charlie squeezes the air in front of my boobs.

"Stop trying to fondle me!" I scream.

"You guys are dorks." Brett flicks a switch and recessed lights illuminate a room only slightly bigger than my bedroom that reeks of chlorine and mildewy wood.

The hot tub sits on a raised cedar platform in the middle of the room. Charlie hangs her coat near a terry cloth bathrobe sagging from a row of hooks on the wall, so I do the same with my jean jacket.

"Time to get naked, ladies!" Brett strips down to his boxers and grabs a beer out of the duffle.

I wish he had left his shirt on. My mind wanders to Joaquin as Brett fusses with the buttons on the wall panel. I think of Joaquin shirtless in his cousin's trailer, how his shoulders were as broad as the couch and how careful he was to keep me from rolling off onto the floor. I miss Joaquin.

Water bubbles to life and music blares into the room. As Def Leppard sings about guys being surrounded by countless pretty women, Brett relaxes into the tub and takes a swig of his beer.

Charlie's been sipping her Big Gulp on the bench near the duffle. She makes a slurpy sound with her straw, holds up the empty cup, and shakes it at me. "All gone!" She belches. She rummages in the duffle for a Purple Passion, unscrews the top, and takes a swallow before kicking off her Keds and rolling up her pants. "I'm comin' in!"

"That's the spirit," says Brett. "At least somebody knows how to have a good time."

I turn down the music. "I'm over Def Leppard."

Barefoot, Charlie wobbles a little on the stairs as she climbs up. She squats down carefully and dangles her feet in the water.

"Give me a massage, will ya, Charles?" Brett closes his eyes and scoots between Charlie's legs. She gulps down more Passion and starts rubbing.

"Mmmm," says Brett. "You have nice hands."

"I bet you say that to all the girls." She smiles, and her eyelids droop.

Kneeling close to Charlie, I grab her Purple Passion.

"Hey! That's mine!" She reaches for the bottle.

"You can have one of my coolers," I promise as I swallow more of the syrupy liquid. It tastes like grape Robitussin.

"God, this water's hot," she says. "My feet are fucking on fire." She starts to get up, but Brett grabs her leg.

"Don't stop rubbing! That feels too good."

"I need to pee," she says, and he lets go. "Where's the pisser?"

"Very end of this hall," says Brett. "*Do not* go back to the lobby, though....You stink like Malibu."

Charlie waves her hand in the air as she stumbles out the door. "I'm not druuuunk." Click.

"Finally," says Brett, "we're alone. Can't you at least get in the water, babe?"

I don't want to submerge myself in that gross water, but I unbutton my Levi's. *How different is underwear from a bikini?*

"Yeah, take it off, baby!"

I slip off the jeans and set them next to a stack of grungy towels.

"Bring me a beer before you get in, 'kay?"

I step lightly down the stairs, tugging the edge of my T-shirt lower, and pad bare-legged across the linoleum to the duffle.

"How about you wrap those pretty little legs around Brett."

I want to take the can and throw it at his prematurely balding head.

He takes the beer and pulls me down, so I'm sitting on the edge straddling his shoulders. My toes burn for the first two seconds before the hot starts to feel good. He reaches back and puts my hand on his shoulder. My fingers press into his neck, half-hearted. He swivels to face me, his head barely above my waist, and starts kissing my inner thigh. He's still holding on to his beer. "You smell good, babe." His face is almost at my panties.

I shove my palms at his forehead. "No."

"Yes." He stands up, sets the beer down, and grabs my wrists.

I slide into the tub. "Stop! Hey! No!"

He snorts as I yank my arms away. I'm up to my thighs in the water, standing on the tub's bench seat, but still he is pulling at me.

"No! *No!*"

Brett laughs beer breath into my face. I hear a knock at the door. "Charlie, help!"

"Is everything alright in there?" It's Fake Boob Lady.

Brett jerks my arm hard. Struggling, I lose my balance and topple in shoulder first.

In one swift motion, Brett drags my whole body down and toward him, clamping a hand over my mouth and nose. I can't breathe. Hot water splashes into my eyes and soaks my shirt. The wet fabric clings, grows heavier. Hands push me under, submerging my body as if I am being baptized—full immersion.

"We're fine, Debbie," Brett calls to the door. "The girls just got a little rambunctious. I'll keep them quieter."

Hot water scalds my face and neck the instant my head goes under. Above the pounding in my ears, the Jacuzzi motor drones deep like a giant hornet. The water dulls my punching and clawing and kicking as if I'm in one of those dreams where you try to run but go all slow motion. My back bumps the side or the bottom, I can't tell. My ankle smacks a ledge—probably the bench seat—and pain radiates up my leg. I *need* to take a breath. *Let go!* My head surfaces. I gasp for air through his fingers and try to bite him.

"Shhh..." he whispers in my ear, one arm bear-hugged around me and the other covering my mouth. "Calm down, and I'll let you go."

I harness all my self-control and stop thrashing. I'm down on my knees in the tub, water up to my chin. Brett loosens his arm, and my shirt balloons around me. He peels his hand off my face, and as I gulp the air, I start thrashing again and chlorine water splashes into my mouth and up my nose. I cough against the burning but try to force myself to breathe normally.

Brett slides back to his bench seat and holds his beer, laughing.

"You're a fucking, *fucking* ass," I say.

"Don't be a baby, Meri." He guzzles the rest of the Miller and crushes the empty in his hand. "It's not like we haven't already done it."

"Real impressive," I say with as much sarcasm as I can muster. My ears are buzzing. It's all I can do to keep from crying as I crawl over and huddle on the Jacuzzi stairs. This is so screwed up. I don't know whether to run out soaking wet to Debbie, who I doubt would take my side, or settle down and try to regain control.

"You're such a drama queen." Brett rises up and out of the water. "These beers are warm." He walks to the duffle, grabs a wine cooler, and sits on the bench. His belly sags over the waistband of his shorts. "God, I'm hot."

I can't stand to look at him. I want to get out of here. I want away from Brett. I just need to go home somehow. But Charlie isn't back yet, and I don't know what to do. Right now the Jacuzzi is the farthest away from Brett, so I sink back in, squeeze my eyes shut, and pretend I'm alone in my bathtub at home. My body feels as buoyant as the day I tested a full-body survival suit.

In puffy orange flotation gear, I lowered myself into the cold Pacific, pushed away from the aluminum edge of the boat, and floated in my insulated suit atop the vast salty ocean. Deep down, invisible sea creatures were swimming and crawling, but I hovered on the surface of an immense and mysterious world, feeling very small. The way I do now.

The platform creaks and my eyelids fly open. Brett is lowering himself back into the water. He wades over to me and reaches out to palm my boobs.

"Get the fuck away," I say.

The door clicks, and Charlie staggers in. "I had to puke a little, and then I think I may have passed out." Her blond bangs have gone flat and are hanging in her eyes. She hiccups and lies down on the bench.

Brett sneers. "What is your problem, Meri? You're being a prude."

"Take me home."

He shakes his head. "Not gonna happen."

"I want to go home."

"No."

I scream. Like I did that day at the bench above the beach. Part release and part battle cry. The sound is strange and echo-y, as if my scream isn't my voice at all, but is rising from a creature deep in the ocean. I close my eyes, take a breath, and start again.

At first Brett only stares, head cocked slightly to the side, but by the second scream, he has hopped out of the water. "Crazy psycho bitch!" He jams his wet legs into his pants as fast as he can.

Someone bangs on the door. Debbie. "I'm coming in!"

Brett is dressed and has the duffle over his shoulder. He flings open the door, barrels into Fake Boob Lady, and takes off down the hall.

Charlie is still passed out on the bench.

"What the hell is going on in here?" Debbie squints at the empty cans and cooler bottles lined up along the edge of the tub.

I'm standing in the middle of the Jacuzzi in a wet T-shirt, screaming. I don't know how well she actually knows Brett. Would she even believe me? I try to formulate a lie that won't get me into trouble. "I thought...I thought I saw something in the water...." Lying on the spot isn't one of my fortes.

"*Something* was in the water?" Her arms are folded under her gravity-defying chest, and her heavily mascaraed eyes squint hard at me. "Girl, is there anything you'd like to tell me?"

I need Charlie to wake up. "I thought it could be a frog?"

She shifts her weight onto one hip. "So you start screaming bloody murder?"

We both know this story is bullshit. "Just let me use your phone."

She gives me one last suspicious look. "You can use the phone out front. As long as it's not long distance."

I'm soaked, Charlie's passed out, and we need a ride to her house. The only person I can think to call is Joaquin.

I peel off my wet clothes and ring them out. I grab my jacket off the hook and button it all the way to the collar. It's hard to squeeze the metal buttons through the stiff denim because I never wear it closed. At least my jeans are dry.

When I get to the desk, the wall clock reads ten after nine. I don't want to get him in trouble. I'll be surprised if he's even there. Debbie makes me tell her the number, dials it for me, and hands me the receiver. I listen to ringing. One. Two. *Shit!* Three.

"Bueno," his mom answers, and I use my sweetest voice to ask for him. I almost die of relief when he gets on the phone. "It's me," I say. "Meri. Sorry I'm calling so late."

He clears his throat. "I'm not doing anything....My cousin's being a dick. What's up?"

"Can you come pick me up?"

The sound of him breathing into the phone distracts me, but I push on. "It's kind of a crisis."

"What happened?" His voice is tight. I can tell he's nervous and concerned, but I don't have time to explain everything.

"Please?" I beg.

"Hold on." He already sounds like a hero.

I wait. Praying Joaquin's mom takes pity on me. She seemed to like me well enough at the beach.

"Okay," he says.

"You can?"

"Yeah, but I gotta be home in an hour. Where are you?"

"Dairy Queen." I'm hungry, and the walk to DQ will help Charlie sober up.

Easy peasy.

My hands and feet have lost all feeling by the time we get to the DQ. Charlie was pissed when I woke her up, but after a few minutes in the icy night air, she started complaining about the cold and Soldotna and forgot she was mad at me.

We are both relieved to get inside, but our toes and fingers throb in the warmth. There are no other customers in the whole place. A guy I don't recognize is at the grill, and this annoying girl from our Ethics in Government class takes our order.

"We close in ten," she says.

I ignore the way she looks at us. I buy sodas for me and Charlie and a large fry for us to split. We slide into an orange-and-yellow booth near the window.

"What's with the bag?" Charlie asks, pointing to the balled-up plastic lump sitting next to me. It's the grocery bag Fake Boob Lady gave me, and in it are my wet clothes. Apparently the woman keeps a stash of used bags behind the counter because I'm not the first person to arrive at Tubs N Fun unprepared.

"The consequences of not having a swimsuit," I say.

"Huh?"

"There's nothing under this jacket."

"What the hell. What happened? And why did we have to walk to DQ?" She looks around. "Where's that asshole Brett?"

Before I can explain, Joaquin knocks on the window beside our booth. Charlie and I both jump.

"What's he doing here?"

"Taking us back to your house." I reach across the table and grab her arm. "And don't say a *thing* about Tubs N Fun. Please. I'll tell you everything later, not here." I really do want to tell her everything.

A minute later, Joaquin slides in next to me and kisses me on the cheek.

"What happened?" he asks. "Are you okay?"

"Long story," says Charlie, as she tries puffing her bangs up with her fingers.

"Let's just go." I slide across and bump my hip against Joaquin. Before he can scoot out, I wrap my arms around him and pull him close. I don't care if Charlie sees me. I nuzzle in between the dangling black strings of his hoodie. He smells minty and familiar.

"Thanks for saving us," I say into his sweatshirt. I hold on for a few breaths before letting go.

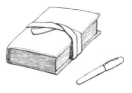

Brett called to apologize for leaving us at Tubs N Fun. I hung up on him, but he called again later. Alex answered. But I heard him say, hey Brett, so I ran to the bathroom and jumped in the shower. I need to break it off for good with that asshole.

I've been checking the mailbox obsessively for weeks and finally my first acceptance arrived today. It was just the one from Peninsula Community College, and they don't even require SATs, but at least I know I'm in and I'll be going to school somewhere next year. Even if it's only here.

I haven't officially broken it off with Brett, but I will. Soon. Joaquin and I are hanging out again. He meets me whenever he can, which is any time he's not working with his dad. I just say I'm hanging out with Charlie or my new fake friend Sharman or that I have to work an extra shift because somebody's sick. Nobody cares where I am anymore. I'm just in the habit of lying. I want to tell Joaquin the truth about dating Brett and what happened, but I don't want to wreck what I have now with him. I like him so much.

Today was a fabulous day because I went sledding with Joaquin and Noah on the hill beside Redoubt Elementary, and then we went to DQ and celebrated the birthday of my favorite poet, Margaret Atwood, who wrote many outstanding poems, including, "You Are Happy," which is awesome, and also the kickass novel The Handmaid's Tale. And also she's Canadian, so we're basically neighbors. When I got home Alex said Brett called.

P.S. I am so falling for Joaquin.

11/21/90

Mom's finally back. One day before Thanksgiving. I was mega relieved that she's home. I'm tired of being the mom. After we picked her up from the airport, we still had time to get a turkey and everything before the stores closed. I don't know how long she'll stay because she says Grandma's getting worse, but I'm glad she's home for now.

19
Break

I hear the church doors open and glance back in time to see a police officer take his hat off in the back of the sanctuary. A deacon, Mr. Wymer, gets up from the last row. He and the officer exchange words in hushed voices for only a minute, and then Mr. Wymer comes straight down the center aisle, striding out with his shiny black oxfords over the blue carpet as if he's Jesus walking on water.

My heart starts pounding with the certainty that they're here for me, that I'm being arrested by a secret, elite arm of the law called the Sex Police. I wish I wasn't sitting alone with Mom and Dad, but Alex stayed over at Ryan's last night on account of today being the last day of Thanksgiving break and my helping convince them Alex's soul would survive missing one Sunday. I'm a goner.

Mr. Wymer bends near my father's ear, and before I know what's happening, my parents are standing. I start to get up, but Dad holds me down. "Mr. and Mrs. Wymer said they can take you home after the service."

My heart races, readying my body to respond to whatever bad thing has brought the police into our church, whatever requires my parents to leave. Alone. Maybe our house is on fire. I imagine our dog whining and barking until his soft body is engulfed in flames. I move to get out of the pew, but this time Mom stops me.

"Your brother's been in an accident," Mom says, "but it's alright." Her eyes cloud as she turns away.

Cleary, nothing's alright. I watch my parents retreat down the aisle, backs stiff. Mom has both her hands around my dad's arm, like she's an old person clinging to a walker. She stumbles. He keeps her up and out they go. The door slams, and I am left alone in our pew on the verge of a heart attack.

Pastor Dan acts as if nothing happened. He keeps going on about original sin and how Eve listened to that stupid snake and was wrong to want knowledge and how she used her feminine wiles to trick Adam. I'm not exactly sure what wiles are, but right now I wish I had a few. I want to get the hell away from church and figure out what's going on.

I try to concentrate on Pastor Dan, even though I've heard the story a thousand times. My tights are scratchy, and my pointy heels are making my toes swell.

I have to get out of this pew.

Just as I start to stand up, Mr. Wyman shoves a double-decker metal tray filled with thimble-sized communion glasses at me. The kind of glasses elves might use to take shots.

"This is my blood," says Pastor Dan.

I take the grape juice and a stale cracker, as we all pretend to eat Jesus's body and drink his blood, which I get is to remember the sacrifice on the cross, but has always felt like a strange ritual. Finally, Pastor Dan closes in prayer. "Thank you, Jesus, in Your name. Amen!"

I nearly leap out of my seat.

The house is deserted when Mr. and Mrs. Wyman drop me at home. Ryan's number is taped to the front of the fridge with the rest of the emergency numbers. His mom should know something.

I start really freaking out when nobody answers. Why did I convince Mom and Dad to let Alex go snowmachining with Ryan? I'm about to launch into full panic mode when the phone startles me with its ringing.

"Merideth. It's Mom." She says she's calling from the hospital.

My mind is whirling, spin cycling through possibilities. "Will he be alright?"

"We don't know, honey."

"What happened?" Whatever happened is my fault.

"He wrecked his snowmachine. He's in surgery now."

"I'm coming down there."

"There's nothing you can do," she says. "We'll call you when we know more."

"Just—could he die?"

"No. He'll live. He..." Her voice cracks. "We don't know if he'll walk."

I slam the phone down. I can't just stay here, waiting around for the phone to ring. I need to do something.

But with Alex in surgery, there's nothing I *can* do. If I go to the hospital, I'd just be sitting there with my parents. Plus, I hate hospitals.

The reality that my only brother—the guy who hikes up mountains and lives for basketball—might never walk again is so big and awful. It carves me out and leaves me empty. This is messed up. All my other problems seem trivial by comparison.

Suddenly, it's obvious what I have to do. My heart pounds with the urge to act. I stuff my feet into boots, throw on my blue parka, and head out to the Bug. If I can't help Alex in this moment, I can help myself.

I sit in the driveway shivering while the Bug's heater loses the battle against the cold. The Bronco's parked out front, so Brett's probably home. His football sweatshirt—the one he gave me after I got barfed on—is wadded in my backseat. I retrieve it and wrap the arms around my legs.

Teeny flakes have begun to swirl outside. Light perforates the clouds in fine beams, sparkling the snow. It's actually really beautiful. I just sit for a while, gazing out my partially iced-over windows. When I glance down at the floor, a piece of white catches my eye. The directions I wrote down to the SAT testing place. I flip the paper over and start writing.

Dear Brett,

Tubs N Fun was complete bullshit.

That's as far as I get before there's a tapping on my window. I nearly jump out of my skin.

"Take a drive, babe?" Brett asks through the glass, his face blocking out my sun. Snow crystals gather in his hair while he waits for my answer. He makes praying hands and mouths, "Pretty please." The effect is more contemptible than cute, and for a second I feel sorry for him. But only for one second. This is the guy who attacked and abandoned me at Tubs N Fun.

Being alone with Brett doesn't feel exciting or safe, and I especially don't like the idea of being trapped with him in the isolated space of his Bronco. But this is my chance to be honest for a change. To end this.

I take a deep breath, grab his stupid sweatshirt from the backseat, and though I'd like to slam him with my door, I just push against the bulk of him until he jumps out of my way. He grins like he's won something.

"Let's get this over with," I say, tromping beside him through the fresh snow. The sun has retreated, and now fat flakes are falling in earnest. The Bronco's handle is icy cold on my fingers, but the door pops open when I pull, and up into the cab I go.

Brett peels out of his parents' drive, leaving a trail of dirty snow. "I've missed you, babe," he says, steering us toward town.

He keeps glancing over, waiting for my response, but I have nothing to say to that. I stare out at the road, edged with gravelly snow berms. Like we're driving on a bowling lane with bumpers.

"I hate this place," I say, but I'm not sure if it's really the place or my present company.

"Come off it, Meri." Wind blasts against the Bronco, hissing in through unseen cracks.

We pass a giant snowblower, and I wish it would just blow snow all over town and bury the Peninsula. "It's like we're living in Narnia's eternal winter." I huff hot breath at the window and draw a peace sign before the condensation disappears. "Hell frozen over."

"Wanna see hell? Go up to fucking Prudhoe Bay."

Dad says Dick Cheney's sending a bunch more of our guys to help in the Gulf War but as long as we keep pumping oil out of Prudhoe, Alaska will stay on top. I want nothing to do with any of it. I just want out of here.

"It's worse. Trust me. Nothing up there but fucking Muks and tundra." He shoves my shoulder, as if he's just made a joke. "Chill, babe. Stop being a fun wrecker."

I drop my voice low. "Racist prick." It feels good to finally call him out.

He slams his palms against the steering wheel. "For fuck's sake! I'm trying to get back together with you."

Now I laugh, because that is probably the funniest thing Brett's ever said. "I don't want that," I say, shaking from anger and adrenaline. "I'm done with you, and I'm done with this town. I can't get stuck in this backwater for the rest of my life."

"Get off your fucking high horse, Meri." We stop at a stop sign, and he turns for a moment to look me in the eyes. "I've been outside. Nothing out there is any better than here. I promise you."

I know he sincerely means every word, but I don't care. His opinion isn't worth shit. "It doesn't matter," I say. "Once I graduate, I'm gone." I'd be happy just to be gone from the fuzzy blue seat so am relieved that he's looped around and is heading back toward his parents' place.

"I'm Meri," Brett raises his voice an octave, "and I think I'm too good for my boyfriend, even though I'm just a spoiled little priss who doesn't know jack crap about the world." He slams the Bronco into park. I'm relieved to be back in his parents' drive.

"You're not my fucking boyfriend. Do you get it? This," I wave my hand between us, pointing to him and to me and back to him, "is over."

His face goes slack. He's not mad, like I thought he'd be. His eyes are big and round and doleful, but there's a realness, like this might finally be the real Brett. He's not sad, exactly. What flashes in his eyes is a look of enduring misery.

"Fine," he says. "Be a bitch. Leaving would be your loss, not Soldotna's."

"Well, lucky for Soldotna *you're staying*." I throw his ridiculous has-been football sweatshirt into his lap. There's nothing more to say. I blast out of the Bronco and dash through the falling snow.

My heart pounds in my ears and doesn't slow even after I'm in the Bug, driving away. I don't expect to hear the voice of reason or God or anything, but with every heartbeat one word pulses in me over and over. Go. Go. Go.

Alex is still in surgery when I finally arrive at the hospital. Mom isn't surprised or mad that I came, even though she told me to stay home.

I sit for a couple hours with Mom and Dad in the waiting room, looking through old National Geographic magazines. There's this one article about a gorilla named Koko who had a pet kitten, but the kitten escaped and was killed by a car, and Koko had a total meltdown.

The story is so sad, I start crying. Mom gives me a big hug and tells me Alex will be alright. She says it wasn't my fault, which it totally was. I'm the one who begged them to let Alex go with Ryan in the first place.

Before Alex is out of surgery, Mom reminds me I have school tomorrow. She says Alex probably won't wake up until tomorrow anyway. I don't want to leave, but she makes me go home.

Nov. 26, 1990

BOY SERIOUSLY INJURED IN SNOWMACHINE ACCIDENT

BY CLARK FAIRCHILD

A 15-year-old Soldotna boy was seriously injured yesterday when his snowmachine hit black ice. The boy was thrown more than twenty feet into a wooded area, according to the Soldotna Sheriff's Department.

The department learned of the accident shortly after noon, and rescue units were dispatched. The boy was taken to the Peninsula General Hospital. No information is currently available on the boy's condition.

Authorities said the boy was riding on Raspberry Road when he lost control and rolled the Kawasaki Invader 440. Speed may have been a factor in the accident, authorities said.

Everyone wanted to know about Alex today. All Mom and Dad told me this morning was that his leg was pinned back together, but there're big spaces where the bone has to grow back in, and the doctors don't know if it will. Mom said his leg is so swollen they couldn't sew his skin closed. I told everyone he was out of surgery and recovering in the hospital.

11/30/90

I think I'm pregnant.

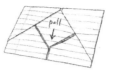

Through every town the beast he will pursue
Till in the depths of Hell she hides her face
Mother Mary!

How's your brother doing? Hope he's okay.
I'm damned to English Lit hell! A long block. Mr.
Banyon is going off about how Dante escaped the
Inferno by climbing through the center of the
earth via Satan's fur. Sounds like a giant vag. If I
start climbing Mr. Banyon, will I get out of Lit?
Banyon is fucking HAIRY. And he could be Satan.
Save me, MerMer!

Charlie Manson (Drink my Kool-Aid!!)

20
Shrink

I'm crying in the bathroom, and even though it's locked, Mom pokes a nail in the knob hole and flings open the door.

I am crouched on the floor, my back against the vanity, holding the pregnancy test.

She blinks and puts her hand over her mouth, as if shoving her shock and disappointment back inside herself. For a moment she just stands there, probably praying in her head, then she bends and gently rotates my wrist to her.

She checks the line in the test's tiny window. "Negative," Mom says, letting out a held breath.

I blink. "But I missed my period."

"Just one line." She falls to her knees and brushes matted hair from my forehead. "Oh, sweetheart...*two* lines mean you're pregnant." She hugs me. "You've been under a lot of stress. That can cause you to skip a cycle."

I collapse against her, sobbing. The test fooled me. Brett fooled me. I am stupid and naïve, and I hate myself. How can I do this to my mom right now? She has so much else to worry about.

"I'm so sorry," I say between sniffs. Mom has been having crying spells at least once a day because she is scared for Alex and still missing Grandma. How can I add my own shit to hers? Especially after that anti-sex letter she sent me from Grandma's, which turned out to be more of an omen than a deterrent. I am the worst daughter in the world. I wish I could shrink down and disappear. "I'm a screwup," I say.

"You're human," she says, wrapping her arms around me. Rocking me like she did when I was a child, her arms tell me things she can't say aloud. She holds me tight until my face grows hot and sticky on her shoulder. When I can breathe again, she stops rubbing my back and sits beside me on the floor. She doesn't look at me. "Who?"

I shake my head. "I can't talk about it."

"That *Brett* boy."

I can't tell if she blames Brett or what, but the fact that she doesn't say I'm awful or that it's all my fault makes me feel a little better. Once a Sunday school teacher said that girls were like sticks of gum—nobody wants you once you've been chewed. My mom's never said anything like that, but still I'm relieved when she doesn't yell or lecture or make me feel worse than I already do. We just sit a minute, backs against the bathroom wall, until finally she pulls me up and tells me to help with dinner.

I'd agree to make dinner every night, by myself, while reciting scripture and singing hymns. That's how relieved I am—giddy even—to not be pregnant with Brett's baby.

"God is merciful," Mom whispers as she flattens the moose burgers.

Clearly, I big-time owe the Great Maker upstairs. Whoever that is.

I expected to be grounded or made to wear one of those medieval chastity belts, but that would require Mom talking to Dad about something she herself can barely accept: not only the almost-pregnant part, but also the fact that I'm doing things—*grown-up* things— and not telling her about them. I've started making my own choices, becoming Head of My Own Life. Apparently, I'm not qualified for the job. Mom has decided to send me to Pastor Dan for therapy until I can be trusted to make "healthy, Godly decisions."

Pastor Dan's office is in a defunct professional building not far from the church. The whole place smells like peed-on carpet, possibly due to the only other tenant, a plumber down the hall. At my first session with my completely unqualified mental health professional,

Pastor Dan says I can call him "just Dan without the pastor" because "we're two friends talking about life."

I hate therapy already.

"I'm going to record our sessions," he says, clicking on an ancient Panasonic cassette recorder. The thing's a brick. I watch the tape swirl around.

First he asks basic stuff. "Do you like school—how's dance team?" Just like that, pushing two questions into one. As if he's trying to get away with something.

I chew my gum and shrug. "Everything's great," I say. *"Dan."*

The office is as hot and muggy as that room at Tubs N Fun, and suddenly I feel Brett's palm pushing against my neck, forcing me under the water. I grab a brochure on attention deficit disorder from the side table and start vigorously fanning myself and rocking in Pastor Dan's big green "guest chair." The oversized rocker recliner is actually pretty comfortable, but things that are comfortable can also be dangerous—boyfriends, stretchy jeans, padded church pews. And definitely this chair.

Pastor Dan puts his hand on the arm of my chair to still it. "You're safe here," he says. "We can talk about whatever you want."

I don't feel safe.

Pastor Dan does this thing where he restates whatever I say but in a way that makes me sound like a jerk. Like I say, "I need my own life," and Pastor Dan says, "You believe your needs make lying to your parents acceptable." Or I say, "Alex is a pain," because he really is sometimes, and Pastor Dan says, "You're saying you're angry and frustrated."

No, dude. I'm saying that Alex is still my annoying little brother, even though he's in the hospital. He may be crippled for the rest of his life because of me, but I have to believe that he will keep on being my annoying little brother, no matter what. Because that's the only thing keeping me sane.

In addition, the one person who has always believed in me, no matter how dumb I am, has cancer. Also, my best friend is ignoring me, and I want to date this really awesome guy who my parents probably won't like, even though they let me date a gigantor dick-head who I just broke up with, so now I'm alone. You know how I feel about all that, Pastor Dan? Really fucking bad.

But none of my shit is dumb Pastor Dan's business. Not my worries. Not my fears. Definitely not my love life. None of it. I wish Alex was better and Grandma Buckley didn't have cancer and Charlie would pull her head out of her ass and Joaquin was my boyfriend—but like Mom always says, "If wishes were horses, beggars would ride," which I guess means wishing isn't worth a crap.

Pastor Dan is an idiot. Really. I could counsel me better. By the end he's just nodding and saying, "ah" and "hm," as if he's evaluating the artwork of a slow kid. Sessions are supposed to last forty-five minutes, but after thirty, he says, "I'm going out to speak to your mother for a few minutes."

Cool air swirls in from the hall when Pastor Dan leaves, though he quickly shuts the door behind him, and I'm trapped again in his muggy, piss-poor excuse for an office. The fact is, I convinced Mom and Dad to let Alex go to Ryan's, he wrecked his snowmachine, nearly bled to death, and now he may never walk again. There's nothing I can do about any of it, and there's sure as shit nothing Pastor Dan can do.

Out in the hall I can hear Mom's voice. Her words are soft and indistinct. I creep over and press my ear against the hollow door, paranoid that Mom has heard everything I just said to Pastor Dan. She waited through the whole session, perched in a folding chair just outside the door. Maybe she passed the time perusing *Reader's Digest* or the latest *Our Daily Bread* devotional she keeps in her purse. Maybe she was praying for me.

More likely she was praying for Alex. She calls herself a Prayer Warrior and believes that the doctor's latest prognosis—that Alex will most likely walk again—is a miracle coaxed out of God by her own persistent efforts.

The hall conversation is muffled by the closed door. I listen super hard to Pastor Dan's low voice. All I hear is something about guilt and girls and pressure.

I wish Mom had just dropped me off and gone to the hospital.

"I'm sorry." Mom is always apologizing. "Are you sure...see her again?" Then, a little louder, "I *know* things like this take time." A hand brushes the door, fingers skittering on dry wood. I back away and resettle myself in the recliner, waiting.

Things like this take time....

Everything in *Slow*dotna takes time, but nothing ever really happens.

I imagine moving to a real city, like New York or L.A. or any city where going to the theater doesn't only mean the movies. Where dancing's an art form, not foreplay, and where wearing a jean skirt doesn't get you called a dick tease. A place where Robert Service's "The Cremation of Sam McGee" and anything ever written by Ayn Rand isn't the sum total of the library's literature section.

When Pastor Dan finally barges back in with Mom close on his heels, I'm day dreaming about being awarded a full scholarship to Cornell and rooming with Charlie, even though I doubt she's applied to any colleges.

Pastor Dan says, "Today was a good start, Meri. We'll meet again over the holidays."

"But if you don't at least go visit your brother in the hospital," Mom adds, "I'll keep you in therapy until you're thirty." If the therapy was better, I'd be on board with this plan. Lord knows I have enough issues to fill a decade of sessions, and she's the cause of many of them. She was an early Brett fan, and she's the one who told me about super hospital brain viruses. But the accident—that was my fault.

Pastor Dan pats the arm of the green recliner. "Be patient. Like I told your mom, you'll get more comfortable."

Before I leave Pastor Dan's office, I lean over and stick my pink wad of chewed bubble gum under the edge of his green recliner. That makes me feel more comfortable.

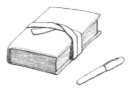

I dreamed I was an eagle up in an aerie and the branches below hung off the trees like lace. I was hungry so I fell into the wind and my wingtips blew wide and my voice echoed back at me and the Great Sky held me. Beyond were the mountains and then something else, but the forest said, "Forget," and the trees whispered, "Home," and the sky said, "Stay." Someday, the river and the salmon, but not today.

21
Ugly Truths

After my second session with Pastor Dan, in which we mostly talked about the upcoming Christmas program that I'm helping organize, I swing by Dairy Queen for some comfort food. I head for the drive-thru, but there's a bull moose blocking my way, devouring one of the tiny landscaping trees around the base of the glowing menu, so I park and go inside.

Therapy makes me feel like I need therapy, so I use the payphone by the bathroom to call Joaquin. I nibble on fries while I wait for him to drive over and meet me. I make it through two more chapters of *Brave New World*, which Mr. Banyon suggested I read over the break.

"What you reading?" Joaquin startles me out of my book coma.

"Just some story about recreational sex and the death of the family unit." I try to sound bored, as if I'm not ecstatic to see him. "It's for school."

He slides into the booth across from me and starts helping himself to my lukewarm fries. "Besides your creepy sex book, what's new?"

"My mom has me going to this counselor guy. For no reason." I heave out a dramatic sigh. "She's the one who needs therapy."

He sits back and lets a fry dangle out the corner of his mouth like a cigarette. "Tell me about your mother," he says.

I laugh, despite my crappy mood. He looks ridiculous—not at all the guarded, all-business guy from that day on the beach. Or maybe he is. Maybe this is just another side of him. There's a lot, I think, under the surface.

"My mom is complicated," I start. "I mean, she loves me and everything and wants me to be happy." I take a soggy fry and start folding it accordion-style back and forth. "But her way to happy isn't my way." I pinch the folded fry hard between my thumb and finger, making grease sponge out. "Right now, she seems singularly obsessed with nurturing my poor invalid brother back to health. And simultaneously ruining my life."

Joaquin nods sagely as he chews.

I let the fry spring free. It doesn't really spring, more sags out and falls wilted onto my napkin. "She's convinced I'm going to get knocked up, and now she's threatening to up my shrink visits if I don't go visit Alex in the hospital."

"Can't believe you haven't already." He half-chokes on a fry. "Gone and seen Alex, I mean." He coughs. "Not the knocked up part."

The image of that fly in Brett's light fixture flashes in my mind, and my gut twists. I try not to think about the Super Big Bad Thing or what Joaquin would think if he knew. I concentrate on the other guilt. "I hate hospitals."

"That's bullshit."

"How about the fact that it's kinda my fault he's in there in the first place. I'm the one who talked my parents into letting him go...."

He air-writes notes onto his palm. "The patient has a God complex."

I slap his nonexistent notebook. "Alright. Maybe I'm a teeny bit afraid. What if he's mad at me? What if he blames me?" My voice cracks a little. "What if he never walks again because of me?" I've been choking on this truth—like a bone lodged in my throat—for weeks. When I'm not feeling gross about the Super Big Bad Thing, I'm feeling like shit about Alex.

He brushes his palm across the back of my hand. "I'm just saying I'd be pissed if my sister didn't come see me if I was in the hospital."

"You're no help," I lie. Telling Joaquin is like getting the Heimlich, which I've only had to endure once, thank God. It felt gross but probably saved my life. I'm already breathing easier. "Your sister's nicer than me."

"But not as pretty." He shoves the last three fries into his mouth. "Don't tell her I said that."

I throw the empty basket at him. "Dude. You ate all my fries."

"Share a sundae?"

I grab his hand when he walks by. "Thanks. You know, for meeting me and hanging out and stuff."

His nose scrunches, and he gives me the smile that makes my December less dark.

When he comes back, he's carrying a huge sundae with two spoons. "Merry Christmas," he says.

"Thanks." I grab a spoon. "We don't even have a tree this year. Christmas is going to suck."

He nods. "Christmas sucks every year."

I scoop out a giant glob of fudge and ice cream. "Stupid capitalist holiday."

Joaquin smiles. "At least the food's decent."

"I liked Christmas when I was a kid. You know, coming downstairs and seeing that mound of presents under the tree. Guessing what everything was." I try to take another bite, but his red plastic spoon blocks mine. I sword fight him until he lets me scoop another bite. "What'th your faforit pard of Chrithmath?" I ask, my mouth full of ice cream.

"My brothers and sister. Everybody trying to find the least expensive gift that's still gonna make the other person a little happier."

"What was your best gift last year?"

"Noah got me a sketch pad."

"Cool. You're an artist?"

"Architect." He leans away. "I mean, I'd like to be. I mainly just screw around and dream up weird-looking buildings."

"Where are you planning to go to school?" I'm secretly hoping he's considering a college in Idaho.

"Never gonna happen," he says, shaking his head. He doesn't say it with any emotion. It's just a statement.

Before I can argue, he cuts me off. "I'm the oldest in my family, and my dad's like a hundred. When I graduate, I'll take over his boat repair business." He grins, but it's all show. There's definitely sadness behind his smile. "I'll put Fiberglass Artist on my business card."

"Screw that! Go somewhere and be an architect."

"I'm the oldest." He shakes his head. "Can't just take off like that on my family."

I scratch at a dried smear on the table—probably from spilled ice cream. "You should be an architect." I concentrate on sweeping the tiny, dried smear shavings into a pile. "You could come to college with me."

He pulls his sleeve up and flexes his bicep. "You think you'd get any studying done with this around?"

He's joking, but the truth is probably no.

"What about you, Miss Miller. What are *you* gonna be when you grow up?"

"I don't know. Taller, I hope. With bigger boobs."

His eyes flash to my chest, but he quickly brings them back up to my face. "I like your boobs."

"I like yours, too." I wish we were in his cousin's trailer.

The booth creaks as he leans back, his arms crossing to hide the pecs I'd love to explore. With my mouth.

I don't know what I want to be or do. I don't have a clue. "I've always wanted to start a band," I say. "But I suck at singing. And I can't play an instrument."

"You're a liar, Meri Miller."

He's more right than he knows about me being a liar. "No," I say. "I really do suck at singing."

Joaquin raises a spoonful of melty fudge as if he's about to flick it at me.

"Okay, okay." I hold up my hands in surrender, fingers splayed in what my fellow Kitties call Jazz Hands. "I want to do something with words, probably. I journal a lot. I write poems sometimes. I guess I want to be a writer. You know, because professional dancer's not a very plausible career choice. I have limited skills." I collapse onto the table. "I don't know what I want to do with the rest of my life. I don't know anything. I'm a mess. Haven't you noticed?"

He lays a hand on my shoulder. "You're kind of going off the deep end here, Mer."

I *am* going off the deep end, but more importantly, Joaquin is calling me by a nickname only my family and close friends use. I want to hug him.

"I want to go to college," I say, sounding all sad and dejected. "But I don't want to go alone. And I don't even know if I'll get in anywhere or how I'll pay for it, and anyway Mt. Redoubt will probably explode and kill us all, so who cares?" I shove the almost-empty sundae over to his side of the table.

"You," he says, scooping the last bite of sundae into his mouth, "are exactly the kind of person who should go to college."

"But this is the only place I've ever lived. I know *here*." The sundae must have been spiked with truth serum because I can't stop babbling all the things I've been feeling but have been too much of a chickenshit to admit. "I know where things are. What time everything closes. It's easy here. I have friends."

"You're smart. You'll make friends."

"I know, but as much as I hate the peninsula—and I do—I still think it's beautiful here. Surrounded by mountains and trees and near the water and everything. This is home to me."

"I know what it's like to make a new place home," he says. "It can be done. But look, I'm not going to talk you into leaving because, trust me, I'd love nothing more than to have you stay here and prance around in spandex." He smiles. "But you, out of every person I know, should go to college."

I'm sick of talking about all of my deepest, darkest insecurities. I slide out from my side of the booth and scoot in next to him. From my jeans pocket I pull a mostly-eaten roll of SweeTARTS. I set a blue and pink in front of him. "What are we?" I know how I feel, but I don't know about him. Not really. I want him to say we are real.

He puts his arm around me and kisses my head. "I'm your secret lover."

I pull back. "I don't want that," I say. "I want..." I stop. What do I want?

He shakes his head. "You don't." He withdraws his arm and stares out the window of DQ at the dirty snow piles at the edges of the parking lot. "You don't want this to be more. If you did, we wouldn't be sneaking around."

His words expose ugly truths, realities I've been avoiding. Am I embarrassed of him? If so, I am every bit as bad as the people I'm hiding us from.

He finally turns back to face me, but I can't meet his gaze. All I can do is watch his jaw flex. He says, "If this was a real thing, you'd meet my friends and we'd hang out with yours and you'd introduce me to your family and we'd hold hands in public."

I'm not ready for this level of honesty. "It's complicated," I say, reaching for him and finding his open palm. I want him to hear the truth of my body, not my lame clichéd words.

"I guess so," he says, staring down at our intertwined fingers, my white hand clinging to his brown one.

I've been lying to everyone in my life, including him. Including myself. How can I explain that? "You have no idea how much I care about you. You're the only thing holding me together right now. You're my most real thing."

He snatches the two SweeTARTS off the table. "Then that's what we are. Whatever that is."

12/7/90

When I'm with him, all the pressure I'm feeling from my parents or school evaporates, and I forget to be sad about Grandma. He doesn't need to do anything special or buy me stuff or pretend to adore me. He just needs to be there, holding me to the earth. My safety cable. Just me being in the same space with him. That's all. He's the ground wire keeping me from short-circuiting.

12/8/90

I got accepted to the University of Idaho! I'm not going to tell anyone, because I don't know yet if I'm going. I haven't received my student loan, and I don't want to leave Joaquin.

12/10/90

If I get through semester finals, it will be a miracle. I've crammed enough this week to make my eyeballs bleed. Joaquin helped me study for my Spanish test, so I probably aced that one. Today was Ethics in Government, which was random but easy. Even the dumbest person knows Wally Hickel is our new governor and we live in the least populated state in the union. More square miles than people. Alaska is a great, big, small state. We only get one House representative and three Electoral College votes.

22
First Real Hospital Visit

Alex is propped up in the bed watching television.

I poke my head in. "Hey, dude..."

He glances up when I walk in, then he goes back to staring at the television mounted on a triangular metal shelf in the upper corner of the room. "Took you long enough, asswipe."

"Potty mouth." The tiny room smells of antiseptic and sick people. I try not to think about deadly brain viruses. "You better hope Mom is down at the vending machine."

"I can say whatever I want. I almost *died*. Remember?"

"You look alive to me." The truth is that Alex is pale and too thin. I recognize the camouflage blanket on his lap as the one off his bed at home. There are other reminders of his bedroom—a stuffed bulldog and his basketball on the ledge under the window. At least this room has a window. Half-turned vertical blinds let in slats of white light. "What you watching?"

"WWF. They have cable here. I can watch whatever, whenever. Pretty sweet." He holds up a rectangular box that looks like a surge protector connected by a cord to his bed.

"Nice." I sit in the chair next to Alex's bed, and the orange vinyl seat cushion hisses. On the television, Hulk Hogan is ramming the Undertaker's head into the floor of the wrestling arena. The Undertaker recovers quickly and uses the ropes like rubber bands to fling himself at his opponent.

We both stare up at the television screen, letting unspoken words fill up the space between us. I want to be touching Alex somehow, so I slip off my Keds, thread my legs through the metal side rail, and lay my feet beside him.

A commercial comes on, and Alex mutes the television with the giant remote. He presses a button. A motor hums from somewhere, and Alex's back lifts so he is sitting more upright and can see me easier. "So what's new?"

"Not much. I aced my Ethics in Government final. Mr. Davies is an old hippie, so we mainly read Kahlil Gibran. As long as we knew basic Alaskan history, the three branches of government, and could recite some cheesy Gibran quote about holding on to your dreams, we were good."

He shrugs. "At least that's good advice."

"I guess." My eyes slide away from him. Get Well cards stand on the bedside table, second-rate proxies of the people who sent them. Each card is a reminder that people are rooting for him, hoping he can keep hold of his dreams.

"So...if not much is new, why haven't you come to visit before now?" Alex isn't messing around with small talk today.

"I did."

"When I was *unconscious*."

"I've had stuff...I'm in like every after-school club, plus dance team and work. Things are crazy with me right now. I'm trying to get into college, not to mention Grandma's probably dying and my brother's in the hospital because I begged Mom to let him go off snowmachining when he should have been at church..." I bite the side of my tongue to keep myself from crying. "Oh yeah, and Mom's making me go to counseling because she thinks I'm an ungodly trollop."

"You *are* an ungodly trollop," he says. "And I mean that as a compliment."

I push my foot at him as if I'm Karate kicking, but I don't actually touch him. "Look, I'm sorry I begged Mom to let you go. I should've just stayed out of it. If you'd never have gone with Ryan..."

"Get over yourself. You don't control the world. Who died and made you God?"

He doesn't know what it's like to feel responsible for another person. I still remember when his pajamas had feet, when he couldn't reach the sink to brush his teeth without me lifting him, and when he needed me to help spread the peanut butter on his toast.

I get up and walk over to the window. The blinds rustle together, swinging as if an invisible person is blowing on them. Above, there's a humming from a grungy central air vent on the ceiling. I guess the cleaning and the bleaching don't extend to hospital air vents. "What even happened?"

"What do you mean?"

Out the window, the sky and the ground are white. Snow is falling. "You wrecked your snowmachine and hit your leg on a stump— that part was in the paper—but...I was in church, and Mom and Dad just left me there. Nobody told me shit. I had to go home with the fucking *Wymers!*"

"Sorry. I'll try not to almost die again while you're in church."

"Good. Also, don't ever do whatever stupid shit you were doing that made you wreck. Ever again."

"Accidents fucking happen. I've spent the last bazillion hours laying here feeling like a pile of steaming scat, blaming myself. I don't need you all up in my junk about it."

I can't believe Alex just busted out the F-word. He never does that around me. *I'm* the bad one, not Alex.

"My life hasn't been a cakewalk lately, trust me. No cake. No walking. As in, I may be permanently *crippled*. Do you not get that?" He starts fiddling with the controller. "Oh, and also, I'm barely passing ninth grade, I don't have a girlfriend, and I'm stuck in a hospital twenty-four seven, which is depressing as all hell. Not that you would know, Miss MIA."

The truth of my brother's misery sucks the air from my lungs. I'm a shit of a sister. But I can't fix this. I can't even fix my own crap. I force myself to breathe and push my guilt down deep. "Sorry. But it's not like you need me to babysit you anymore." I walk back over and slump into the uncomfortable orange seat. "Besides, Mom and Dad are already here with you every damn second."

"Right." He pushes a button, and the bed lays him back.

I grab a random Get Well card off the table—there's a picture of an open Bible on the front and some scripture written in loopy letters: *The prayer of faith shall save the sick, and the Lord will raise him up. James 5:15.* It's from some old lady at our church. I'm not sure how I feel about scripture or church or God these days, but in my head I say a quick prayer anyway. I beg God for the millionth time to let Alex walk again.

Alex stares up at a brown water stain on one of the white ceiling tiles. "This dump needs a remodel," he says. "Bad."

I'd like to forget we're even in our gross hospital. The place is giving me hives. I want to talk more about the accident, as if knowing all the details will somehow make it possible for me to change the outcome. "Were you showing off or something?"

"What? No. I mean, we were driving fast, but we always do. I wanted to get out to Sterling—to get my Hot Grips."

"Your what?"

"You know, heated handles you wire up to your battery."

I blink and shake my head.

"Are you even an Alaskan? Nevermind. Anyway, we had to go back to Ryan's house first—he forgot something—I don't even remember what—but Ryan just jumped on his machine and took off. I couldn't let him *beat* me, so I hauled ass down the road, right. As you know, my Kawasaki is far, *far* superior to his piece of junk Polaris, so I'd almost caught up when I hit this stretch of black ice. We were still on Carver Drive—you know where it bends and becomes Raspberry Road—well, there was no way I could make that corner. The machine did a bunch of barrel rolls and landed on its track—Dad said it still runs fine, just bent up the frame and a ski. I wasn't so lucky."

"Were you scared?"

"What do you think? I was pissing in my pants. Literally. I couldn't move, I was stuck in the woods, and I peed in my snow pants."

"Gross."

"Nothing hurt at first—I didn't know I'd hit a stump—but I knew something bad had happened. When I lifted my leg, the boot stayed on the ground. My foot was hanging straight down off the end of my leg—ninety degrees. I almost puked. Ryan says, 'Holy shit!' then takes off. I was like, *that asshole left me here!*"

"He was going for help, right?"

"Yeah, but I didn't know that. I wasn't really thinking straight, you know? I thought he didn't want to get in trouble. My best friend...I thought he'd left me." Alex looks down at his leg, which is in a cast and hanging in a sling. "After I had lifted up my leg the tendons and muscles started stretching out. That hurt like hell. I tried to crawl to the road. I thought I could save myself, you know, like one of those dramas in real life from *Reader's Digest*. I pulled my body like a foot and couldn't go any further. I just sat there and yelled, screaming for someone to help. I wasn't that scared, really. I didn't realize my leg was bleeding all over inside my snowpants."

"Shit. I'm gonna kill Ryan. Why did he leave you so long? What the hell?"

"He was having his *own* drama in real life. I found out later that he had to knock on a ton of doors. It was Sunday, remember? Everyone was at church. Ryan was totally spazzing out. Then he found this stoner guy who answered the door in a bathrobe. The guy was really slow and for some reason didn't want Ryan to use his phone. The guy didn't want to help at all. Ryan said he was watching *Family Feud* and eating a frozen dinner off a TV tray. The dude finally gave Ryan a blanket and called the cops. When the ambulance came, the paramedic was like, 'You only could've lasted another twenty minutes or so.' I guess I had severed arteries and was bleeding out. The paramedics pumped me full of fluids and stopped the bleeding. But when we got to the hospital, the doctor was like, 'Son, we'll probably have to amputate your leg.'" Alex's voice dropped to a deep register that I didn't know he had. "And I was praying my ass off, 'Please, God, don't let them take my leg; I just started getting good at basketball.' That's when the minor miracle occurred."

"You were kinda due for a break at that point." I push out a laugh. "Get it? A break?"

"Hilarious. There just happened to be an expert bone guy—an orthopedic surgeon from Anchorage—who was already down for another operation. A lady's hip replacement, but she got rescheduled."

"Poor lady. Jacked by a dumbass kid."

"Dr. Bone Guy decided to try and salvage my leg instead. For ten hours he lined up the pieces of my leg bones—the ones he could find—then held them together somehow with this little beauty." He pointed to the metal cage on his leg. "My external fixator keeps the old leg from moving so hopefully the pieces grow back together."

"Whoa. So now what? Will you be able to walk?"

He shrugs. "Remains to be seen. At this point, I'm happy I didn't die or get my leg amputated. They're already trying to talk me into redoing ninth grade, but I'm not gonna. I've been doing homework, and honestly, here is better than high school."

"Didn't know you were so anti-school." We've both had a crappy year, but I was only paying attention to my crap. There's probably a lot more going on with Alex that I don't know.

"Well now you do," he says. "I suck at school bullshit. It's painful...not as painful as having my leg x-rayed—that was *excruciating*—but high school's close."

"Listen, drama boy," I can only take so much of his self-pity, "high school's not that bad. You're not even in a relationship. *Those* are excruciating."

He laughs at me. "Boy troubles, little sis?"

Over the summer Alex grew more than six inches and now is taller than me. He loves pointing it out. I look him up and down. "All boys are trouble."

"Listen," he says, yawning. "You not coming here until now was a complete cop-out and has ruined your odds of being awarded Sister of the Year, but I'm not mad. I'm glad you're here now." He sounds strangely grown up. I guess you'd expect that from someone who just cheated death.

"I'm still pissed at *you* for driving like an idiot and almost killing yourself."

"I'm mad about that, too. And I've had 'a lot of time to think about it,' as Dad would say."

"So would you say you've been 'using your head for something other than a hat rack'?"

We both smile.

The smell of hamburgers wafts into the room just as Mom bustles through the doorway carrying a white paper sack. "Brrrr!" Her face and hair are damp, and she is bundled in her turquoise parka with the hot pink lining. Alex and I call it her snow bunny coat. "Fresh from Little Skeemo!" She holds up the bag. "Best burgers in Soldotna for the two best kids in town."

"You mean the best *kid* in town," says Alex. "We both know Meri is fast becoming a delinquent."

"Alex, cut your sister some slack. She braved her hospital phobia to come see you. And unlike a certain unnamed person, Miss Meri made the honor roll."

It's nice to hear Mom bragging about something good I did for a change.

He huffs. "Well, *she* wasn't maimed in a tragic accident."

Mom rolls her eyes. "Your leg is injured, my son, not your brain." She walks over and sets the bag of burgers on the table. I help her gather up the cards and stack them neatly toward the back of the table so we can spread the burgers out on napkins.

After we eat, Alex is exhausted. He's on a bunch of meds, I guess, for pain and stuff. I bend over and give him a little hug before I go.

"Carpe diem," he whispers, because that's deep for a ninth-grade boy, and he's not about to tell me he loves me.

12/15/90

I'm so glad I finally visited Alex. It wasn't as scary as I thought. Joaquin was right. If only everyone else could see how great Joaquin is. How he makes me a better person.

12/16/90

The sessions with Pastor Dan aren't helping—even Mom can see that. I can hardly stand to look at him on Sundays when he's giving his sermons. After the service today, I stood on the bluff's edge thinking how one slip—a tilt too far or a loose stone under my sole—could send me plunging to certain death. I imagined myself falling and hitting the water. In my mind I transformed into a beluga and swam away.

12/17/90

Joaquin called today and wanted to know what I thought about him taking a business class at the community college. He said it would help him run his dad's business, and if he takes it this next semester, the high school would pay for it. I said it sounded great and tried to be excited. But it sucks. I had thought maybe I could convince him to study architecture at a university. Maybe even the University of Idaho. But he's definitely staying here.

12/18/90

Today last year the sky darkened and dumped Mt. Redoubt's ash everywhere. Color no longer existed in the world. Buildings, cars, snow—even the air—turned gray. Schools were evacuated, and we were all pretty sure the end was near. Looking back, that feels like a small crisis compared to the disasters of this year.

23
The End of 1990

December is a dark, grueling month. I drive to school in cold blackness, sit all day under fluorescents, and by the final bell, the sun has already abandoned me. I'd punch Mr. Sun right in his big fat face if I didn't need him so bad. By winter solstice, I'm light-starved and on edge. Everyone is. We become zombies. Half-human. Any unusual behavior is generally categorized under the catch-all of "cabin fever." As in, "Woman duct tapes husband and hides him under the bed" or "Man accidentally cuts off his own leg while using a chainsaw in his living room." That's just cabin fever.

Thanks to the Christmas shoppers and the shortage of retail stores in Soldotna, Pam schedules me for extra shifts at Jay Jacobs. I'm mostly just straightening sweaters or cleaning out dressing rooms, but it's better than hanging out alone in my room writing terrible poetry or reading Aldous Huxley's depressing predictions for the future.

After Alex got in his accident, tons of people wanted to know how I was doing, if Alex was going to walk, and how things were at home. Random teachers and students would send cards. A few ladies from church brought casseroles and goopy potatoes and other weird potluck food by our house. But that stopped after a few weeks. Once word got around that Alex had responded almost miraculously to the surgery and that he wasn't going to be a cripple, he was old news. He's still in the hospital, but hardly anyone asks how he's doing anymore. *I* don't even know how he's doing. Mom and Dad have forgotten I exist—they're tuned in to the Alex Channel, all day, every day. My life feels darker than a normal December.

Charlie doesn't want to hang out anymore, we never see each other outside of school, and she even messed up our after-school tradition by inviting Kenny to join us—the *worst*. Since ninth grade, Charlie and I have had our own special way of coping with this miserable month. At the close of every December school day we rush out of our respective classes, meet at the front double doors, fling them open, and yell the number of days left until break. Then we bust up and flip off what's left of the sun. One day last year, we were like, "Eleven!" and this hockey guy was all, "*What?*" because he just happened to be out in the parking lot in his jersey, which was—*true story*—number eleven.

"Why?" I asked Charlie. "I thought it was our thing?"

"You don't have to get all pissy," she said. "It's just a stupid countdown."

Now Kenny meets us at the door every day to yell numbers at no one. He really isn't into it, and even Charlie and I don't yell as loud as we used to.

Joaquin is the only person who hasn't completely abandoned me. Since the Tubs N Fun rescue, we talk almost every day. I'm grateful Brett hasn't called since the breakup.

Yesterday Joaquin called to say his dad is taking time off for Christmas, which means he can see me over the break. While we were talking, Mom breezed by and said, "Say hi to Charlie." I nodded and pressed the receiver closer so she couldn't hear Joaquin's voice. I want to tell Mom about him, but I don't want to risk not being able to spend time with him. Because he is amazing and means everything to me.

I guess in all fairness the Bug is hanging in there for me, too. Pretty sad when my car is one of my only two real friends. I leave her plugged in at night so her engine doesn't freeze, and she burbles to life like a champ in the mornings, even when it's thirty below.

Today the temp's up to a balmy two degrees, so when I bail after lunch, I'm not even the least bit worried about the Bug starting.

Maybe I'll regret it, but I leave without saying goodbye to Charlie. She and Kenny can yell, "Zero!" this afternoon sans yours truly. They'll be too busy making plans to go ice-skating at the Sports Center and tubing down the Redoubt Elementary hill to miss me. Screw our stupid tradition.

I meander along K-Beach Road with no real destination, singing along to John Denver on my AM radio. My breath puffs out in little clouds. The Bug's heater is worthless when the weather's this arctic, but I'm bundled in my parka and favorite burgundy scarf.

The Kenai Flats are frozen and desolate—not even a caribou wandering out there. I keep driving, and the dark orange sun dips nearer the horizon. A couple more hours and the light will be gone. Before most of us even eat dinner.

When I get to Kenai, I follow the highway past town to the bench overlooking the beach. Before I get out, I grab my beat-up copy of Margaret Atwood's *Selected Poems 1965-1975* from the glove box.

My boots crunch against the packed snow. Though the path is clear, deep drifts shroud the dead grass. Only the taller stalks peek above the snow, and the setting sun turns them gold. My hand tingles as I whack the spent husks. They are encased in sharp, frozen crusts, and each blow causes tiny ice flakes to explode into the air. I feel as small as one of those ice shards.

Someone has pushed the snow from the bench—it's piled along one side—and I stupidly wonder if it was Joaquin. I think of him standing next to me last summer on this very bench, and I wish he was here with me now. But there's no one. Just me and Margaret. The sea below is flat and indifferent, and the beach is hidden under slush and giant, dirty blocks of ice. Lonely chunks of frozen inlet.

A breeze hisses through the grass, and icy air seeps through the seams in my coat. I hunker down on the bench and open Atwood's collection to "You Are Happy." Among other things, the poem is about being very cold, which at this moment I am, and about how sharp the world becomes when it is very, very cold. How singular.

We ate TV dinners and opened a few presents. We didn't have a tree, but Alex was there, officially out of the hospital, and Mom said I don't have to go to therapy anymore. Best Christmas gift ever. BITE ME, PASTOR DAN!

12/25/90

Charlie called today to say Merry Christmas and that she got me a present. I felt super bad because I didn't get her anything. But I will now. She's still my best friend. I just wish we could go back in time to when we shared more with each other. I don't think she realizes how pissed I've been at her lately. When she calls or I see her, she acts like everything's fine. It's like she's not even tuned in.

1/2/91

Happy New Year to me. I didn't get into Cornell.

1/4/91

I always wondered if Charlie Bucket had regrets about taking over Wonka's chocolate factory. When he found that golden ticket, he was hungry. It was winter. He wanted a better life, and the dream of endless chocolate seemed a nirvana. He didn't yet know about the creepy tests or Veruca Salt or those psycho Oompa Loompas. The story never says if the factory made him happy, but when my own letter, gold-stamped with the official State of Alaska seal, arrived saying I was being awarded twenty thousand dollars from the Alaska Student Loan Program, I immediately wrote and accepted the loan, with all its unknown conditions.

24
This Is Home

I've never been inside Joaquin's trailer, and I'm more nervous than I expected as I stand shivering in my puffy blue parka outside on his wooden steps. The stairs have been swept clean, and a path has been shoveled from the road to here, but about two feet of snow has collected everywhere else, including on their roof. Spiky icicles hang from the eves like walrus tusks.

I promised Joaquin I'd come by to help with his first assignment for the business class he's starting at the community college, and I secretly hope he's the only one home. I'm trying to be a part of his life because I want us to be a real thing, but what if his family doesn't like me?

I take a deep breath. The cold air helps clear my head. I can do this. Easy peasy. I knock, two dull thuds, and hear footsteps from inside. The door opens, and a girl about my age stands and appraises me.

"You must be Meri." She crosses her arms but doesn't invite me in. The girl has delicate features, soft brown eyes, and straight, coppery black hair down to her waist. She's so pretty I can't stop staring.

Joaquin pushes in between us, bumping the girl gently out of the way. "Chill out, Eva," he says to her. His face breaks into a wide smile. "Hey."

I pound the snow off my boots one last time and follow him inside. His house is warm and smells delicious, like chicken soup and pumpkin pie. My stomach growls. "Somebody cooking?"

"Me," says the girl, hovering too close to us as I shed my winter gear. "Just so you know, I'm taking boxing classes."

"Settle down," says Joaquin, taking my coat and hanging it in a closet near the door. "Meri, this is my sister, Eva. She's every bit as weird as you."

She clearly doesn't want to shake my hand or anything, so I give her a little wave.

"I'm already helping him with his essay," Eva says, straightening a row of already orderly books on a shelf near the closet. "I got an A plus in Honors English last semester."

When Joaquin told me he was stressing out over the introductory essay he's supposed to write, he didn't mention he was already getting help from his superstar sister.

"I can get help from more than just you," he says to Eva. "Go check your soup."

She huffs into the kitchen. Joaquin takes my hand and leads me into the living room where we sit together on their floral sofa. The colors and pattern remind me of Grandma Buckley's couch—there's even an afghan folded over the back. The place has a good vibe. "I like your house," I say.

He shrugs. "This is home."

The wide wooden coffee table in front of the sofa is littered with papers, pens, and a notebook. Joaquin hands me a paper—the assignment sheet—which directs students to write five paragraphs describing themselves and why they're interested in business.

"How much have you written so far?" I ask, glancing toward the kitchen. Eva's pretending to busy herself by stirring something in a crockpot.

Joaquin tosses me his notebook. One paragraph is written in neat print:

My name is Joaquin Santos. I was born in Tijuana, Mexico, but my family moved to Kenai when I was seven. My dad runs Santos Fiberglass & Boat Repair. I've helped with the business since I was a kid. I'm the oldest in my family, and

I'll take over one day. I'd like to learn more about how to run a business, so I can grow ours and help more with the books. Right now, my mom does the books, but she hates it.

"Good start," I say, impressed by how much he conveyed in only seven sentences. "Maybe consider adding a few specific personal goals or describing something you're passionate about?"

"Hm," he says. "There is this one girl..."

"Not essay-worthy," I say, shaking my head. "But later I'd like to hear more."

He leans in and kisses me. Eva shouts from the kitchen, "Not much writing happening out there."

"Mind your business," he says, sliding his arm around my shoulders.

He's not chewing gum today, but he still smells minty. I snuggle closer and ask him brainstorming questions, jotting down his responses on a blank sheet of notebook paper.

When he's thinking of answers, my eyes wander around his house. I'm surprised by how familiar the house feels. There's the picture of the white-haired man praying over his bread—we have one just like it in our dining room—and on an end table sits a plain, black Bible that looks just like the one my mom has had since forever.

"Whose Bible?" I ask.

"My mom's," he says. "She drags us to the Nazarene church as often as she can."

I didn't know his family was religious, and I want to ask more about his feelings about God and church, but the phone rings and a second later Eva yells, "Dad wants to talk to you!"

"I'll grab it in my room." Joaquin jumps up and lopes down the hall.

I stare at the notebook, trying not to glance into the kitchen, but I feel Eva's eyes on me and can't help looking up.

"Wanna try my soup?" she asks, holding up a bowl.

As if on cue my stomach growls, and she brings me the steaming bowl of chicken soup. "Perfect winter food," I say, raising a spoonful to my lips and slurping a taste.

"Do you like him?"

At first I think she's asking about the soup and am about to say, delicious, but realize she means Joaquin, so I nod and gulp down another swallow of soup.

"I heard you were with Brett Hale," she says.

Heat creeps up my neck. This girl is bold.

"If you don't already know," she says, "he's a pushy jerk, and I'm only telling you this because my brother really likes you."

"How old are you?" I ask.

"Sixteen, but I'm a junior." Eva's voice drops to a whisper. "Brett and I were hanging out last year—mostly at the parties Mikey has—and Brett did some bad things. Joaquin knows but swore he wouldn't tell." She glances down the hall. "He hates Brett, by the way."

My mind is spinning. I can't believe Brett was with Joaquin's sister, but now I see why Joaquin was trying to warn me about Brett last summer. I want to hug Eva for having the guts to confide in me, and even though her warning comes too late for me, I am grateful.

"Thank you," I say, searching for the right words to convey how sorry I am that she had whatever experiences with Brett that she did and wanting to comfort her and commiserate with her and be angry all at the same time.

Before I can reply, Joaquin reappears from down the hall and perches beside us on the armrest of the sofa. "She makes a mean soup, doesn't she?"

Eva smiles at him. "I need something sweet. Let's cut into that pie you made."

She follows him into the kitchen, and as I watch the two of them serving up our slices of pie, I think how lucky Eva is to have a big brother like Joaquin—someone who she can trust with her secrets and who always has her back. It makes me like Joaquin even more.

2/2/91

Happy birthday to me! I can vote and go to jail! My actual presents were lame. Dad changed the oil in the Bug, and Mom got me an ugly scarf with rainbow hearts on it. Charlie got me a lame Cherry Pie T-shirt from the Warrant concert she went to with Kenny. Joaquin was the only exception. He gave me a wishbone for luck and a paper bag full of SweeTARTS but only my favorite flavors. He said there were eighteen rolls worth in there. He'd opened them all and removed the gross pinks and blues. BEST GIFT EVER!

2/14/91

At school Kenny gave Charlie a bouquet of pink roses. Joaquin met me at the mall and surprised me with a heart-shaped chocolate chip cookie that he made himself. He said he was giving me his heart. I felt bad for eating his heart, but it was so yummy, I couldn't stop.

2/24/91

During church I decided to ignore Pastor Dan completely. I sat there the whole time and just chatted up God, mainly about my life and all the things that scare me, but also about how I'm grateful that Alex is getting better and that I met Joaquin. I thanked God for how lucky I am to be with a person who is so kind and thoughtful and hot. I prayed that my mom would see those things in Joaquin, except for the hot part. I prayed that Grandma would miraculously recover and that Charlie would stop being such a jerk and that my life would work out the way it's supposed to. I felt so peaceful at the end of the service, like God had given me a big hug or something. It turned out to be the best day I've ever had at church.

2/27/91

Warmed up today above freezing. I'm so ready for spring.

3/1/91

Alex went back to school today. He's on crutches, but at least he can get around. The doctors say his leg's healing better than they expected.

25
Popped

The thing about spring in Soldotna is that it smells like dog shit. Strong and rotten. You'd think dogs spent the entire winter shitting their brains out and burying the piles under the snow for the express purpose of ruining summer's rite of passage, the season Alaskans call "breakup."

Despite the unpleasant odor, melting snow means winter is on its way out. Crusted-over heaps hunker here and there like old men clinging to life. It will be months until we've seen the last of the snow, and more depressing whiteness likely will fall before summer as temperatures drop and rise like a fishing bobber. But today the sun is warm and bright. For now it's above freezing, and shit-smell be damned, I'm happy. Even happier when Joaquin calls to say he's free and can be at the DQ in ten.

I tell my mom I'm meeting my new bestest friend and girl-from-church, Sharman, for pizza and a movie. It's just easier, letting Mom operate under the delusion that Sharman and I are two Christian girls going to drive-in movies and sock hops. The lie works better for both of us.

When my SAT scores came back and Mom saw that I did well enough to get into a good school—easily good enough for the University of Idaho—she reminded me I could live at home for free if I stay in Soldotna and go to the community college. She said it really nice, too, like she was doing me this huge favor. People are always willing to be there for you if you're doing what they want. I wish she would just be happy for me, instead of trying to control me.

I'm taking my frustrations out on a large order of fries and giant pop when I see Joaquin drive up in the minivan. From the booth we now call ours—the one by the window and closest to the door so we can evacuate fast if Mt. Redoubt blows again—I watch him park and get out. He swings his keys around his middle finger and jogs toward the door in his slouchy black boots, tight jeans, and white tee. His hair is pulled back, and his shoulders look suddenly broader.

He sees me watching him, so I hold my fry like a cigarette, take a salty puff, and blow fake smoke at him through the glass. He waves his hand in front of his face and goes into a convulsion of fake coughs.

I'm still laughing when he scoots in on my side, shoves a handful of fries into his mouth and swallows after almost no chewing. "Starving," he says reaching for more.

I take another drag off my cigarette fry and shake my head derisively.

"You know those things'll kill you," he says.

I smirk. "Then I better make now count."

He cocks his head to the side. "If you only had a day to live, what would you do?"

I suck soda through my red straw, buying time to think of a clever response. "Can't it be a week? I can barely drive to Anchorage in a day."

"Fine," he says. "A week to live."

I think about faraway places I've read about in books. "I'd go to Spain," I say. "For the castles."

He narrows his eyes all judgey-like. "You're such a princess."

"How about I let you come along as my interpreter?" I drop my voice. "Or my sex slave."

He shakes his head. "They speak weird Spanish in Spain. Let's go to Mexico."

I heave a dramatic sigh. "Fine. But will you still be my sex slave?"

"I'll be your sex slave right here and now. In Dairy Queen." His elbows are on the table and his biceps are filling out his short sleeves nicely.

"Prove it," I challenge.

He leans in and nuzzles my neck—lips first then teeth. His soft bite snakes a shiver up my spine. My head tilts, and he kisses his way across my cheek to my mouth. He moves slowly, as if cherishing each time his skin connects with mine. As if my body is a temple.

"Holy," I say, tossing my limp cigarette fry. I need both hands free. Dairy Queen fades away, and all I see is Joaquin. I pull his face to mine until our noses touch and his deep brown eyes nearly swallow me up. I squeeze my lids shut and kiss him hard like he might disappear if I don't.

He pulls away first.

"Let's go to your cousin's," I say, panting a little.

Joaquin hesitates. "He's having a huge a party tonight. Mostly assholes getting high."

"That's cool," I say. I just want to be with him in a less public place.

"You sure?" he asks. "Didn't think you were much of a partier."

"I'm gonna die in a week anyway, right?"

I park behind the minivan at Joaquin's, and we walk over to his cousin's trailer. When we get inside, first person I see is Sharman—my "bestest friend" from church—except her eyes are circled in heavy makeup and her normally close-cropped hair is spiked with gel. Her black jacket is covered in safety pins and zipped tightly over her bigger-than-I-remember-from-church bust. She's sitting cross-legged on the velour couch where Joaquin and I first made out.

"Hey," I say because it would be weird if I didn't.

She takes a slow hit from the joint she's holding. How very church girl of her.

"Yo, Meri!" Matt says, slouched next to Sharman, his blond hair greasy and his pupils huge. "You're a real little tease, aren't ya?" He laughs, "Huh-huh-huh."

"Piss off," I say and swallow hard to slow the adrenaline.

"I hear you're a natural red head," he says. "Huh-huh-huh."

Joaquin steps between us. "I don't wanna have to throw your sorry ass out, Selanof."

Sharman exhales a big smoky breath at Joaquin. "Heeey Saaantos." She sounds like a cat purring. "You going to prom this year, baby?"

He glances quickly at me then shrugs. "Dunno."

"Let me know. When you know," she says.

I suddenly want to scratch this church bitch's face off, but instead I grab Joaquin's hand just as the trailer door bangs open. "Fuckin' A!" says an unmistakable voice.

"Hale!" says Sharman.

I let go of Joaquin's hand. "I want to leave," I whisper. "Now."

Brett hasn't seen me yet, but he's standing between me and the door.

"Hey, Shar," Brett says. I didn't even know they knew each other.

He grabs the joint out of her hand and takes a drag. She leans forward, her face at his hips, and I'm shocked when she makes a biting motion at his crotch.

His hand covers his fly. "Maybe later, babe," he says. Behind Brett, ducking in the doorway, is Kenny, holding Charlie by the hand.

I can't believe Charlie's here. "No way," I say louder than I meant to.

Joaquin pulls at my arm, but I'm frantically looking for another way out.

"C'mon," says Joaquin, his voice soft. "Let's just get out of here." But it's too late.

Brett looks up. His face goes slack for a flash then recovers. "Hey, babe," he says, as if that name is all mine. As if he didn't just call Sharman "babe" two seconds ago.

Joaquin threads insistent fingers through my slack ones and leads us closer to the door. Closer to Brett.

Brett's eyes track to our hands. "What the fuck?"

Charlie sees me, runs over, and hugs me. "Hey, girl!" She reeks of rum. "God, I love you," she kisses me on the mouth. "You didn't say you were coming out tonight!"

I wipe my mouth. "Neither did you."

"Kenny wanted me to come," she says. "And I'm glad because I've missed you so much." She lays her head on my shoulder. "You better be coming with us to prom."

Brett glares at Joaquin. "Get some beers, will ya, Santos?"

Joaquin's hand tightens on mine. "They're in the kitchen. We're heading out."

"We?"

"Meri and I."

Brett cracks his knuckles. "Don't think so."

Charlie puts her arm around mine and pulls me toward the kitchen. "I'm thiiirsty."

Joaquin holds tight to my hand so that our arms have to stretch as Charlie drags me away. When our hands pull apart, I hear Brett say, "She's pretty good in the sack, eh? Even sloppy seconds?" He puts his finger in his mouth, makes a popping noise against his cheek.

The sound of my heart exploding.

"Shut your fucking mouth," Joaquin fires back at Brett.

"What? She didn't tell you?"

Joaquin's eyes are almost black, like the drops of crude oil encased in glass on a shelf in our living room. I can't hide the truth when he looks at me. The truth I should have told him.

Joaquin shoves Brett out of the way, but Brett just laughs.

"C'mon, dude," says Kenny. I'm not sure if he's talking to Brett or Joaquin.

"Hey Shar," Joaquin says extra loud.

"Yeah, sweeeeetie?"

Joaquin stares hard at me, his eyes spitting at me. "How about that prom?"

"Why, yes," she coos. "I would very much like to accompany you."

"I hate that skank," I whisper.

Charlie burps beside me. "She's got great hair, though."

I shake free of Charlie and push my way out the door into the bitterly cold March night. I hate everything about this place. My mouth is as dry and salty as last year's smoked salmon. I can barely hold it together as I run to the Bug.

"Wait, MerMer!" Charlie yells after me. The trailer door slams, and her footfalls tap-tap-tap down the steps behind me.

My car door sticks, and I yank and yank on the handle. Charlie's getting closer, and I'm tugging with my all my strength so when it finally flings open, I almost knock her out.

"Wha's the rush?" she slurs. "I needs you here."

"Are you fucking kidding me?" I whip around to face her. "I've needed you all year, bitch."

She tries to come in for a hug. "Me loves you."

"Don't." I push her off.

The moment I slam the door, a sob bursts out. My windows are fogging and tears are heaving out so I can't see Charlie, but I don't care. I slump against the wheel, start the Bug and back out. My headlights find her face, light her wide eyes for just a second before she turns back toward the trailer.

I cry so hard on the way home that I can barely see the road. My whole body is shaking, as if I'm having a seizure or something. I find a napkin in the glove box and try to fix my makeup so Mom, if she sees me, doesn't ask questions. I keep telling myself over and over, "It'll be okay, it'll be okay." Because I have to believe it will, even though I just lost a really super important something.

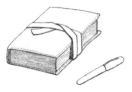

3/10/91

Charlie called when I got home from church and was being really nice. She kept saying how wasted she was last night. She wanted to know why I left the party in such a rush and what was going on with me. I told her I fucked Brett and now we're over and things are majorly screwed up and I'm probably going to hell. Also, I have no one to go with to prom next month. She got quiet then said we need to talk more often and that I should come over, but my mom wanted me to go to evening church. Charlie said I could go with her and Kenny to prom, but I don't even want to go. I think she's hurt that I've been keeping secrets, but I'm mad at her for being the worst best friend in history. She's practically married to Kenny.

3/12/91

Charlie has been acting like a best friend again. She waits for me after class and at my locker. She asks me about how I'm doing. I like that she's trying so hard, but it feels weird. Like we were watching a show together and she missed a bunch of episodes. Now she's trying to get caught up. I told her I'd been hanging out with Joaquin, and she wanted to know if I had any other secret boyfriends.

3/18/91

Neither Charlie nor I are doing anything for spring break this week. Today Charlie came along with me and my mom to the mall because we both need new shoes. She said she didn't want to spend a lot because she was saving for an emergency, and I was like, you mean like when we move? It was stupid of me to think we'd still be leaving together, but I guess I just want that so bad. She said no, she didn't think she was going anymore. I'm so pissed I could scream. We had everything planned, and now all because of Kenny she's bailing on me. She didn't even say she was sorry.

26
Stupid Prom

On Saturday, the week before the Stupid Prom I Will Not Attend, I refuse to get out of bed. I'm curled up in protest against the cruel world, listening to Dad stomp around the kitchen barking about how no daughter of his is allowed to laze around all day.

Five seconds later Mom knocks on my door.

"How about we go shopping for a prom dress?" She steps over clothes mounds and stacks of books on her way to my window. "Your dad says we should get you a brand new store-bought one." She flings open the curtains, blasting my room with light, and rushes to add, "But you know I'll make a dress if you want."

"I'm not going to prom." I pull the covers up over my face.

She rubs the top of my head through the thinning softness of my old rainbow comforter. "This is your senior prom, honey."

The air beneath the blanket is growing stuffy with my exhalations, and when I say, "I'm having an existential crisis," it sounds whinier than I intend.

"I'm not sure what that means," says Mom, "but I think you'll regret it if you don't go."

I burrow out from under the covers, take a deep breath of cool air, and pronounce that dances suck. My next breath morphs into a full body sigh that nearly becomes a sob. "Also I don't have a date."

Mom stands and crosses her arms. "Yes, you do."

I squint up at Mom. "I don't."

"Linda the Hairdresser's son is tall, handsome, smart, and very responsible," says Mom. "He graduated last year, but she said he'd love to take you."

"What?" My mind begins working this coded equation as it relates to prom and me.

Generally, Mom refers to her friends according to how she knows them. As in, Linda the Hairdresser and Bowling Team Jacquie, Trudy from Bible Study, and her best friend, Your-Aunt-Lily-My-Only-Sister. Otherwise a homebody, Mom rarely does stuff with friends outside the activity they share, I guess because she's too busy with her sewing projects and Mom things and yakking on the phone with Aunt Lily (which pisses my dad off because it's long distance).

I think back to yesterday when Mom said, "Oh, I had a nice lunch with Linda, you know, the Hairdresser," I should have suspected something was up—it was too soon for her to get a trim—but was too flummoxed over the drama that led to my datelessness to notice Mom had stepped outside her normal routine.

She shrugs. "I said, Lee would love to take you to your prom."

Newsflash: Linda the Hairdresser is Linda *Johnson*, mother of Lee, the Sporty-Hockey-Guy, Johnson. "Really?"

Mom becomes braver. "He didn't go to his senior prom—he had the flu or something." She waves her hand, not wanting to get sidetracked from her mission. "And like I told you, Linda said now he regrets it." Her voice drops to a conspiratorial whisper, "She also said he has a little thing for you."

"A thing?"

Mom raises her eyebrows and nods. "I know this has been a tough year for you, and even though I've worried about you dating, I can't stop time."

"Huh." Not sure whether to be more surprised about my mom's change of heart or Lee's "thing" for me. I think back to the party at Matt's and relive the memory of Lee and shot pong. Did I get a tingle when Lee wrapped himself around me? I don't think so, but it's hard to remember anything beyond the part when Brett went all apeshit.

As prom dates go, on the OPA scale (Other People's Approval), Lee rates at least an eight. He's blandly attractive, out of high school, and hangs out with people way cooler than me. Plenty of girls—popular girls, even—have a thing for him.

Maybe I should give him a chance. "Okay."

"You'll do it? You'll go?" Mom smiles so wide her lips stretch above her gums. "You deserve a good guy."

I swallow down the urge to cry again over Joaquin. I had a good guy.

"I love you," she says, her eyes as glassy and dilated as Sharman's were at that party. "I just want you to be happy."

I hug her. This isn't how I had hoped my senior year would go, but sure, I'm happy.

Prom night is here, and despite how much I resisted the idea, I'm excited. Mom and I made an emergency trip to Anchorage to buy my tea-length-off-white-almost-wedding dress with poufy sleeves and a lacy underslip. She calls it the Gown and has been working on my coordinating hairdo for most of the afternoon. Big reddish-brown curls are piled and pinned on top of my head, and a few fall loosely around my face. My scalp has lost all feeling.

At least I wasn't forced to suffer the indignity of Alex's teasing. Dad took him out to pizza and a movie. Alex is getting pretty good at hobbling around with his bum leg in the external fixator these days. There's a good chance he may even walk normally someday.

When Lee shows up at our door, he's wearing checkered Vans—no socks—a black tux, and a cream satin cummerbund that almost matches my store-bought dress. In typical hockey-guy style, Lee has a wad of chew bulging out of his lower lip. "You look great," he says as I float from the kitchen to the living room wearing the Gown. He hands me a clear plastic box, and inside is a giant pink carnation. Mom goes gaga and helps him pin the corsage on my dress. I can't tell if it's pretty or gaudy, but at least it smells sweet.

We head toward the door, and he offers me his arm, as if he is the Disney prince and I am Cinderella. As if we are both just actors playing roles we are expected to play.

"Your chariot awaits," he says.

Our plan is to meet at Charlie's first, go to dinner with her and Kenny, make a showing at prom, and end up out at Kenny's uncle's cabin way the hell in the boonies off Swanson River Road. Kenny's been stockpiling liquor there for the past two months.

But now panic is rising in my throat. I feel locked into this agenda, trapped in an overly scripted evening, and Lee's not the guy I want cast in the role of my prom date.

Before we're even out the door, I begin editing. "Mom, I was planning to stay at Charlie's tonight..."

Mom hesitates. She doesn't want to ruin the moment, but she's suspicious. She knew I'd be out late, but she was expecting Lee would drop me home before morning. I'd told her only that he was taking me to dinner then prom. "Charlie's?"

It *has* been a while since I've stayed over at Charlie's house.

"What about Sharman?" she asks.

I keep forgetting that Sharman and I are supposed to be tight. Sharman, my imaginary church buddy who I've been using as an excuse to see Joaquin but in a cruel twist of fate is now going with him to prom. She is my mortal enemy.

"Sharman's date doesn't like Lee." I'm tired of lying to my mom, but this is as close to the truth as I can devise on the spot. "Anyway, Charlie and I are still best friends, and we've been waiting for senior prom, like, our whole lives." This last part is kinda true.

"Okay. What time should I pick you up tomorrow?"

"Actually, how about I just drive over to Charlie's?"

Lee looks as confused as Mom.

I hurry and continue. "Then I'll have the Bug for morning. I'll just follow Lee over there now, leave my car, and he can drop me at Charlie's tonight."

"Fine by me," says Lee.

Mom's smile is tight, but she agrees and relaxes again when I bring her back into the moment by reminding her she wanted to take pictures. She positions us in a zillion different bride-and-groom–like poses, and I'm relieved when the camera finally runs out of film.

Before we leave, Mom hugs me twice, saying over and over how beautiful I look, as if this prom is more for her than me. Then we are out the door.

I follow close behind Lee's sleek Toyota 4Runner on the way to Charlie's. His mom may be a divorced hairdresser, but his dad, as it turns out, is a bigwig out at the Tesoro refinery.

Charlie's ready when we show up. First time in the history of the universe. She's standing on the porch in an electric-blue, spaghetti-strap number that identically matches the vest under Kenny's white tux. Charlie's wrist corsage is delicate: two white roses tipped in blue. Mrs. T.'s taking pictures.

I slam the Bug's door and yell, "We're burning daylight!"

The two turn and Charlie waves. Kenny grabs her hand and leads her to the passenger side of his new car, a sporty Geo Storm, also electric blue. That plumbing gig with his uncle must pay a shit ton more than what I'm making at Jay Jacobs. I can barely afford gas.

The night begins at Garden of Italy, and I hate that it reminds me of Brett, especially when Lee says how much he loves Garden of Shitaly. I opt for the bland alfredo, even though spaghetti and meatballs is the best thing on the menu, because I don't want tomato sauce staining my new dress. While I concentrate on keeping the dress stain-free, Kenny and Lee small talk about their cars.

Charlie's unusually quiet, so I'm guessing something's up with her. I wonder if she's still angry with me for not telling her about Brett. Or maybe there's something wrong with her mom—she seems more anxious than mad. She's biting her fingernails like crazy, which she hasn't done since we were in ninth grade. I have no idea, and I'm not going to spend all night trying to read her every gesture like tea leaves. If she wants me to know, she can tell me. I've got my own problems.

Stupid prom was a bad idea. My palms are sweating, and my deodorant's failing. I poke at my alfredo with the silver fork and eat a few bites of salad before I excuse myself to the ladies room to pat my armpits with paper towels. Charlie doesn't come find me.

Lee blasts a mix tape of his favorite Rush songs the whole way to school. They all sound identically horrible. By the time we pull into the SoHi parking lot, I want to burst out of his 4Runner and make a mad dash for home in my stupid satin heels. But I want to see Joaquin. Even though knowing he's going to be there with Sharman is driving me crazy, at least I'm showing up with a date.

We somehow arrive before Kenny and Charlie, and because I can't think of a reason to hang out and wait for them, we don't. Lee doesn't offer me his arm this time, just stands there watching me flounce out of his 4Runner. I concentrate on staying upright and do my best runway saunter to the double doors of the SoHi commons.

The song playing when we step into the dark foyer is "Human," that one about being human and making mistakes. It's a slowish number, and because we don't know what else to do, Lee pays our five dollars to the pep squad girl at the table, grabs my hand, and leads me out into the center of the swaying crowd under the mirror ball. Already there's a swampy mugginess permeating the dancers in their penguin suits and fancy dresses.

Lee pulls me close. He smells freakishly like my dad, except his deodorant is fainter and his own musky sweat is more pungent.

"You glad I brought you?" he asks, as if escorting me to prom deserves the Nobel Prize.

"I'm glad I'm here." That's the best I can give him—I'm glad I'm not missing my senior prom.

"You look good," he says for the third time. "You smell good, too." He presses closer as we rock back and forth, a millisecond off the beat.

Like a swimmer gulping in air, I turn my face to the side for a breath, and there, a few couples over, is Joaquin. He's staring straight at me. Our eyes lock, and in that moment, I want to tell him I'm sorry and that I wish we were here together and that if I've ever loved a boy it's him, but he looks away.

That's when I notice Sharman. She's wearing the exact red strapless dress Charlie wore to Homecoming. Charlie must have loaned her that dress. They must be hanging out.

"Bitch," I say.

"What?" asks Lee. I push away from him and weave through the crowd until I catch a flash of electric blue.

The last notes of the ballad fade, and my heels click-click faster on the commons floor. Kenny's arms are still wrapped around Charlie's waist, as if the song isn't ever going to end.

I grab Charlie by the arm, swing her around to face me. "Something you want to say?"

She pulls away. "Hey, Merido. What's the undie bundle all about?"

An undanceable hard rock tune slams out of the tripod speakers near my head. My voice rises, becomes a shout. "Don't act dumb! I see you lent Sharman that red strapless."

"Chill already." She twists her mouth and loops her arm through mine. "Come to my office." She drags me toward the girls' bathroom.

The lights in the bathroom seem bright, dizzying. A junior girl is leaning across a sink, her face against the mirror, pinching a zit. She jumps when she sees us.

"Out," says Charlie.

The girl puts her hand over the red spot and tosses her hair, but leaves.

"Just, why?" I plead, bending to check for feet under each stall. I've long taken for granted that Charlie and I know everything about each other, as if our thoughts flow back and forth by osmosis. But now I realize we don't have any special mind-reading powers. She doesn't know how I feel about Joaquin. Maybe she doesn't know how I feel about Sharman, either. "You know I hate that two-faced bitch."

Charlie pulls a tiny turquoise hair pick from her wrist clutch and starts fluffing up her bangs in the mirror. Finally, she says, "You have no clue about the shit storm I'm dealing with right now."

Anger surges in me again. "Like you know what *I've* been going through?"

She sucks in her cheeks so her face looks thinner. "Get over yourself. I'm talking about something big."

"Oh, and I guess my crippled brother and my grandma dying of cancer, that's just regular teenage drama."

Her eyebrows push two vertical creases into her forehead. "I'm sorry."

Her apology sucks my anger out. "So what's your thing?"

She turns to the side so I can see the profile of her thin waist, wrapped tightly in silky blue. "Nothing."

Our friendship's turned to crap, and I'm realizing that it's because neither one of us has been confiding in the other. "I haven't been the greatest friend to you."

"No, I'm the dick." She slumps against the wall and stares at the ceiling. "Sorry I wasn't there for you with all the shit happening with your family."

"Did I tell you my mom put me in therapy?"

She snaps her chin down, and her eyes go all buggy. "Lydia wouldn't do that."

"Yep. With Pastor freaking Dan."

"Holy balls! Why didn't you tell me?"

"It was awful, and I already stopped going." There's so much more I want to tell her, but this bathroom doesn't feel big enough to hold all my shit. And if I'm being honest, I'm still a little angry with Charlie. "Why did you want me to get together with Brett so bad? He was a serious dick."

She shrugs. "I thought you liked him."

I shake my head and almost don't say anything more about it, but I want her to know. I want to stop lying to the people I care about. "Brett was a serious asshole. Like the worst boyfriend in the history of boyfriends. And no matter what you think of Joaquin, I like him. Really, really like him."

"Of course you do." She sighs.

"What's that supposed to mean?" I prepare myself for her judgment, ready to defend Joaquin by telling her everything I love about him. I want to throw every blissful thing I've ever done with him right in her disapproving face.

She shrugs. "You never tell me anything anymore."

Though not what I expected, I can't dismiss the truth. She's been distant this year, but so have I. "Is that why you're hanging out with Sharman now?"

She shakes her head and pulls a tube of lipstick from her clutch. "That's not my dress. I bought it at Jay Jacobs, remember? God! You work there!" She smooths frosted peach across her lips and shoves the tube back into her clutch. "They had like seven of them. Sharman's got huge tits—I'm sure her dress is at least two sizes bigger."

This fact immediately seems obvious. Blood rushes to my cheeks.

"I've been with Kenny like every second I'm not with you. I couldn't give two shits about Sharman."

She's really twisting her lips now.

We've grown apart this year, but she's still my best friend, and my Charlie spidey sense tells me something's wrong. "Is something going on with you?"

She bangs open each stall's flesh-colored door, rechecking until she's satisfied we are definitely alone. Her eyes catch mine in the mirror. "I may be preggers," she says.

"Shit."

"*Maybe*," she says.

"How do you know?"

"Missed Aunt Flo this month. Over two weeks late already."

I shrug. "Maybe you're just stressed or something."

"I bought a test," she says, "but I don't have the guts to take it. Not by myself."

I want to hug her, but I just touch her arm. I am still her best friend. "I'll do it with you."

She waves me away as if there's a bad smell in the restroom. "Let's not talk about it anymore. Tonight's prom. Let's have fun."

Fun? "Lee's an idiot," I say.

"But the cabin's gonna be awesome. You're still coming, right?"

The thought of spending all night with You-Look-Good Lee is unbearable. "Probably. I don't know."

Disappointment flashes in her eyes, but she bobs her head up and down like it's no big deal. "Whatever. I better get back to Kenny."

27
Mudding

"Hold on!" Lee screams. The 4Runner lurches. I reach up and grab the oh-shit handle as we slam into a rut and bounce sideways. A row of wiry aspen scratches against my window. This trail is too narrow for Lee's truck.

"Hey!" I yell because he keeps gunning the engine. "You sure this is a shortcut to the cabin?" Something bangs under the floorboard. A log. Please be a log and not a crushed animal.

He wipes the back of his hand against his forehead. "Absolutely."

Big, juicy rain drops splat against the windshield, clearing a tiny space before the wiper blades re-smear the glass with a glaze of mud. I've been following Lee's lead all night, trusting the idea I had of him: a sweet, goofy guy with a thing for me. But who takes a girl in a prom dress fourbying?

Everything that seemed quirky at the beginning of the evening—the checkered Vans with his tux, the giant pink corsage, and the wad of chew bulging out his lower lip—have all become idiotic. Reality check: Lee is a small-town hick, and I am trapped in his truck.

The 4Runner dips low as we splash into an extra deep puddle. Brown water sprays onto my window. I'm hanging on to the oh-shit handle, gripping it with both hands while my shoulder braces against the door. The wheels screech, or maybe it's something in the engine. All I know is we're bucking up and down, the motor's groaning, and we're not moving forward.

"Aw, shit," says Lee. He rolls down his window, and for the first time tonight, spits what looks like wet coffee grounds into the rain. He must have been swallowing this whole time. What a gentleman.

Lee guns the engine again. The wheels make a mucky, whirring sound. "Fuck me!" He bangs the dash.

This is not the sedate guy from math class. But then, what did I really know about him? He sat there every day, barely saying a word. Sometimes you mistake getting used to someone's face for knowing the person.

"Don't tell me we're stuck," I plead.

"Fine. I won't tell you." His window is still rolled down, and I see at least that the rain has lessened to a fine spray. A sliver of moon shines through the clouds. Lee sticks his head out and screams into the night. Which only makes him into a bigger, louder idiot.

I hate you, Lee. I hate him like I hate Brett and Matt and Sharman. They all act like they know some big secret, like they're golden, like the world's their big, fat, fucking oyster. What a bunch of liars. "What do we do now?"

"We get us unstuck."

"Um?" I wave my hand down the length of my creamy satin bodice and skirt. The store-bought dress shimmers in the moonlight.

Lee shrugs. "You steer, I'll push."

"Fine." I go back in time and trace the flawed logic that brought me here. My mom and her meddling...But even as I think it, I know the real reason I'm in this 4Runner with Lee instead of slow dancing with Joaquin. The reason is me.

Lee opens his door, leaving it swinging wide, and leaps down into the muck. Rain beads on his forehead and collects on his seat. Lee jogs out of view as he yells, "Go when I tell you!"

I quickly scoot over into the driver's seat and try adjusting it forward so I can reach the pedals, but Lee is already barking, "Ready? Are you ready?"

I sit on the edge and tighten my fingers around the black, leather-wrapped steering wheel. My feet find the pedals.

"Okay, go slow."

I carefully push the gas, and we start rocking the 4Runner, back and forth, a gentle rhythm that feels like teamwork but is only a desperate synergy, as fleeting as a one-night stand. We lose momentum just as I think we are going to make it out.

"Shit!" Lee screams from behind the 4Runner. "Goddamit," he says, like it's my fault.

"Let's try again," I say. Raindrops stain my dress in dark bursts.

He glares. "Work with me this time, will ya?"

We start again, but now I'm determined. I press hard and long so that greasy mud splatters off the front tire. Into the cab. Onto my dress. But I don't care anymore. I only want to get out. To get unstuck. To be free. Lee whoops when we crest the lip of the rut. I slam on the brakes just in time to avoid crashing the 4Runner into a tree.

Lee runs up next to me, out of breath but flush with victory. "Scoot!"

I don't move. "Take me back to my car."

"Why? We said we'd meet Charlie and Kenny at the cabin."

I stare at him with the hate I can no longer contain. "Take. Me. Back."

He puts his hands up. "Fine."

We make our way out of the woods without getting stuck again. The intense silence on the drive back to Charlie's is awkward, but the trip is mercifully short.

"Don't call," I say, slamming his door. Easy peasy.

He peels out and is gone before I've even opened the door to the Bug.

I can't think of anywhere to go, so I just start driving. Staying at Charlie's without Charlie, with just her mom—that would be weird, and I don't want to go home. After driving around aimlessly, I end up at the Kenai 7-Eleven. The Bug's gas needle is on empty, so I quickly fill up, not caring if my dress gets messier—it would hardly be noticeable at this point—and head inside to pay and buy something sweet.

It's not yet eleven. I'm hoping anyone I know will either still be at prom or already at an after party somewhere. But just as I'm walking up to 7-Eleven's glass door, a Probe with racing stripes and a blue Bronco speed into the lot next door, kicking up gravel. The Bronco parks alongside an empty Civic hatchback, and a sophomore girl I recognize hops out. Beastie Boys pounds the air behind her. She gives Brett a cutesy little wave and blows him a kiss before climbing into her Civic. I want to run over and warn her that Brett's a giant creep, but I doubt she'd listen. I jerk open the door instead. *Ding-dong.*

Inside, everything looks exactly the same as always. Except the lights buzz too loud and the floor beneath me is slimy. Fish sticks—which smell vaguely rotten—are tonight's hot case main attraction, growing more inedible with every minute spent under the heat lamp. I make a beeline through the candy aisle, grabbing a roll of SweeTARTS. I am standing in front of the fountain pop dispenser, trying to decide if I should get a cola, when I see him. Beautiful and mesmerizing in his black tux and red cummerbund.

I launch myself behind the chip display, wishing I could shrink down and crawl into a Frito until he leaves. But there he is at the counter by the tide charts, his hair smoothed back into a low ponytail.

Sharman is probably outside in the minivan fixing her makeup or getting high or checking to make sure she has a condom, just in case, and I can't even think of her with Joaquin. What I'd give to be in that stupid minivan tonight. I flash back to the night at the trailer, and my stomach tightens when I get to the part where Brett makes that sound as if to say, "I popped her," like I was a party balloon. A toy bag of air that's no longer fun.

I crouch lower behind the chips. If I'd been honest with Joaquin, would tonight be different? I remember Joaquin's eyes, but now looking back, I see more hurt than anger in them. I was the angry one. At myself for lying. At Brett for being a douchebag.

Fuck Brett. I'm still *me*. I'm not damaged. I'm smarter. So what if I didn't tell Joaquin every gory detail about my sex life? This is my life. I get to make my own choices, and I don't owe the world an explanation. This is me learning. Like a scientist conducting experiments. Brett and Lee are only two points on my dating graph. Test failures, not regrets.

I march up the aisle toward the counter where Joaquin is standing, his back to me. My dress is splotched with mud, and my mascara's making a mad dash down my cheeks, but my job isn't to be a perfect princess. I'm a girl—a person—with every right to have my own experiences. Joaquin knows me, the *real* me, and I have to trust that.

I dump my handful of comfort food on the counter near the register. "Hey," I say.

He startles at my voice and looks confused when he sees my dress. "What happened to you?"

I shrug. "A mudding trip gone wrong."

He starts laughing.

I look up, mortified, but Joaquin's laugh is real and easy, not cruel. "We should have gone together," he says. "I'm sorry about the other night. I just—I felt like you lied to me, and I just reacted."

"I know." My cheeks warm. "I'm sorry." I'm close enough to touch him. I want to reach out, maybe take his hand. "The thing is," I say, "I want to be with you. Like all the time. I've liked you since last year, but I wasn't sure you liked me." It's such a relief to finally tell him.

His smile is wide and real. "My prom's in two weeks." He grabs my hand, "And I do like you."

I let out the breath I didn't know I was holding. "Serious?" I sputter.

"As a heartbeat."

"Cool. Yes. Definitely." I give his hand a squeeze, and we just look at each other for a second or two.

"You should get back to Sharman." I don't know why I say it.

He shakes his head. "She's so stoned, she wouldn't notice if I was in here all night."

"Can I call you?" I know things are alright now. Better than alright. And I'm determined to be better than alright, too.

"You've always been able to call me." He leans in, and his forehead bumps mine.

"Sorry," he says.

Adrenaline pulses through me. "Not sorry," I say, and though I want more than anything to feel his lips on mine, I'll wait until he doesn't have another girl sitting in the car.

4/13/90

This was the worst best night of my life. Nothing can keep me from going with Joaquin to his prom.

4/14/91

We skipped church today and all slept in. That was nice. Mom didn't fight me when I told her I was going to prom with Joaquin. I'm not sure it's because she's fine with it or if there's just no fight left in her. Now that we know Alex is going to walk, Mom's preparing for the next crisis. She says Grandma's really bad and is talking about flying back to help Aunt Lily with "the end." I wonder if Grandma's really dying or if she's just going to be sick forever. She hasn't written for a long time, and Mom hasn't let me talk to her on the phone, so maybe she really is dying. I hope not, though.

28
First Us

The upstairs bathroom in Charlie's house cramps in on you, even when you're alone just doing your business. The sink is so close that the edge of the laminate scrapes against your arm when you're sitting on the toilet, and on the other side, your knees knock against the baby blue tub that doubles as a shower.

Whenever Charlie and I are in her bathroom together, one of us has to be sitting somewhere, and we both usually want to stand in front of the mirror. But today the door is locked, and neither of us is standing or looking at ourselves. Charlie's perched on the plushy toilet lid while I have to hover on the edge of the counter with my ass half hanging into the sink.

It's Monday. I had to skip Dance Team this afternoon so Charlie and I can do this in private before her mom gets off work. My mom's at physical therapy with Alex, and Dad's at work, so nobody will notice if I'm late getting home.

She shoves the little box at me. "Read this," she says. "I can't concentrate." Her thumb is covering the letters P and L of FirstPlus, so the package looks like it says "First us," and I think, yeah, at first there was only us: me and Charlie. I stood by her against the wall in junior high when no boys would dance with us. I slapped that guy in the face in tenth grade for calling us lesbo-brainiacs and almost got beat up by his girlfriend. I'm the one who's here now.

Her hand is shaky, or maybe the bathroom light is flickering. The box trembles in the air.

"Take it, bitch." She stretches closer. *"Please."*

Gripping the faucet with one hand, I reach toward Charlie with the other, but at the last second she tips her arm back and throws, landing the package in my lap. I teeter, nearly pulling out the faucet to right myself.

She smirks. "So, Graceful, what do I do?"

"Pretty much just pee on it," I pretend to scan the directions on the back. "And wait."

She twists her lips, as if still deciding whether she should take the test. "Open it."

My fingers rip the glued flap. There's no turning back now. We can't reseal the box and return it to the store. We can't rewind to BK—Before Kenny. Whatever happens, whatever we find out, barely matters. Because what we were Before Kenny—best friends...*girls*— already feels like old song lyrics. Kenny's what's playing now.

I reach inside the box and feel only air and paper. Dark empty space surrounds a folded page of more directions. Then my fingers find the thing, barely bigger than a tampon. I slide it out and tear the wrapper. "Here."

She cups her hand and waits until I drop the white stick into her palm. I let it go and make a wish. That Kenny's little swimmers are slackers. That he's shooting blanks.

She scrunches up her face. "I can't do it while you watch."

I swivel as best I can on the teeny countertop. My knee bangs the wall. "Ow!" Tiny bouquets of pink roses and five-petaled, blue flowers float in lines up and down the wallpaper. I rub my knee. "Damn, that really hurt." My voice drowns out what Charlie is doing. Pee dribbling into water reminds me of the mall restroom or school locker rooms, places where nothing is private. I pick up a pack of decorative soap squares wrapped in dusty plastic. Inside, they're probably still perfectly good. I scratch at a corner. "No matter what," I say, "I still want you to come with me."

"What?"

"You know, leave here. Together. Like we talked about. I know you'll get in. We can go to college. Be roommates." I already know this plan is the old song, but I want to keep singing it. I want to stop time, stay here with Charlie in her bathroom.

"Turn around already." Charlie's sitting on the edge of the tub now. The toilet lid's up, and there's yellowish water in the bowl.

"Flush, weirdo," I say.

"What if I need it?"

"What?"

"What if I didn't get enough pee on here?" She's cradling the stick in toilet paper.

"I'm sure it's fine. Anyway, toilet water pee would probably contaminate it." I scoot closer and watch the blue tide roll slowly across the tiny white window. We wait for two lines or one.

"This is it," she says. "Life or no life."

Charlie doesn't know I've done this before. Doesn't know about me sitting in *my* tiny bathroom, waiting. I had to skim the directions on the box myself, watch the tide roll across and leave a line, my life colliding into a blue wall. Would she have been there if I'd asked?

We wait in Charlie's bathroom for the blue to fade away and leave the answer in the white window.

Charlie holds the stick, her lips twisting and untwisting. "I could be a mom."

"What?"

"If I *am*, I mean. I like kids."

"You *want* to be pregnant?"

She shrugs. "Why do you have to say it like that? Like I just said I'm gonna become a whore and sell drugs."

"I...sorry."

"I don't even know if I'm ready for college. I like it here. With Kenny. My mom had me at seventeen, and I'll be eighteen in August. Kenny's a good guy. He has a job...."

"He works part-time with his uncle as a *plumber*."

"Fuck off." She acts dismissive, but I can tell I've hurt her.

"Hey," I say. "You don't even know if you're going to *be* a mom."

We both look down at the white window. That's when I see the shadow. Something barely there. One blue line like I had, but crossed by another, a soft echo. A plus. "Two."

She squints. "Really?"

"Yeah. That means yes."

She nods. "Wow."

"How do you feel?" I ask. Because I feel awful. I feel sorry. I feel all the things I would have felt for me if I would have been pregnant, only more. I feel like punching Kenny.

Charlie says softly, "I'm gonna be a mom." She stands and looks at herself in front of the mirror, smoothing her hand over her still-flat belly.

I don't know how she's keeping calm and not drowning herself in the toilet. I turn toward the mirror and see my face has gone all splotchy and red, especially around my nose, and my hair's a tangled, greasy mess. I look like shit.

Charlie reaches over, uses her fingers to rat my bangs back into shape. She smiles. "Wanna go shopping for baby clothes tomorrow?"

I nod, forcing my lips into a half smile. "Sure." It's all I can manage.

A part of me hates her for not being more upset. A big part of me. She won't be going to college with me. She won't be going anywhere. She's going to stay in Soldotna—maybe forever—and she seems just fine with that.

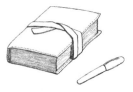

4/20/91

Charlie and I went shopping for baby stuff today. I bought a Baby Smurf blanket and a sleeper thing that was really soft and green and looked like a long nightgown with elastic on the bottom. It said Alaska Baby on the front. Super cute.

4/22/91

Joaquin

Rain is inevitable.
It starts slow, ticking
and tapping the birch leaves.
Unhurried, the way he walks,
rolling in from far away.
You know his swing,
feel the pressure change,
the patter sounds like footfalls
quickening with your heartbeat,
as he closes the space between you.

4/26/91

Kenai's prom is tomorrow, and I'm so excited I can't sleep.

29
Sweetlove

I've been dreaming about Joaquin arriving at my door like a prince or a superhero to whisk me away, but when the doorbell sounds that hideous refrain from the Dukes of Hazzard car, I cringe.

My hair hangs in boring curls down my back—the braided updo I'd planned didn't work—and Charlie's red dress isn't the greatest shade against my skin. Mom added a few strategic darts, so at least it hugs my waist and hips. This is the same dress Sharman wore when she went with Joaquin to the SoHi prom, but it was convenient and free and Joaquin already had the matching bow tie and cummerbund. I just hope I look better than she did.

When the bell goes off again, Mom comes barreling into the living room. Alex is lounging with his leg up on an ottoman. There's no chance he'll be dashing to answer the door. His bones are healing quickly but are still pinned.

"Mom, do you mind?" I say. I don't want Joaquin's first sight of me to be at the door. I want to make a grand entrance.

"You look pretty," Mom says, eyes glassy. "I wish your dad were here." Dad's never around for my big things, but today I'm glad he's gone. He'd just make it awkward, or worse, make me stay home. Mom's not sure about this whole Kenai prom thing either, but she's letting me go. I guess she's starting to trust me. Or maybe she's just resigned.

She heads toward the entryway as our General Lee doorbell invades the living room once more. I pretend the trumpet is a regular door chime. I can't let stupid details get in the way of my perfect evening. Not when everything else in my life has gone to shit.

I dash up the stairs and wait at the landing, imagining myself descending with the poise and grace of an angel. Or at least a well-bred lady from *Dynasty*.

Behind Mom, Joaquin strolls into our living room in a simple black tux. His features sharpen against the crisp white shirt and red bow tie. His thick black hair is tied back, but as usual, a few baby curls escape around his face.

The room must be filling up with water, because I can't pull in my breath. Oh dear God. Oxygen in and carbon dioxide out, you stupid breathing organs.

Mom tilts her head toward Joaquin like I should move in his general direction. She grabs the Polaroid camera off the coffee table. "Picture time."

How is she doing that? Speaking and acting normally. Does she not see him? He looks like one of those guys on her romance novel covers.

My mouth is so dry, and my limbs aren't letting me budge from the stairs. I can do this. Easy peasy.

He waits with one hand in his suit pants pocket and the other holding a dainty, white rose wrist corsage.

I force my feet down the stairs, one shaky, high-heeled step at a time.

"Not bad," he says, grinning.

I take the corsage, loop it onto my wrist, and bring its spicy sweetness to my nose.

"Red is, I mean, you look very...bright...nice. I mean, nice." He covers his face with his hands. "Can I start over?"

I laugh and shake my head. In that moment Joaquin turns from a magazine model back into himself. The person I see is as awkward as me. He plays solitaire when he's lonely. He collects wishbones. He is the guy who showed me how to dipnet and helps me with Spanish.

Mom stands us against the wall and arranges us like flowers. Joaquin's arm wraps stiffly around my waist, and his hand holds my wrist. I stand rigid, hoping Mom doesn't notice how nervous being this close to him makes me. How much I want to devour him.

"Relax," Mom says to me. "He's not going to bite." She smiles at Joaquin, "Right?"

I remember the feel of his teeth on my neck in Dairy Queen. A girl can hope.

"No, Mrs. Miller." He shakes his head, his expression unreadable, almost blank, but when I meet his eyes, there's a flash of knowing, as if maybe he's remembering the same moment I am.

Joaquin escorts me to the Kenai prom in his mom's minivan that, if I'm honest, smells a bit like fish guts and campfires. We hold hands at first while he drives, but then it feels forced, so he lets go and grips the wheel until we're parked.

Inside, the commons is stuffy, and mostly I don't know anyone. The theme is Under the Sea, and it looks like a fabric store threw up with all the shimmery blue material draped everywhere. We stand around and drink punch until a slow dance plays, and it's the song about dying in someone's arms. Joaquin holds me gently as we sway around under the mirror ball. He's already a little sweaty, and so am I, but I cling to him anyway. He rubs my back, and I think maybe I could just die right there, in his arms, but too soon the song is over and a new one with a hip-hop beat starts playing. It's about a girl being poison.

Thanks to four years on dance team, my sense of rhythm and ability to shake my booty has become a source of personal pride. I break into my signature version of the Running Man, lifting my knees and feeling my bounce groove.

"White girl's got moves," he says, though his are far more cool than mine. I'm just grateful he's not steering me off the dance floor toward the punch bowl.

His body is so controlled. As the music thrums, each of his muscles flex in a coordinated and athletic, but understated, way. His arms and legs—even his pelvis—shift in time to the beat, hypnotic. How can he be such a good dancer? He's like the unicorn of boys.

I step it up, thinking I'll try a kind of Running-Man-meets-Roger-Rabbit, but the result is more spaz-meets-aerobics-instructor.

He hides his eyes, but beneath his hand, he's smiling. Seeing the familiar gap in his teeth, that dimple—these make my embarrassing antics worth it.

"Too much?" I yell over the music.

He's fully laughing now. Also nodding, and I should feel more embarrassed than I do.

The throng of sweaty dancers presses against us. I'm hot and breathless, and I'm ready to get out of here.

As if he can read my mind, he says, "You want to go somewhere else?"

I flash him a guilty smile.

The forest hangs around us. Spruce branches, like curtains, turn the evening darker. We've come to the literal end of the road: Captain Cook State Park. Beyond the campground, the land ends and there is only the inlet, the narrow arm that leads to the ocean.

"I brought snacks," he says, throwing me a box of crackers. "And more SweeTARTS." From the back of the minivan, he pulls a Ziploc full of all the colors except pink and blue.

I grab the plastic bag and start munching. "How about a heater?" The van doors are open, and the invading night air is cool. All I have is a worthless lace shawl to drape over my bare shoulders.

He shrugs off his suit jacket and hands it to me. His warmth lingers in the sleeves. I want nothing more than to feel that warmth coming directly from his body to mine. "What's the plan?" I ask, hoping it has something to do with making out.

Joaquin rummages around in the van. "Brought a tent," he says, holding a cylindrical black bag. He pulls out a smaller yellow one. "But only one sleeping bag."

A thousand questions collide in my mind. Does this mean we're going to have sex? Does he have protection? Should I stay and go to community college? Why didn't I bring a change of clothes? I don't ask any of them. Instead I say, "Can I help?"

He reaches into the black bag. As if he's a magician pulling scarves out of a hat, a pile of bright blue nylon emerges on the ground in front of him—much more than I would have thought the bag could contain. "This is a two-person operation," he says.

I've camped before, but always with my parents in their camper. Never in a tent.

Mixed in with the fabric are aluminum dowels that snap together. He shows me how to piece them into long stays that, he says, serve as the structure.

Twice I nearly stab Joaquin in the eye with a tentpole, and after the second ocular near miss, I come clean. "It's my first time ever pitching a tent!"

"That's hard to believe," he mutters.

Operation Tent Pitch goes faster than I expect, and once assembled, the tent is surprisingly feather-light. With one hand, Joaquin easily moves our tent to a softish, mossy patch of ground. We've parked in the best spot—nearest the trees that edge Discovery Campground and the beach.

The night is soundless, save for waves breaking faintly in the distance and hungry mosquitos buzzing around us. These microscopic carnivores are already taking advantage of my exposed skin.

I'm relieved when Joaquin shows me how the bug netting works. "Great. Let's just get inside," I say, slapping at my neck and my legs and the backs of my hands. Mosquitos are wetter than you'd think. They're so scrawny, but smashing one leaves a moist blackish-red scramble of tiny wings, legs, blood, and that sucker thing they use for a drinking straw and poison injector.

Joaquin unzips the door and throws in the yellow bag. "Quick," he says. The second the door is wide enough, I scramble through. He dives in after and zips the door closed. Inside, the tent is dim, but he's brought a small battery lantern that clips to a carabiner at the apex of the tent's ceiling. When he flicks it on, the tent fills with buttery light, like it's being lit with candles.

Aside from the suit jacket, I'm still wearing Charlie's red dress. The stays are pokey, and the bodice is cutting into my waist. "I'm not being slutty right now," I say, "but I need this dress off. What do you have in terms of extra clothes?"

"Would it be horrible if I lied and said nothing?" He asks, grinning. That damn dimple's impossibly cuter in the lamplight.

"How about you give me your shirt," I say, unlooping the rose wrist corsage and shoving it into the jacket pocket, "and I'll give back the jacket?"

"Deal." His fingers nimbly untie his red bow tie and unbutton his oxford. I want those fingers on me.

The space is cramped, even with just Joaquin and me in the tent, and I have to hunker to accommodate the slope. I reach behind and unzip the dress, halting and awkward, like those people who open presents one piece of tape at a time.

Joaquin pretends to focus his attention on fluffing the sleeping bag, but I can feel each time his eyes flick onto me. My skin heats despite the cold.

Finally, I get the dress undone to the waist, and my bodice falls forward so that my strapless bra is all that is between my boobs and the world. I quickly pull the jacket across my front.

"I like seeing you," he says, but I keep the jacket pulled tight.

His shirt is unbuttoned and hanging open, I stare through the narrow window at his exposed chest. Joaquin's pecs and abdominal muscles are actually visible. There's no layer of thickness beneath the skin. I reach out and touch his stomach, and his muscles contract.

"The coat," he says, reaching out his hand, "and I'll give you my shirt."

I want to see more of him. "Why me first?"

"We switch together on three?"

I nod.

"One, two," he slips out of his shirt, and on three we are both essentially topless.

I'm already shivering. "I'd be warmer if I had your body heat." It's a bold thing to say, but every square inch of my skin wants to be touching his. He drapes his oxford over my shoulders. Still shirtless, he hugs his arms around me, so my chest and stomach warm against him.

The sleeping bag is zipped open like a butterfly, one side red and one side yellow. Joaquin spreads the sleeping bag over the tent's tarp-like bottom, and I snuggle down into the up-facing red side, pulling the edge around me.

The shirt and the jacket drape over us like blankets. I shimmy out of my dress entirely. He scoots so that I can fully lie down—he still has to bend his knees—and motions for me to cuddle up next to him, which I'm already on my way to doing. My skin heats against his; our arms and legs twine together.

With almost no distance between our faces, kissing just happens without me having to think about it. No awkwardness, just his mouth to mine. Or maybe my mouth to his. My hands on his shoulders and down his back. His hand over my stomach and around my back and up over that strapless bra I wish I'd thrown into the inlet. My body transforms into a holy thing, a temple I want to inhabit fully.

Nobody is in charge. His tongue leads mine, then mine leads his. There is nothing in the universe better than how we kiss. Soft and imploring, but confident at the same time. We make out a while longer, then talk a bit. Then make out some more. I'm so blissed out that I'm trembling.

At first I think I'm shaking from all the hormones raging through me, but then I realize I'm actually freezing cold. It's well past midnight, and the temperature has dropped in earnest. As much as I'd like to stay and make out until dawn, as a practical matter, I don't want to get hypothermia.

"It's colder than a witch's tit out here," I say.

Joaquin's eyes are only half open, and since I pulled my mouth away to speak, he's trailing kisses along my jaw. He puts the lobe part of my ear in his mouth and sucks a little bit.

The blood drains from my brain and funnels to my pelvis—in the best way. My head doesn't need to intervene because my body, as it turns out, knows exactly what it's doing.

But I'm seriously trembling from the cold.

"Sweetlove," I say, "much longer and you'll be feeling up frozen boobs."

He smiles in a way that makes me think he likes that I called him sweetlove. I'm not sure where that came from, but maybe it's a substitute for wanting to tell him that I do.

I love him.

He kisses me one last time before we untangle, and as much as I don't want to, I struggle back into Charlie's dress.

Already I regret not going further, and even as I tell myself we still have time and still can someday, I realize I've been harboring this stupid idea that if I have sex with Joaquin, it could somehow erase—or at least supersede—my first time with Brett. Guilt tightens my stomach as the ugly reality hits me. How could I use him like that?

I slide my freezing arms into Joaquin's suitcoat, resolving that whatever future intimacies Joaquin and I share, I won't let my selfish desire to nullify unpleasant past experiences drive me. Joaquin deserves better. Whatever we do will be about us sharing something real and good.

The tent takes longer than I think it should to take apart and stuff into the pack, but finally we are back in the minivan with the heat on full blast. Thankfully, his heater works much better than the one in the Bug.

Joaquin has left the top part of his shirt unbuttoned, and this pleases me immeasurably. He holds my hand as we drive back into town. I rest my head against the passenger side window and keep nodding off. As the lights of town come into view, he asks, "Want me to take you home?"

"Would that be awful?" I don't want to go home, but I'm so tired. The clock on the dash says 2:38 a.m., and I just want to crawl under my covers and sleep forever. I'd love him to be with me, but I know there's no way that could happen. "I just want to go to bed."

"Not awful," he says, and as if he can read my mind. "Better if I was with you." He lifts my hand to his lips and kisses the back. "This was the best. Thanks for being my date."

Tonight was the best for me, too. Despite nearly freezing to death, my dress sucking, several mosquito bites, and many awkward moments, Second Prom far surpassed Stupid Prom. Second Prom doesn't erase the first one, but it doesn't need to.

There are no do-overs. The Super Big Bad Thing will always be what it was—mediocre at best, regrettable at worst—and who knows if I'll get a second chance with Joaquin to do it better. But tonight, an infinitely more significant first has eclipsed my sex milestone. Something much sweeter.

4/28/91

Aunt Lily called, and Mom is flying back tomorrow. Just her. She says it's too expensive for all of us to go. I'm praying my student loan check gets here early. I'll use it to fly down. I want to say goodbye.

4/29/91

Drove Mom to the airport tonight. I told her on the way that I'd been accepted by the University of Idaho, and that's where I plan to go. She just nodded and started quiet crying. I told her how awful I feel about everything—what happened with Alex and Grandma's cancer and how badly I've acted this year. She said nothing was my fault. Not Alex or Grandma or even me. She said I'm a normal teen, and she's just had a hard time letting me grow up. I wasn't expecting that and started quiet crying, too. She hugged me when we got there and told me to please just drop her off because she needed some alone time. I hugged her like ten times before I let her out of the car.

4/30/91

I've kept my acceptance letter from the University of Idaho in the top drawer of my nightstand for months, but today was the deadline for me to commit to going there. Saying yes to them means saying goodbye to Joaquin. I didn't break down until after I got off the phone with Admissions.

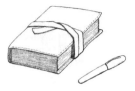

Dad came home today. I told him that I was going to college in Idaho in the fall. He said he always knew I'd do great things. I wanted to say that would have been a nice thing to hear once in a while, but I just said thanks, and he went downstairs to watch television.

30
Goodbye Ceremony

"She's gone," says Mom, hiccupping into the phone. "My mother is gone."

You think when a person you care about dies, something will happen. Like a trumpet will sound and everyone around you will start wearing black and will give you space and you won't have to go to work or school and for a while the promises you made won't matter. Everyone will say sorry, send flowers, and feel sad with you.

But that's not how it works.

After I hang up, I turn invisible. The digital numbers on my radio clock rearrange themselves into infinite combinations, blinking their way through the dark. Night stretches on and on until, well before the sun arrives, the numbers announce morning.

I get ready for school like usual. The Bug idles in the driveway, trying to get warm, like any other day. I shiver into the vinyl seat just like I did yesterday.

Except this is nothing like yesterday.

I drive through town. Buildings rotate around me as if in discrete orbits. The Dairy Queen is dark and dingy. The 7-Eleven is small. The tiny spring snowflakes and that woman walking alone mean something sinister.

Inside my car planet, I turn up the AM radio. Steve Perry is belting out "Separate Ways." I used to think this guy was a poet, but clearly he doesn't know what the hell he's talking about. Love can't find you if you're dead. I know everybody's dying, but a person you've known your whole life dying is totally different. A person being dead who should be playing cards with you and listening to Patsy Cline with you and reading books with you makes no sense.

Charlie tells me on our way to first period that the baby's bigger than a bean.

"Cool," I nod. Then I tell her about Grandma.

"Holy shit!" she says. "I'm so sorry." She hugs me and that's nice, but I end up not going to class. I just drive around in slow motion until school's out then wait at the bus stop near our house for Alex to get off the school bus. I ache to be around another person who loved her, someone who's feeling what I am.

A neighbor and his son are waiting at the bus stop, too. I watch from inside the Bug's fogging windows as the little boy stares up at a tall spruce, tilting his head back farther and farther. All he can possibly see is sky, the vast, clouded mystery beyond where he stands. He giggles. He looks dizzy.

I mastered the back handspring when I was twelve and have since done about a million, so the feeling of flinging my head backward and the little flashes I sometimes see in the air when I land are sensations I anticipate. A familiar disorientation. I can bring it to mind when I shut my eyes.

So many things like that you have to experience to really know. Like people. You know them or you don't. I blink and see my grandma in her overalls drinking iced tea. I blink again, and she is teaching me to play cribbage; we count our cards and move painted nails along the wooden board she made. With every blink, memories swell inside me and water seeps out the ducts of my eyes. The body can only hold so much. This is just science.

The boy waiting with his father at the bus stop is leaning so far he starts to fall backward. But his face never changes. He keeps smiling, like maybe he doesn't know he's falling. Or he's not afraid. Maybe he trusts his father will catch him. Maybe he doesn't mind falling, or he is so pleased with his profound, incomprehensible moment that he is holding on for as long as he can. I turn away as the father swoops in to catch the boy.

That kid doesn't know jack crap about life. I open the Bug's magic box and rummage around for my pack of Big Red. The gum burns sweet in my mouth.

An announcer on the radio says Kuwait is free, but Saddam Hussein's still a threat. I think of the girl in my Ethics in Government class who said her cousin was killed last month during Operation Desert Storm. She was the only one of us who could point out Kuwait on the wall map. That tiny black dot may as well have been Jupiter.

I don't know a damn thing about the Middle East or Saddam Hussein. I wore peace signs and laughed like an idiot back when Brett said we should nuke 'em. Every night I see clips of tanks on the news, but none of it makes the Gulf War—or any war—mean anything. War is like outer space. Big and cold and inexplicable. Like death.

Death has no edges. You can't master it with practice. Someone dies and you feel this horrible feeling that fades slower than the half-life of carbon. Then you lose another person and you start all over. A new horrible. Big and cold and inexplicable.

A squirrel scratches at the frozen dirt near my front tire. He acts like he can't see me. I guess maybe he can't. But even through the fogging glass, I see him, and that makes it worse because it's obvious he's doing something important. The brown hairs on his back tremble. He is focused and alive.

A kitten froze once in our barn. Dad butchers our chickens and kills unwanted cats. One time I sprayed hairspray on a bee and set it on fire. That was stupid.

I don't know what it means to die. I don't know if we go somewhere or just go away. I look up, but even the sky is too heavy. Too risky. All that space, white clouds, full of what? Too much carbon dioxide and humanity's eventual demise. My death. What is there beyond that stupid sky, anyway? Is Grandma up there? Is she gone?

Brain tumor. Maybe Grandma is in heaven and someday I'll see her again. That's what Mom said.

When Alex finally hobbles off the bus, the red lights blinking, he smiles at me like I am the sky. The world speeds up. Sounds are loud. He makes me real again.

Alex actually hugs me and cries, too. I let myself ugly cry, and he acts like it's no big deal. Just finds an old DQ napkin in the Bug's magic box and hands it to me.

Outside, big, wet flakes drift down around us and melt into puddles. That's May in Alaska for you.

"Been a bitch of a year," he says, staring out the window. "Fucking snow."

We grab a bag of chips at home, collapse on the couch, and zone out in front of the boob tube. Geraldo Rivera is shouting at a black-robed man who claims to be a Satanist. Dad won't be home for another hour. I want to stop time and just sit here with Alex for days.

"Let's do a Goodbye Ceremony for Grandma," he suggests during the commercials. He grins. "I just made it up." His mangled leg is propped on a bean bag. It's healing but still held in place with screws and a metal contraption that I call his chastity belt.

I punch his good leg.

He grabs my fist and twists until I squeal. "Just because I made it up, doesn't mean it's a bad idea. We could have a kick-ass Goodbye Ceremony."

I yank my hand away.

"Tomorrow we'll go to the beach." He adjusts his leg and winces.

I shrug. "I don't know what I'd say."

"It's a *Goodbye* Ceremony. Duh."

The beach is covered in dirty ice and desperate patches of melting snow. Now that I'm here, I feel forced into this ceremony thing. It feels fake. "This is dumb."

"You're dumb," says Alex.

I kick down into the snow until my toes go numb and my white Keds turn gray, but I don't stop until I see sand. I need to know that the beach is still down there. "Lead the way," I say, but Alex doesn't move. He points to his leg.

It's true the frozen ruts are hard for him, but he's gotten good at hobbling. He could make it, if he wanted. We're only like twenty feet from the waves. "Don't be a wuss," I say.

"Screw you." His face turns hard.

I look out at the inlet as the sun hunkers down toward Mt. Redoubt. "Sorry," I say. "I'll stay here, too."

We gaze out at the water, neither of us talking. I think about Grandma and how much I'll miss her. I know she's dead, but it doesn't seem real. I try to remember the last time I spoke with her. Did I say goodbye?

I feel like one of us should say something ceremonial and profound. "Death sucks," I say.

He whacks me behind the leg with one of his aluminum crutches.

I kick at the offending crutch. "For a guy who nearly died," I say, "you're contributing very little here."

"When you're the one dying," he says, "it's totally different." He dislodges a rock from an ice rut with one of his crutches and smacks the rock like a hockey puck. "It's also different when you're the one who screwed up."

I go back to kicking the snow.

He swings at another rock but misses. "You're so lucky you're a girl."

He's being stupid, so I start walking down toward the waves.

"You're so freaking lucky," he repeats, and something in his voice stops me, turns me back.

The top half of his face is in the shade of his hand, blocking the setting sun from his eyes. "Everything you do is golden," he says. "Nobody expects you to be a leader or land the high-paying job or take care of a wife and kids. You don't even have to leave home if you don't want to, and nobody would think less of you. Anything you do exceeds expectations."

My cheeks grow hot despite the fact that the temperature is just above freezing. I stand there, stunned. Who is this? He takes my silence as an invitation to keep going.

"You get to do whatever you want. College or not, either way, Mom and Dad will say, 'Good job, Meri.' You date who you want. Everything comes easy for you. School. Boys. Gymnastics. I had one thing. *One thing*. Basketball." His whole body is trembling. "And now I don't."

A sob is bubbling up in my chest, but I fight it down. "I didn't do this to you!" I fling my arms wide like by "this" I mean the whole frozen-over beach. "I'm sorry about the accident, but I've always worked my ass off, just like you, for everything I get. I started gymnastics when I was seven. Almost *ten years* and the best I ever got was second in state, and for your information, Mom and Dad are every bit as hard on me as on you. I'm the oldest. I have to do everything first. So fuck off." I almost push him, but stop myself. "Shut up and give me a minute."

"You've got as long as you want." He starts back toward the car. "You'll be gone soon anyway, and you'll forget this whole place even exists."

I shout after him. "Who says I'm leaving?"

He stops, turns so his head makes an ugly silhouette. "You've always been leaving."

"This goodbye thing isn't for you, dickhole," I say. "We came to the beach for Grandma."

"I'm done saying goodbye," he says. "I'll be in the car."

5/19/91

Found out Grandma willed her house to my Mom and Aunt Lily, but I guess she told them I get to stay there, if ever I want. Aunt Lily is moving in but said I could come live with her in the room Grandma was fixing up for me. I don't know if I can get along with my Aunt Lily, but I'm willing to give it a try if it means leaving Alaska. Knowing I have a place, even though it's with Aunt Lily, makes it easier somehow. Plus, Grandma willed me a little money for school. My plan is to leave here in June so I have the summer to get settled. I haven't told anyone, but I used some of my savings and bought my ticket today.

5/20/91

Some days I miss Grandma so much I can't concentrate, can't stop thinking about her. It's like the grief of losing her is a monster all curled up inside me and then suddenly for no reason it unfurls. Grief yawns, stretches a paw, and drags its claws down the inner walls of my chest. It doesn't mean to hurt me, just wants me to know it's still with me.

31
Scared Is Okay

Mom always says I'll be late to my own funeral, and I always say, who wouldn't want to be late to their own funeral? But when I run into the gymnasium on graduation day, I can almost feel her being pissed up there somewhere in the bleachers. While the principal drones through her welcome speech, I find my empty seat.

Charlie gives me a little wave then signs, "shame, shame," with her fingers.

Under my gown I'm wearing my Cornell sweatshirt, so by ten minutes in, sweat is trickling down my back. The gym is stuffy, and I can't stop fidgeting in my folding chair.

Finally, my name is called—*Merideth Miller! Come on down*—and I know my show's officially over. High school and dance team and sneaking out and pretending like I have all the time in the world to grow up, *done*. I can either go out there all by myself in the big world and risk failure *or* stay in Soldotna and live with my parents.

I don't really have a choice.

I'm standing in front of the Borough Administration Building, regretting the decision to confront my fear. This two-story concrete monstrosity houses the Mayor's office and school district administrative staff, as well as the headquarters for the Kenai Peninsula's Borough government. What is most important about this building, however, is that it has a public elevator, and I am terrified of elevators.

Joaquin squeezes my hand. "You got this." He believes facing your fears builds confidence, but I'm feeling the exact opposite of confident.

"This is stupid," I say. "I don't need to do this." I've lived with my phobia this long, why tempt fate?

"You're stronger than you let yourself be," says Joaquin. "Just trust yourself."

Parking garages, hotels, malls, and dorms all have elevators. These are places I want to go, and even though I could take the stairs most of the time—and probably will—I want to get over this stupid fear. If I can't even step into a safe mechanical contraption with a 0.00000015 percent fatality rate, how will I muster the courage to leave everything I know, including this guy I love, and make my way in the world?

Joaquin lets go of my hand and jogs across the parking lot toward the main doors.

"Wait," I say, because inside is the dreaded people-lifting box of doom. "Did you know the Kenai Peninsula Borough is about the same size as Massachusetts and New Jersey put together?"

He stops at the glass door and turns. "You coming or what?"

I hustle up three cement steps, feeling in my pocket for Joaquin's wishbone—I need all the luck I can get—and pull my jacket tighter. The morning is brisk, even for late May. Doubtful we'll hit fifty degrees today, but blue violets and yellow pansies valiantly dot the flower boxes on either side of the door. They give me hope.

When we get inside, the wall heater is blowing warm air, but somehow the building still feels cool. The plain white walls and gray carpet aren't helping, nor is the dank mildew smell. I don't want anyone to ask what we're doing, so I grab Joaquin by the arm like I know what I'm about and head straight to the big metal door trimmed in black.

Joaquin doesn't waste any time. "Up or down?" His finger hovers over the call buttons. Second floor or basement?

Most people who are scared of elevators are afraid of falling. For me it's the going up. The shooting like a rocket out of control into the unknown stratosphere above. "Down," I say. "Let's go to the Assembly Hall. There're vending machines down there."

He hits the button, and we wait.

"Why do they scare you so much?" he asks as we both stare at our indistinct selves reflected in the metal door. His door self stands tall and steady, with a blob of black hair, blue jeans, and a silvery gray tee. Mine is shorter and shiftier.

"Being lifted in a box, hurtling up out of control should scare everyone," I say.

"Not out of control," he says. "Out of *your* control."

I hate and love that he knows me so well. My real fears center around control and my fear of not having it. There's a ding and the door slides open. He enters and holds the button so the door stays open. "You got this, Meri."

My heart is pounding. I don't want to ride the elevator. "Why do you want me to do this so bad?" I don't want to go to college. I'm scared to leave home. I can't leave him.

The elevator buzzes, like it's pissed we're keeping it from its business. He shakes his head. "Whenever you're ready." He lets his finger fall. "This has to be your call." Before the door rumbles closed, I hear him intone, "I'll be back."

"I love you," I say to the metal door. My lonely, distorted reflection stares back, judging me.

Encouragement is a tricky business. Some people love to be cheered on, and others prefer absolute silence before attempting a challenge. For me, it's a little of both. Joaquin has done everything right, coaxing and giving me space, as if he is naturally suited for me, like he is my one.

When the door opens again, he is standing there holding out one hand. He presses the button with the other. His grin and that dimple are irresistible, and all I want is to get in there with him.

So I do. I grab his hand and he pulls me in.

"I'm scared," I say. I wonder if we'll stay together, even while I'm gone.

"Scared is okay," he says as we ride down.

I squeeze his hand in mine, and my heart beats steady. I can do this. Easy peasy.

The door opens with a ding, but I push the button for floor two and hold him in. "This is the part that really scares me," I say, as we speed upward toward the oblivion of the second floor. My breath catches, and I wonder if Joaquin and I will be together someday in the future or if this will all become a distant memory from our past. Or if we'll both die today in this elevator.

Suddenly he pulls me close and wraps his arms around me. "I already miss you," he says, his voice shaky. "So bad." He buries his face in my hair. "Sorry."

The door opens, and I press the down button. "Why am I going?" I ask into his soft shirt.

"Because it's who you are," he says. "You want the whole world. It's why I love you."

He's never said it, and I am so overwhelmed to hear it that I actually wish the elevator would break and strand us between floors so that I can hold on to this moment, but of course it doesn't. "Thank you," I whisper as the door opens. "I love you, too."

Charlie picks me up in Kenny's blue Geo. It's weird being the passenger. Her belly is starting to stick out a little, but today she's got on a tailored jacket over a black flouncy top, so you can't even tell.

"Nice shirt," I say. I purposely wore my ratty Cornell sweatshirt not only for luck, but also so that Charlie would look more put together than me.

Charlie's hair is pulled back in a banana clip—she looks as professional as I've ever seen her—but she's twisting her lips like crazy.

"Don't be nervous," I say. "Pam needs you as much as you need her."

"That bitch better hire me," she says, "or she can go straight to hell."

I laugh. I love when the old Charlie comes out. "Pam doesn't believe in hell."

"Oh, she will if she doesn't give me that job." She pulls the Geo into a front-row spot near the double doors closest to Jay Jacobs. The Peninsula Mall parking lot is nearly empty. Who feels like shopping on a sunny Tuesday morning?

"The moment of truth," Charlie declares, cutting the engine.

I feel like we're planning an ambush. "Pam's scheduled to open alone, so let's wait until five minutes after. She'll be in a better mood if she's settled in." She likes to count the till and get the music playing.

"Fine by me," she says. "Thanks for...you know." She pulls down the visor and checks her makeup in the mirror.

I nod. "You'd do it for me."

"And hey, I'm sorry I'm making you go to Idaho alone."

"You're not making me do anything."

She smiles. "Let's do this."

There's no one in the mall. The place is completely dead except for Pay & Save, which is always busy with summer tourists and old people getting prescriptions. When we walk into Jay Jacobs, the music's thumping and Pam is near the back singing along as she straightens a clearance rounder.

"Hey, Pam," I say.

"What are you doing here? You're not scheduled to work until tomorrow."

"You know my friend Charlie."

Pam nods. "Hi, Charlie."

Charlie waves then wanders over to the earring display.

"Can I talk to you a sec?"

Pam stops straightening.

"I decided about college. I'm going outside—to Idaho."

"Congrats," she says. "We'll miss you."

"Thanks. You've been a great manager, and I don't want to leave you guys shorthanded, so what do you think about bringing Charlie in to fill my position?" I say it all too fast and instantly want to suck the words back in so I can try again.

"I can't promise anything...."

"Please," I beg. "She's awesome, and she'd fit in really well—look at her—she'd be perfect."

Pam sighs. "I'll at least make sure she gets an interview. When's your last day?"

I know once she's hired they can't fire her for being pregnant. But I know they won't hire her if they know in advance, so I say, "Next Friday," because I don't want her to be showing any more than she is already.

"Usually it's two weeks, but whatever," says Pam. "I'll list the position in the paper—that's company policy. I can interview her next week."

When Charlie drops me off, I feel like it's the end of something.

"Wait," I say. "I'll get your hairspray. I've had it for forever."

"Aw shit, just keep it. I owe you."

I pull my Cornell sweatshirt over my head. "Will you at least take this?" I straighten the T-shirt I'm wearing underneath and hand over my good luck charm. "Don't forget me."

"How could I?" says Charlie. "You're my best friend, dumbass."

"Just take the shirt already. It's got good juju."

She grabs it. "Fine." She balls the shirt up on her lap and stares at it a minute. "I'm naming the baby Taylor," she says.

"Taylor Taylor? That's weird."

"For fuck's sake, Merinator!" She slaps me. "No. Taylor *Clark*. She'll have her daddy's last name." She rubs her belly. "And so will I. Someday."

"Right." I've decided to keep my last name, even if I do get married someday. I used to hate Miller, but I've spent my whole life making the name mine. I don't want to start over.

Charlie's face goes soft. "Meri, I'm happy with Kenny, you know. We're scared, but we want this baby."

"Scared is okay," I say, and this time, when I'm the one saying it, I believe it.

"Kenny said he'd never leave me the way his dad left his mom," says Charlie, "and I know he means it. Taylor will be better off than me—she'll have a dad."

"She?"

"I just have a feeling."

6/4/91

Baby Taylor,

You looked like a little fish in the sonogram picture. So teeny. Hope you're born while I'm home at Christmas so I can meet you.

I was the first person your mom told when she thought she was pregnant, which basically makes me your aunt or godmother or something. I wasn't super psyched back then, but now I see how you are everything she's always wanted. You're lucky. Your mom and dad really love you.

It's weird to imagine you growing up and being a teenager right here, like me and your mom and dad. You'll probably think Soldotna sucks, too. It's actually not that terrible. Maybe you'll even think this town is the place for you. But listen, if you ever feel like you need to bust out, like the only way you can be who you were meant to be is to leave, don't let anything stop you. Your ocean is out there.

Good luck growing up, little fish.

Meri

6/10/91

When someone you love dies, nothing hurts at first, like when Alex broke his leg. You're in shock. But once it hits you, it's like waves over and over. You think you're going to drown. Sometimes there are moments you feel like you're okay. You think maybe it's lessening, like how fog burns off or a smell dissipates, but really, it's in there, gathering itself, getting ready to slam you again.

6/11/91

I wonder if after I leave I will miss Joaquin the way I miss Grandma. At least I can come back and see him.

6/12/91

In the dream I was a red salmon following the Kenai River away from the tight tuck of rocks to the inlet. I was new. Sides slick. Bump, bump, brush. Back and forth made the motion of being. I shone when the sun found me, his face reflecting in me over and over. I jumped up suspended in dead air then fell back into the cold I knew. Life. My body pushed through, following the map inside me toward the Great Blackness that would rise up and around. Rush to me, said the sea, I am your tomorrow. Forward, forward, forward. Home is an ocean.

32
The Most Important First
of My Life So Far

Joaquin glances out the DQ window. This is our last day together, and though he doesn't want me to go, he's as resolved to it as I am.

"Don't worry," he says, scooping a bite of the hot fudge sundae we're sharing. "I'll keep you up on what's happening here."

"Great," I say. "I'll look forward to opening envelopes of blank paper." We both know his letters will be my lifeline. I'm terrified to leave here, but I'm excited to see what I can do and who I can be in a new place.

"Eva says good luck, by the way." Joaquin's doing everything he can to help me. He wants me to make it out there, to become the person I was meant to be, and that makes the idea of leaving him even harder.

"Tell her goodbye for me," I say, wondering how her senior year will go.

"You'll be glad you left," he says.

I'll never be glad I left him. I kiss him softly on his cold, chocolate-sweetened lips. It takes all my willpower to pull away and let that be enough. "Of course I'll write," I say, "because I'll be sad and lonely and won't have any friends." I can't fail him. I have to survive in a world I've only visited twice. "But you'll be going out and having fun. You won't write."

"You know I will," he says. He leans forward but thinks better of it and sits back. "In Spanish. I'll make you work for it."

I whisper one of the few phrases I know. "Te quiero."

"Te quiero," he says.

I want him. But I want my own life more.

I'm giddy to get on the plane. I will fly first to Anchorage, then to Washington, and finally one more flight will land me in Idaho. I want to go, but there is a twist in my belly.

Dad stands beside one of the giant dead-animal display cases in the Kenai Airport, glaring at the empty runway. His green British Petroleum hat has faded to the yellowish shade of a Mr. Yuck sticker, yet still it's the brightest thing in this waiting area. Within the glass case, a shabby stuffed brown bear is frozen upright in the midst of stepping forward, paws stilled at his sides, as if the bear was caught in the act of pretending to walk like a man.

Dad's stance is similarly unmoving, except his feet are planted wide apart, weight on his heels, and his hands are half-tucked into the front pockets of his Sears dungarees. A wooden toothpick rolls back and forth along his lower lip—the only sign that, unlike the bear, my dad is not a wonder of modern taxidermy.

I imagine what Dad might be thinking. If he will miss me. I wonder if the next time he is welding, mask down and sparks flying, my father will see me in the private sanctuary of his mind walking the grounds of a university he's never seen. I wonder if he will feel proud.

I see Alex through the glass pane that separates the waiting area from the airport café—Mom made him come along. He's hunched over a table reading some fantasy paperback by Raymond E. Feist, sipping what I know is a Dr Pepper. He acts like he doesn't see me.

A row of black vinyl seats connects Mom and me. She's explaining the calling card. "Punch in this code before you dial the phone number." She points to a line of tiny digits running along the bottom of a gray, plastic card.

I already know how it works, but I let her explain.

Out the giant picture windows, past the runway, dying grass

blends into thin spruce. These are the last images I will see of my home until winter break. My fingers work in secret to undo the metal button at the suddenly too-small waist of my jeans.

Mom holds the card out to me. "See? This is your code." She brushes her fingertip back and forth under the string of numbers. "Should I write it on a separate piece of paper, just in case you lose it?"

I shake my head and take the card. I'm past needing a backup.

A low, intensifying buzz makes us both look up. Taxiing toward us is a small, white-and-burgundy plane. *Glacier Air.*

"Twin-engine turboprop Beechcraft Super King," announces Dad without turning from the window. "That's yours."

The aircraft rolls to a halt, and even before its two propellers have stopped spinning, the curved side opens and a stairwell folds out. A dozen people—mostly Slope workers in Carhartts and unseasonably heavy jackets—make their way down the metal stairs. They blink and look around, as if confused. These burly, unshaven men have spent two weeks or longer on a rig, making their livings in the brutal Prudhoe Bay Oil Fields on Alaska's North Slope. They probably dream of this moment: when they get to come home.

A woman's voice calls my flight number over the airport loudspeaker, but I can hear her actual voice because she's standing six feet away behind a little podium, and now that she has my attention, she looks familiar. I try to place her. Her tanning-bed bronzed face is pretty, and I think she's not much older than me. She tucks a loose strand of black hair under her slim felt hat, and just like that I remember her—a cheerleader. Tara *Raymond*...or *Brayden*...something like that. A senior when I was a freshman. She was at Matt's party.

Tara's lips move behind what looks like a CB radio microphone. I hear both her delayed voice, a tinny echo through the PA system, and her real one announcing that boarding will now begin. The way she says it, so calm and sure, reminds me of Charlie. I wish Charlie were here.

Out the window a tall guy in navy blue coveralls is pushing a metal cart piled with suitcases. I only see him from behind, but his movements are familiar. He stops next to the plane's open baggage compartment, and when he slings in a duffle, I catch his profile. Matt Selanof. Guess this is his big job in the aviation industry.

I turn back to Mom, who is trying not to cry. Her face has grown splotchy and little tides are rising along her lower lids. She hugs me. "I love you. I love you. Keep God alive in your heart. I pray that you find your way in Him." This is how she lets me go. I hear the *I love you* part and I add, *You're amazing. You will do great things.* When she blinks, the tears wet little paths along either side of her nose. "I'm a watering pot," she says.

I kiss her cheek, and she smiles before she starts digging in her purse, deep down, where I know there is a pink refillable tissue dispenser because I gave it to her when I was twelve—on her birthday—and she always carries it with her, filled.

My leaving will hurt her most. She will cry alone in the kitchen. If Dad walks in, she will cut an onion as an excuse or say her eyes are irritated. She will think nobody knows how lonely she feels, but already I know. I'll feel it, too. I stare hard at the bear and will my eyes into tearless marbles.

Dad steps closer and unexpectedly pulls me to him. My face presses into his scratchy Woolrich shirt. It smells like diesel and mayonnaise. This isn't the first time he's hugged me—I've seen pictures of me on his lap when I was a kid—but my insides feel like they are collapsing. I wish he would let go.

"Be good," he says, still not releasing me.

My back stiffens. What does he expect? "I will," I say, pushing away. His words summon old sins and sins I have yet to commit. "Take care of Mom and Alex."

I've checked my luggage so all I have left to grab is my green Jansport. It feels familiar, but heavier. Inside are my journal, two pens, my old gymnastics tee, Charlie's hairspray, a deck of cards, my yellow Walkman and favorite mix tapes, the lucky wishbone Joaquin gave me for my birthday and the remaining half-bag of SweeTARTS, my grandma's unsent Grand Canyon postcard, the copy of *As I Lay Dying* I took from her house, and Margaret Atwood's *Selected Poems 1965–1975*.

I hoist the pack up over my shoulders, but one nylon strap whips against my head, and the plastic adjuster twists into my hair. I am caught like a fish, my head pulled into an awkward angle as I try yanking free. I tug harder until my scalp burns.

Suddenly the pack magically lifts off my back and hovers above me. I snake my head to the side and see Alex is holding the Jansport while carefully untangling my hair. I hadn't noticed he'd left the café.

"Thought you were reading," I say.

"I was."

When all the strands are loose, Alex gently resettles the pack on my shoulders and hits me with his book. "This is your big moment." He hobbles a step back, sizing me up. His leg is nearly healed but still protected by a plastic boot. "Attention everyone," he says, as if he's introducing me to the airport, "my sister is leaving Alaska!"

I fake-kick his leg before I lean in and wrap my arms around my walking-miracle brother. His chin clears my head now the way my chin used to clear his. The accident didn't keep him from growing.

Our hug is quick, but still I have to squeeze my eyes to hold in the water works. I can't even say the word. There's nothing good about this goodbye. "Your time will be here soon enough," I say. "Take care of the Bug while I'm gone." I tap my toe against his boot. "And try not to get yourself killed."

"Worry about yourself." He can't even look me in the eye. "You're about to miss your plane, college girl."

I punch his arm then hurry to the podium where *Glacier Air* Tara checks my ticket.

She doesn't look up, just nods me to the glass door that leads to the runway. I shove the metal handle too hard, so the door jumps away from me. Outside, the air is cold for June.

When I get to the plane's metal steps, I climb. I don't look back, not even to wave goodbye to Alex and my parents. I know they are all watching me. I'm not sure God is paying attention, but I pray that Alex will be alright.

Beyond the runway, the scrubby spruce trees wobble in the

breeze. I remember that kid and his dad waiting at the bus stop the day Grandma Buckley died. Part of me wishes I could be more like that little kid, just fall into the next moment believing everything will work out. I duck my head and find my seat—7A. Lucky.

Charlie is right now working a shift at Jay Jacobs as a fashion consultant. I'm still a little sad she's not sitting next to me, but I'm also happy for her. Kenny has his plumber job, plus he picked up a night shift stocking at Pay & Save. He wants to save up for diapers and stuff.

My pretend friend, Sharman, has been hooking up with Lee. At least she's not dating Brett. I wouldn't wish him on my worst enemy. He's with that poor sophomore girl. I left an anonymous note in her locker, but who knows if she'll take my warning seriously.

I settle myself into a seat sized for a toddler, pull Joaquin's lucky wishbone from my backpack, and jam my pack under the gray-haired man in 6A who reeks of week-old sweat and maybe a little pee. He swivels to see who's behind him. The brown cap that sits high on his head says, MUSH! Dad has the same hat hanging on a nail in our—*their*—arctic entry.

The plane starts to shake as the propellers spin up. The engines are even louder than the Bug's. I wave to the airport as we creep slowly toward the runway. I wave to the house I can't see and the bedroom I've lived in my whole life. Mom has plans to put her sewing machine in my room—just temporarily. I doubt the room can distinguish between the whir of Mom's new Singer machine and the sound of me breathing.

The tiny airplane bumps and rattles down the runway, and suddenly we are sloshing from side to side. I'm nauseous and we haven't even reached the clouds. My head spins like the moment before I passed out on the university campus with Brita.

The ground below is obscured as we rise through the turbulence. The spruce along the runway transform from trees into black clumps, and the airport looks like it's made from gray Legos.

The wing outside my tiny portal window bends and bounces like the big diving board at the SoHi pool. I grab the seat-back in front of me as we heave skyward then drop fast and jagged.

The pilot warns us to keep our seat belts fastened as the plane begins jumping wildly around in the air. My stomach's now as queasy as when I rode the Zipper, but I know this time the ride won't stop until either we're on land or at the bottom of the inlet.

Through the crack between the seats ahead of me, I can see the guy with the MUSH! hat gripping the armrest, tendons raised on the back of his hand. I reach up and twirl the pearl earring I took from Grandma's house. I try to slow my breathing by picturing Grandma Buckley's face. I wonder if she can see me now, flying out into the world.

I hope I made the right decision to live with Aunt Lily for the summer before moving into the dorms. I've already been assigned a roommate. The girl is only a name on a notecard today, but for ten months I will sleep above or below her every night. What if she snores? What if she thinks I'm stupid? I think of the movies I've watched in preparation. Like *Dead Poets Society*. Maybe she will listen to the Cure before bed and tell me things she's never told anyone. I think of everything I've never told anyone.

The airport road shrinks below us, but still I can trace it back to town, to the gas pumps and 7-Eleven's distinct orange and red on white. To the Kenai Believers Church and Anchor Court, the place Joaquin and I first kissed. I close my eyes and see our legs twisted together in his cousin's trailer, mere yards from where the land falls away and the river becomes the inlet.

Every day the Kenai bluff erodes a little bit more. Maybe while I'm gone, those trailers and the rusty anchor and my church with its neon cross will all tumble into the water and wash away. Or Mt. Redoubt will blow again and cover the whole place in lava.

Even if that happens, this place—where I learned how to love and be loved—will always exist in me.

The pilot banks and heads us along the Cook Inlet, our path to the north. Below the inlet's surface hide the belugas. The whales will swim out to deeper water soon, feed on hooligan in the spring, and follow the salmon back in the summer. Each year they leave only to return again.

When salmon swim out as fry, they stay in the ocean. Nobody knows for sure where they go. It's as if they hear a distant calling, and they follow it. They find their way to the ocean and spend years out there, maybe under ice caps or off the coast of countries thousands of miles away. They swim, feed, learn—do whatever salmon do—until they are ready to swim back to their river, their birth home, and leave their second home, the entire ocean.

I don't know if I will come back every year like the whales or leave for my lifetime like the salmon, but I know I will be back. I miss Joaquin already. The thought of him—his dimpled cheek and baby curls—makes my chest ache, and I cough to keep from crying.

Grandma said, "Love is letting every day be new." I think that's what I'm doing. Someday, maybe Joaquin will leave with me or I'll return and stay with him. Or maybe not.

I hold the wishbone he gave me tightly in my hand.

Out my window the Kenai Peninsula blurs, and patterns emerge like hieroglyphs. The land becomes language, decipherable. I read: *Home*. This place and these people are what I know. They are all I know.

All I *knew*.

About the Author

Meagan Macvie was born and raised in Alaska. She received her MFA in fiction from Pacific Lutheran University. Her work has appeared in *Narrative*, *Fugue*, and *Barrelhouse*, as well as the short story anthology, *Timberland Writes Together*. Meagan lives with her husband and daughter in Washington State. For more information, visit her website at meaganmacvie.com.

Acknowledgments

The character of Meri first appeared to me at a community writing class back in 2010, and *The Ocean in My Ears* grew from that original spark. To those who have fanned her flame all these years and helped bring Meri's world into existence, I am deeply grateful.

Much thanks to my talented friend and mentor, Carrie Mesrobian, for the marathon phone calls, stellar advice, excellent humor, and steadfast belief that this could be a real thing. To my Hotchix and fellow writing warriors, Dawn Pichon Barron, Grace Campbell, and Carmen Hoover, thank you for believing, critiquing, editing, rabblerousing, conference going, and sharing the love. To Karen Irwin and Suzanne Shaw, thank you for your friendship and wisdom, your writerly feedback, and for going with me on Adventures of Great Consequence. Thanks to the Pacific Lutheran University Rainier Writing Workshop crew, especially the fearless and hilarious Potty Mouth Girls, the class of 2014 fictioneers, and my fantastic mentors Scott Nadelson, Mary Clearman Blew, and Jim Heynen. Grateful also to Tina Foriyes, Clark Fair, Teri Zopf-Schoesler and Marky Maughan, my first creative writing teachers, for showing me that I could; to Off Point Writers for the early oomph and marvelous perspectives; and to Amy Benward, Keith Eisner, Melissa Graves, and Brandii O'Reagan for insights, suggestions, and encouragement along the way.

Extreme gratitude to all my readers. That means you! Thanks to early young adult readers Hanah, Emma, Astrid, Owen, and Sonrisa, and special thanks to the amazing and talented Taylor VonHeeder for reading many times, providing vital feedback, and being the heart of the book in so many ways.

To the good people at Hedgebrook, Hypatia-In-The-Woods, and the Vermont Studio Center, thank you for allowing me creative space to work. Thanks also to the experts at the Alaska Department of Fish and Game who patiently answered my bear and salmon questions.

Big thanks to all the brilliant people at Ooligan Press, especially my project team kicked off by Hayley Wilson and led by Margaret Henry and Emily HagenBurger, for taking care of the details and making sure this book was the very best it could be. Honored to have the Pacific Northwest Writers Association name an early version of the novel as a young adult finalist in their 2016 literary contest.

Much love to my friends and family for encouraging and supporting me despite not always getting me. Thanks, Mom, for reading a zillion times—I love you more than there are stars. Thanks Dad, for teaching me how to fish, weld, and go my own way. To my brother (aka HH), who broke his leg just so I could write about it. To my amazing husband, forced to listen to every word—hold on—I'm changing that part—wait—okay. You're a saint and I love you. To my smart, vivacious, writer, observer, videographer, crafter, and artist daughter. Thank you, Bunny, for always waiting up for me. Stay kind, keep reading, and continue making your own incredible stories.

That goes for all you beautiful people. Be kind. Read. Tell your stories.

Ooligan Press

Ooligan Press is a student-run publishing house rooted in the rich literary culture of the Pacific Northwest. Founded in 2001 as part of Portland State University's Department of English, Ooligan is dedicated to the art and craft of publishing. Students pursuing master's degrees in book publishing staff the press in an apprenticeship program under the guidance of a core faculty of publishing professionals.

PROJECT TEAM
Emily HagenBurger
Margaret Henry
Hayley Wilson
Terence Brierly
TJ Carter
Taylor Farris
Elizabeth Hughes
Melina Hughes
Gloria Mulvihill
Laura Nutter
Brianne Robinson
Joanna Szabo
Theresa Tyree
Pam Wells

ACQUISITIONS
Molly Hunt
Bess Palares
Emily Einolander
Alyssa Hanchar
Camilla Kaplan
Chelsea Lobey

DESIGN
Leigh Thomas
Maeko Bradshaw

DIGITAL
Stephanie Argy
Emily Einolander

EDITING
J. Whitney Edmunds
Olenka Burgess
Alison Cantrell
Mackenzie Deater
Kaitlin Fairchild
Michele Ford
Emily HagenBurger
Alyssa Hanchar
Elizabeth Hughes
Camilla Kaplan
Hope Levy
Chelsea Lobey
Hilary Louth
Amanda Matteo
Gloria Mulvihill
Amylia Ryan
Alyssa Schaffer
Joanna Szabo
Theresa Tyree
Pam Wells
Desiree Wilson

MARKETING
Jordana Beh Wathey
Morgan Nicholson

SOCIAL MEDIA
Elizabeth Nunes
Katie Fairchild

Colophon

The Ocean in My Ears is set in Fanwood, an open-source digital typeface designed by Barry Schwartz and distributed by The League of Moveable Type. Based on the designs of Rudolf Ruzicka's Fairfield (1940), Fanwood is a modern version of the Venetian Oldstyle designs of the Italian Renaissance.

CPSIA information can be obtained
at www.ICGtesting.com
Printed in the USA
BVHW01s1514210118
505899BV00013B/325/P